Eileen MacDonald journalist and auth including THE KEEPER.

Also by Eileen MacDonald

The Sleeper
The Infiltrator
The Keeper

CLOSE
TO HOME

EILEEN MACDONALD

**POCKET
BOOKS**

LONDON • SYDNEY • NEW YORK • TOKYO • TORONTO

To Cathy and Harry

First published in Great Britain by Simon & Schuster UK Ltd, 2003
This edition published by Pocket Books, 2004
An imprint of Simon & Schuster UK Ltd
A Viacom company

1 3 5 7 9 10 8 6 4 2

Simon & Schuster UK Ltd
Africa House
64–78 Kingsway
London WC2B 6AH

www.simonsays.co.uk

Simon & Schuster Australia
Sydney

A CIP catalogue record for this book is available from the British Library

ISBN 0–671–01796–9

Typeset by SX Composing DTP, Rayleigh, Essex
Printed and bound in Great Britain by
Cox & Wyman Ltd, Reading, Berkshire

ACKNOWLEDGEMENTS

I wish to thank the following for their invaluable help: Dr Nicky Foulds, Specialist Registrar in Clinical Genetics at St George's Hospital, London; Ron Thwaites QC for his excellent legal advice and Catherine Davidson, Assistant Professor of English at the American International University in London for her careful reading of the text. I would like to add that any errors in the manuscript are mine, and not theirs.

CHAPTER ONE

The telephone rang.

It wasn't meant to. During Conference, all calls were supposed to be switched through to the Editor's secretary.

The meeting had just started and over by the floor to ceiling windows that peered far down to the Thames below, the magazine's editor, Roz Clayton, was talking.

It was her first conference since her return from maternity leave and her five heads of department, grouped around her on easy chairs, were showing rapt attention. But on her desk that telephone kept ringing.

Stop it, Roz thought desperately, talking on. Answer it, she ordered her secretary silently. It showed her up. Forgetting to divert the phones suggested a lack of care. It hinted that her mind was not properly on her job, but still half at home, befuddled by hormones, dreaming of baby smiles.

For the sixth time the telephone shrilled its double note. It couldn't be ignored any longer.

'Shall I get that?' asked the young health editor, helpfully rising.

'No.' Roz crossed swiftly to her desk. Mindful of everyone's eyes upon her, she resisted the urge to snatch up the handpiece and bark into it. She let it ring once more before she took it, only to hear the dialling tone. She identified her mistake at once: that it was her other line, her newly installed personal line that rang. Hardly anyone had that number. Her husband, Hugh, but he knew not to ring then.

It rang again and she grabbed it.

'Roz?'

A young female voice which for a moment Roz didn't recognise. 'Please can I speak to Roz?'

That twangy New Zealand voice. It was Alice, the nanny. Roz's heart began to pound. Please God don't let there be anything wrong. Let Charley be all right . . . 'What's wrong?' she asked tightly.

'Charley . . . he's having some kind of fit. He won't come out of it. I'm on my way to the hospital . . .'

They lived right in front of the West Brompton Hospital in Chelsea; their garden backed on to it. Roz had told Alice that if there was ever anything wrong with Charley, to run him round there. Don't even think of calling an ambulance.

Alice was running now; Roz could hear her breath bursting in gasps. If she closed her eyes she could see her baby convulsing in the nanny's arms . . . A fit? Why would Charley have a fit? 'Is he breathing?' she cried. 'Is he conscious?'

'I . . . I don't think so. He's . . . sort of stiff. I'm at the hospital now—' The line went dead.

She couldn't cut her off like that. She couldn't leave her not knowing. Beside the window, everyone had stopped talking. One stood up, the others followed, they began making for the door, single-file, eyes averted.

She felt the suck of airlessness, and pulled herself together. She must not faint. She got the hospital number, and dialled it.

A recorded voice told her to key in the extension she required or wait for an operator.

Why were they torturing her like this? She gave a little whimper.

'Roz?'

The health editor had stopped beside her. She was a mother herself, Roz remembered, a kindly woman. 'Is it Charley?' she asked softly.

'Yes. He's had a fit.' Roz felt how her jaw ached, saying that.

The woman's brow creased but her voice remained soothing. 'It's quite common. Has he got a fever?'

'No. At least not when I left him this morning.' The words reverberated in her brain. Why had she ever left him? Didn't she love him?

'High temperatures can come on really quickly,' the journalist murmured. 'Try not to worry. I'm sure he's going to be fine.'

At the other end of the line, a voice finally drawled, 'West Brompton.'

'Paediatric Casualty, please.' She sounded like a doctor, she thought, surprised at herself: cool and efficient. Perhaps there was no need to panic.

'A and E,' announced a nurse.

'My baby's just been brought in by my nanny. He's five months old. Charley Eastwood.' She punched the words out. They would say he was fine, that it had been a false alarm. Already Roz could imagine herself telling Alice she had done the right thing, but my goodness, what a scare she had given her!

'Oh, yes.' There was hesitation in the woman's voice, and the terror returned to Roz, whumping into her guts. 'The doctors are with him now,' the nurse continued carefully.

'With him?' Roz pleaded, desperately wanting and not wanting to know more.

'Yes. Perhaps you'd like to come in,' pressed the nurse gently.

It was that serious. Of course it was. 'Yes,' she said, 'I'll come straight away.' She replaced the receiver. Her secretary entered the room to say that the driver was bringing the car round now; it would be waiting once Roz got downstairs.

'I'm calling Hugh first.' She dialled his number without thinking what she was going to say and when he came on the line, she couldn't speak. 'It's Charley,' she managed.

Hugh's voice rose in query and then quick panic.

She forced herself to explain.

'I'll meet you there,' he said. He was a Home Office minister, a clever and ambitious man, who intended to be the next leader of his party. He had an office in Whitehall. He would reach the hospital far quicker than Roz at Canary Wharf.

The traffic was kind to her until they reached Tower Bridge where it stood still. Without a word from her, the driver began to snake through the side streets; in the back of the car, Roz kept trying the hospital. The reception was poor and when she did get through, no one senior enough could be found to talk to her.

A sob cut sharply in her throat.

The driver swung out of the road into another. Horns blared behind them, and she saw familiar landmarks. The restaurant where she and Hugh had gone the night before, leaving Alice to babysit. The Italian deli, the newspaper shop – they were close to home now, only they weren't going home. The car slewed to a halt outside the hospital entrance. The driver offered to accompany her, but she refused.

Inside the foyer, a receptionist gave her directions to Paediatric Casualty, twice. She walked, then started to run, her open coat flying out behind her. She pushed open double doors and collided with a man in a wheelchair. 'Stupid bitch,' he swore, but she was gone.

She saw the Winnie-the-Pooh stickers on the wall that she had been told led to the children's unit. In the waiting area, there were five or six families sitting, but no sign of Hugh. From a room with its door closed, a child screamed.

A nurse came forward and Roz gave her name. Did a mask come down? 'He's in PICU,' said the nurse quietly. 'I'll take you up.'

'PICU?'

'Paediatric Intensive Care.'

The name hit her like a blow. But perhaps all babies who had a fit went there? She didn't like to ask; she didn't want to know. She wished she'd asked her health editor more questions when she'd had the chance.

She followed the nurse into a glass lift and they rose in silence, looking down upon fantastic sculptures: a clown balancing a red ball upon his nose, a couple in bronze holding a child in the air. The hospital was an NHS flagship, Roz remembered, designed to be beautiful as well as good. Charley was in the best possible place. Chill tears ran down her hot face. He would be all right, she told herself, and saw the nurse watching her. The nurse's eyes looked moist. Quickly Roz looked away. She couldn't stand anyone else's tears.

Inside PICU, Hugh was stationed at the foot of a bed with his back to her, his blond head bent. A doctor was talking to him but he didn't appear to be listening. When Roz approached he didn't look up. She couldn't bring herself to follow his gaze.

'Hugh,' she said.

He looked up then. Dead dark eyes into hers, no word for her, and his gaze returned to where it had been before. She took his hand, but he didn't return her pressure. His unresponsiveness terrified her. Finally, there being no other option, she followed his gaze.

A baby lay splayed on the bed like a frog, the legs falling away from the hips, head turned to one side, eyes shut, a tube up his nose, another one in his mouth, tubes snaking everywhere from the body, hooking him up to machinery and drips.

'He's being ventilated,' the doctor murmured, but she didn't hear him. She was thinking, as she continued to stare, that it wasn't a baby on the bed, certainly not Charley! There'd been a mistake, thank God. Horror for somebody else but not for her.

'We've had to anaesthetise Charley to stop him convulsing,' continued the doctor.

She find her mind yawn open. She looked again at the bed, and saw that of course, it was her baby. The golden fuzz of hair sprouting on his head, his fat little feet. Such a thing could not be happening to her. She felt herself slipping and put out her hand to grasp the metal bar of the bed. She glanced wildly at Hugh, but he was beyond her still. She turned to the doctor. 'Charley's going to be . . .?' Her heart failed. 'I mean, is he going to be all right?'

'Mrs Eastwood, it might be better if we go into my—'

Strings snapped inside her head. 'I'm not going anywhere!' she screamed. 'Charley?' She lunged forwards. If she could touch him, she could make him well. But hands restrained her.

'Mrs Eastwood, Charley is very sick—'

'He's my baby!' What did this stranger have to do with her? How dare he interfere? And why did Hugh just stand there, blankly staring?

Hugh croaked, 'Tell her.'

There was a silence, except for the ventilator's soft sigh. A nurse adjusted a syringe on one of Charley's tubes. The doctor said finally: 'We're waiting on the results from the MRI scan . . .'

'Tell her,' barked Hugh, coming to life.

The man cleared his throat. 'The preliminary findings indicate there has been considerable contusion to the brain.'

'Contusion?' echoed Roz.

'Bruising.'

What did that mean?

The doctor went on, 'We believe there has been significant damage to the substance of the brain itself.'

She grappled to understand. The worst: Charley was going to be brain-damaged. Their perfect baby for whom she had waited so long, whom she had loved so passionately even before his birth, wasn't going to be as other little boys. He was going to be different, abnormal. A shudder ran through her. But it didn't matter, she told herself, she loved him still. How dare anyone suggest otherwise?

'We believe the seizure was as a result of the injury.'

'What injury?'

Looks like darts shot forth. 'That's what we need to find out,' said the doctor quietly.

'They're interviewing Alice now,' Hugh said in the same flat voice.

'What for?' queried Roz faintly.

Hugh looked at her properly for the first time. 'They're saying Charley was shaken,' he said.

Alice Bishop. The wonder nanny, so highly recommended by the agency that in turn was meant to be the best in London. Roz had meant to check every one of her references but after the third, she had stopped: everyone had been so glowing in their praise.

Why hadn't she bothered? Would it have taken so much more effort to have called New Zealand? What was she, a professional journalist or a mousey housewife, afraid of the phone bill?

But Alice was super. She loved Charley. Charley loved her. Roz was jealous of her.

The doctor was saying that they needed to speak to everyone who had been in contact with Charley in the last twenty-four hours. It would help them build up a picture of exactly what had happened, and when. Would Roz go with his colleague? He indicated a female in a white coat. And Hugh with himself?

'What for?' Roz asked again.

'They suspect us,' said Hugh.

'Us?'

'They suspect everyone, don't you?' he smiled. How could he smile at such a time, she thought with another shiver? How could he jest? She saw the medics thinking the same.

'I can't leave Charley,' she bleated, clinging more tightly to the bed's bar. Surely they could see that?

'We'll call you at once if there's any change,' promised the doctor.

She clung on. 'Can I touch him?' she begged pathetically.

He hesitated. 'Yes, of course.'

To be given permission to touch her own son . . . But approaching him as he now was, was so different from any other time she had touched him. She was afraid of him. So fragile did he seem, so alien to her. 'Charley,' she whispered, bending close to his face, 'it's Mummy. Mummy's here. Wake up, darling. Please wake up.'

His eyelids didn't flicker. He didn't move.

It was as if he was already dead. She heard a moaning sound and realised it came from herself.

'Roz . . .'

She put out a trembling finger, and with a gossamer touch, both not to hurt him and to avoid the plastic tubing, she placed it upon her baby's cheek. He was warm. She felt a surge of hope; he was going to be all right. He only had a bruised brain! Bruises healed. They would get the best specialists, the best education. They could afford it. Charley would soon catch up, and if he didn't, so what? What did it matter if he was a bit slow?

She let a tear drop on to Charley's cheek. If he could no longer cry, she would cry for him. Then she wiped it away.

She let herself be led away into a room and questioned by the watchful female doctor.

How had Charley seemed that morning? The previous night? Who had had charge of him? Who normally had charge of him?

Roz answered as best she could, although suddenly she felt enormously tired. During the week, Alice had sole charge of Charley from eight o'clock in the morning until seven in the evening. Roz always made sure she was back by then. After that, except on babysitting nights, she and Hugh looked after him, no matter how weary they were, or how many times he cried in the night, and he was fretful at night. The night-care was a bone of contention between them, not that Roz shared that with the doctor. Hugh argued that now Roz had returned to work, they both needed their sleep. They had highly demanding, stressful jobs: Alice would have to be on duty at night, Hugh said, or they could even employ another girl.

Privately Roz knew that Hugh was right. To herself she admitted that probably in the end she would have to concede the point, but it had only been three weeks, and they had just about managed it between them. One night's sleep, one night's caring for Charley, and soon, hopefully, he would reach an age when he began sleeping through the night? . . .

She was his mother, she wanted to do something for him, not hand over his whole care to a nanny. Last night, Hugh had been on duty.

'Did your nanny babysit?' the doctor asked, breaking in on her reverie.

'Yes.'

'How was Charley on your return?'

She thought hard but there was nothing to remember. 'Fine. Sleeping.'

'Did he wake in the night?'

'Yes. But that's not unusual.'

'How was he this morning?'

Roz cast her mind back. Picking Charley up from his cot, unzipping his little sleeping bag, prising him out soft and warm for her precious morning cuddle, before reluctantly handing him over to Alice.

She hadn't wanted to leave him that morning, she remembered. She hadn't wanted to say goodbye. She had been ten minutes late setting off and Keith had broken all records to get her to work on time. Tears stung her eyes. 'Charley was fine this morning,' she rasped.

The doctor wrote that down.

There was a white electric clock above the woman's head. Roz watched an hour seep past. Time seemed to have both speeded up and slowed down. The doctor was replaced by a social worker, another woman. Roz felt quite bemused. The questions came and went like waves, at times it seemed to Roz that they were the same questions. Sometimes she answered them, sometimes she didn't. She was floating.

A nurse came in to say there was no change in Charley. The questions began again. Suddenly it was two o'clock in the afternoon. Roz came to: she had had enough.

'How much longer is this going to go on?' she snapped.

'I'm sorry?'

'These bloody questions.'

The social worker gazed at her. They suspect us all, Hugh said. 'Where's Alice?' she demanded.

'She's in another part of the hospital. Please, Mrs Eastwood, it won't do any good to—'

Roz got up, opened the door and started walking. She tried the first door she came to, but it was locked. She saw the Intensive Care Unit up ahead. Around Charley's bed clustered a squad of medics. She recognised one of the doctors from that morning.

'Massive bloody bleed,' commented one of the team, gazing at a scan picture.

A greasy student bending over Charley sniffed: 'The bruises on the upper arms are becoming more evident.'

'No skull fracture though.'

'In twenty-one per cent of cases it's the dad. The dad here is that Minister for Families who's always on the telly . . .'

Somebody whistled; somebody else snickered.

'He's not giving anything away.'

'Cool as a cucumber.'

'So's she.'

Roz went cold. She snatched at the nearest sleeve and the man jumped when he saw who she was.

'How much longer has Charley got to stay here?' she asked.

'I'm sorry, Mrs Eastwood?'

'When can we take him home?'

They were staring at her as if she was crazy. 'Charley needs to be here.' The doctor spoke softly.

'Being poked and prodded by you lot? Experimented upon?'

'No one is experimenting on him, Mrs Eastwood.'

'No? Don't you think I should have seen this first?' She snatched the scan picture from his hand. She saw the greys and blacks of her baby's head, clouds oozing into each other. His poor damaged brain. Her own mind felt it would break. She started to cry. 'I want to take him home.'

'I'm afraid we can't allow—'

'I am his mother!'

'Mrs Eastwood—'

'He's my baby!' Her breathing became short and hard. She felt herself getting smaller and smaller. She put out a hand to stop herself from falling and was caught by others as she sank to the floor.

Machinery kept Charley alive for two more days. During that time, a battery of tests were carried out to determine his brain function. Throughout, Hugh and Roz were at his side, taking it in turns to sleep. They were never left entirely unsupervised, a nurse at least was always hovering, a presence they were both aware of, but chose not to refer to.

On the morning of the third day, the consultant appeared at

the foot of the bed and asked them to accompany him to his office.

Roz knew what was coming. She and Hugh both did. They sat side by side, unable to look at each other. The consultant spoke to a point in the air midway between them. Roz heard his voice in snatches.

There had been a rebleed in Charley's brain. There had been further extensive subdural haemorrhaging. Charley had slipped deeper into unconsciousness . . .

Hugh broke in. 'He's braindead, that's what you're saying?'

A hand seemed to snatch at Roz's throat, cutting off her air supply, but she vowed she would not faint again.

The consultant was saying quietly to Hugh, 'Yes, I'm afraid that is the position. Charley's brain has died.'

'But he's still alive,' begged Roz. 'You can see on the screen. His heart is going.'

The man's eyes filled with tears, and detachedly Roz felt pity for him. 'He is being ventilated and his vital signs supported, Mrs Eastwood, but I'm afraid—'

'Switch him off,' interrupted Hugh.

'No!' she choked.

Hugh turned on her savagely. 'D'you want him to be a vegetable?'

'Stop it!' she cried, putting her hands over her ears, but he prised them away. His eyes bulged with anger. His spittle landed on her face. 'My son is not going to be kept alive when his brain has gone, d'you hear me?'

'Mr Eastwood,' protested the consultant.

Hugh shook her. 'D'you agree? Do you?'

'But he's my baby,' she whimpered.

'Not any more. He's dead.'

Something broke inside her. 'All right,' she said dully. She was no longer Charley's mother, but his executioner. She began to cry again, and now Hugh's arms enfolded around her. 'All right, my darling. There's my good girl, my brave girl.' He rocked her to and fro, and the consultant left them alone.

An hour later, Charley was moved into a side room and the tubes supplying him with medication and nutrients were removed. His ventilator was switched off.

He died shortly after in Roz's arms. Hugh stood behind her, seemingly unable to touch or even look at his son. They spoke no words to each other, but left the hospital together, going out by an underground exit in order to avoid the media crush at both the front and rear of the building. Even so, a paparazzo snatched them, and their faces, white and stunned in the back of the car, appeared on that night's news programmes.

Hugh was very much in the news at that time. He had just been appointed Minister with Special Responsibility for the Family. The death of his own only son, the manner of it, while undeniably tragic, was also the hottest story around.

For that reason, he and Roz were not driven home, but to a remote Sussex farmhouse belonging to a colleague. There, Roz was sedated; Hugh went walking all night.

Two days after Charley's death, one of the tabloid newspapers splashed on the story that a previous baby whom Alice Bishop had cared for in New Zealand had died under suspicious circumstances. A local police chief believed she had suffocated the infant, but there had been insufficient evidence to charge her, and in the absence of it, the coroner's verdict had been cot death.

On that cool May morning in England, however, the police officers who had been interrogating Alice for several days decided they had all the evidence they needed. Alice Mary-Ann Bishop, aged twenty-six, from Hastings, New Zealand, was arrested and charged with the murder of Charley Wilfred Eastwood.

CHAPTER TWO

I t was the first 'Killer Nanny' case in Britain for six years. That, coupled with Hugh's political position, ensured that the Old Bailey trial held five months later received mass-media coverage. Nothing more about Alice's background had been published since her arrest, for fear of prejudicing her trial, but the New Zealand case stuck in the public mind and branded her guilty.

On the first day, people queued inside and outside the building for seats. Alice's parents and younger brother, not allowed into the courtroom itself, were reserved places in the public gallery from which they viewed the proceedings below. They were there every day, for the most part silent witnesses.

The case had been underway for two weeks and the prosecution had already presented its evidence. Roz and Hugh had each given their testimonies, namely that when they had left Charley on the morning of May 14th, he had been healthy; three hours later he was dying.

The defence suggested they had rowed on the night before he had been injured; they denied it.

From medical experts, the court had heard of the extent of Charley's injuries. His head had been slammed against a softened hard surface, probably the carpet that was fitted throughout his home. His skull had impacted on the floor, but his brain had carried on travelling, resulting in extensive deceleration damage. It was a classical 'Shake and Impact Injury'. Sickening photographs had been shown and two members of the jury had cried.

Additionally, police had revealed that a vital piece of evidence was missing: a tape from a video camera hidden in Charley's nursery. The camera was one of two secreted in the house; a measure suggested, and installed, by a security company as a favour to Hugh, in the hope of eliciting more business from his government department. The camera in the kitchen/family room had developed a fault and was due to have been replaced, but the one in Charley's bedroom had worked well. The missing tape would have shown what had happened in the nursery eighteen hours before the baby was injured. In its place another tape had been found, showing an earlier week. The prosecution alleged it had been a clumsy attempt by Alice Bishop to hide what she had done. The missing tape had not been retrieved. Bishop, it was claimed, had destroyed it.

On that bright Monday morning in October, she was due to give evidence for the first time. At twenty to ten, as Hugh's ministerial car drew up at a side entrance of the Bailey, a media mob hurled itself upon it. Cameramen crushed each other to get the best and tightest angle on the parents. Microphones were jammed into their faces as they emerged from the car.

'Mrs Eastwood, is there a message you'd like to give Alice Bishop this morning?'

'How do you feel towards Alice?'

'Is is true you're pregnant again?'

Roz spun round to deny that, but Hugh, tight-lipped, kept her going towards the building and in through a doorway. Inside, the barrage ceased. The Family Liaison Officer greeted them, and led them to the oak-panelled courtroom. It was already beginning to fill.

Hugh detached himself to speak to a police officer. Roz went forward to join her best friend seated beside a solicitor's clerk.

Like herself, Mady O'Neil was a journalist, although Mady worked as an investigative reporter on a national newspaper. They had known each other for eleven years, having met at a newsagency in east London, Mady's first job. Roz was six years her senior but their friendship had withstood job changes, Roz's far more glamorous career, house moves and husbands who didn't like each other or the friendship itself very much.

Without Mady's support, Roz knew she would have gone under in the past five months. Mady had been her rock: always there, always understanding, even at the funeral when Roz had been the only member of the congregation to remain dry-eyed.

Mady had been Charley's godmother. A mother herself, her son, Archie, had been born six weeks after Charley. She and Roz had made plans of how the boys would spend their childhoods together: playing in the London parks while their mothers picnicked; outings to the museums, the zoo, jaunts to the countryside. 'Of course, they'll probably hate each other,' they had laughed. Now Archie was nine months old, curly-headed and crawling . . .

'Hi,' Mady greeted her with a quick peck on the cheek, while her eyes sought out the true state of Roz's mind. 'How are you doing?'

'Not bad.' Which was true, Roz thought. She felt neither

high, or especially low. The antidepressants helped blur the edges. Thus far they had been enough for the trial and she hoped she would not have to resort to the stronger medication she had taken at first, and which had turned her into a zombie.

She glanced over at the witness box. She had got used to the presence of Alice Bishop sitting behind her in the dock, but very soon now she would be standing in the box in front of her, pleading her case.

Hugh took his place beside her. He looked grey and tense, there were bruises under his dark eyes through lack of sleep. She touched his hand and he responded with a fleeting smile. The jury of seven women and five men came in. The judge entered and the court rose and sat.

'The defence calls Alice Mary-Ann Bishop.'

The name rang out in the hushed chamber. Then a door clicked open in the side of the dock and Alice was brought forth into the body of the court. She was tall but walked with a stoop to hide it. She kept her eyes down. As she passed the row where Roz and Hugh sat, Mady saw she was trembling.

Good, she thought viciously. Fear at least could not be put on. Or could it? Daily, it seemed to her that as the trial progressed, Alice had got younger and more vulnerable.

There was no trace now of the lively, confident blonde whom Mady first remembered meeting at Roz's. Then Alice had worn hipsters and quite a bit of make-up. Now her hair was a dull, lifeless brown parted severely in the middle and dragged back into a ponytail. Her face was scrubbed clean and her clothes – today a knee-length navy skirt, pink blouse and low shoes – were plain, almost frumpy, and served to emphasise her skinniness. She looked about fourteen years old. Scarcely more than a child, hardly a baby-killer.

Alice's voice quivered as she swore the oath and gave her full name. She caught Mady's eye and, for a moment, there was a pleading look on her face. Mady looked away, thinking: once she had liked that girl, had trusted her to hold her own son . . .

The defence barrister rose to his feet. He was a well-regarded QC, arguably as eminent as the Crown's.

'Alice,' he smiled across at her as if they were friends, 'you babysat for Charley on the night before he was injured?'

Alice took a deep breath and launched into her story. 'That's right. Hugh and Roz usually went out on a Wednesday . . .'

She spoke in a quiet, low voice that tended to tail away at the end of sentences. Twice, the judge asked her to speak up.

Mady saw his irritation mirrored in the faces of several members of the jury and was glad. Dislike her, she told them silently, find her irksome, difficult to believe.

The barrister stopped her. 'Let me just clear up one matter, Alice. The prosecution rightly pointed out that when first interviewed by police officers you maintained you had been in the house alone that morning with the baby. It wasn't until two weeks later that you altered your statement?'

Nervously, Alice admitted doing so.

'To include the fact that a friend of yours, Kate Armstrong, a fellow New Zealander, was there as well?'

Mady's pulse quickened. Kate Armstrong had been with Alice when the New Zealand baby had died. As a journalist, Mady knew that, but the jury weren't allowed to, not until after they had reached their verdict, for fear of prejudicing them against her. British justice, Mady thought bitterly.

Alice agreed that Kate had been there.

'The prosecution alleged all sorts of reasons as to why you changed your statement, but I ask you, why did you lie to the police?'

Alice coloured. 'I . . . I was in shock, confused. I couldn't believe what I was being charged with. I didn't see why I should drag Kate into it . . . I kept thinking they'd realise it was a mistake, they'd let me go.' She took a deep breath. 'And I was trying to cover it up. I hadn't Roz and Hugh's permission for Kate to be there that night.'

'Why not?'

'They might have said no.'

'Why did it matter so much if they did?'

'Kate was leaving the country the next day. She was an overstayer; Immigration was on to her, and she had to get out fast. Her money had run out. She'd nowhere else to go. My room was in the basement, and Roz and Hugh always went out on Wednesday nights. I thought if Kate came after they had gone out, and left after them in the morning, they would never know.'

'I see. Was Charley perfectly well, as far as you could tell, that evening?'

'Yes. As far as I could tell.'

Roz and Hugh had returned home at eleven o'clock. Kate was already hidden in the basement bedroom; Alice retired there also. To her consternation, Hugh and Roz then came down to the kitchen. She paused.

'Tell us what happened next,' asked her lawyer smoothly.

'They rowed.'

'You overheard them?'

'Yes, I . . . we, Kate and me, couldn't help it. My bedroom was at the end of the corridor beside the kitchen. My window was open. It was a hot night.'

'I see. What was the row about?'

'About who'd see to Charley that night – go into him when he cried. I wasn't on duty at nights. It was Hugh's turn, but he said he was so tired. He hadn't been sleeping well . . .' Alice reddened.

'How do you know?'

'He was coming down to the kitchen to get himself a drink at two or three in the morning. I used to hear him sometimes.'

'Was this his regular practice?'

'It was that week.'

Several members of the jury looked over at Hugh. They had already heard about the row and the alleged drinking, during Hugh and Roz's cross-examinations, but now they were getting the details. Out of the corner of her eye, Mady observed Hugh staring straight ahead. Was Alice telling the truth, she wondered suddenly? Had Hugh been in trouble that week? He had denied it but that didn't mean it wasn't true . . . She caught herself. Roz and Hugh were the victims, and they were telling the truth. Alice was a clever liar, hoping by whatever means to muddy the waters.

'You say Mr Eastwood would get himself a drink. Do you mean an alcoholic drink?'

'Yes. You could smell it. The empty glass would still be on the table in the morning.'

The barrister raised his eyebrows. 'Please continue.'

'Roz said no way would she see to Charley. She said she'd only been back at work three weeks, she needed to be fresh, and anyway she'd been on duty the night before.'

'That was it?'

'More or less.'

According to Alice, Roz and Hugh had left the kitchen

separately. She and Kate had talked for a short time before falling asleep. During the night, Alice claimed to have heard Charley cry at two o'clock, 'about five', and then at six-fifteen.

Hugh and Roz claimed Charley had cried just twice, at two and then at five.

Alice's lawyer stuck his hands under his armpits. 'You heard the baby cry three times?'

'Yes.'

'You're sure?'

'Yes.'

'Your room was in the basement, two floors below Charley's?'

'Yes, but his window was open and, as I say, mine was too. The way the house was laid out, my room was in a kind of well. Noise travelled down.'

The lawyer nodded. 'Are you certain that it was his cry you heard? Not a dog or a cat, or a shriek from the street?'

'No, it was Charley. I was attuned to his cry.'

'Yes of course, you were Charley's main carer, weren't you?'

Roz stiffened. Don't rise to it, Mady begged her silently. Amongst the sackfuls of supportive mail Roz and Hugh had received, there had been some hateful letters, blaming Roz for what had happened. She had chosen to work, had chosen to leave her child with a stranger. What did she expect? Women like her shouldn't have babies . . .

Alice told the court that she worked eleven hours a day during the week, plus babysitting two or three evenings a week.

The lawyer paused, letting the court absorb exactly how many hours Roz spent parted from her child, by choice: she didn't have to work; she didn't have to go out in the evening to enjoy herself.

But Roz loved Charley, Mady wanted to protest. No mother ever loved a child more. Just because she wasn't cut out to be a full-time mother, didn't mean that she loved him any less. It was Alice that was on trial, not Roz.

Finally, the lawyer spoke again. 'You are convinced that you heard Charley cry three times?'

'I am,' said Alice.

After Charley's first crying spell, she had heard Hugh go down into the kitchen. She heard him pour himself a drink, then she fell asleep, waking again at around five when Charley cried again. Hugh was in the kitchen. She presumed he'd been there since the earlier cry.

'Did Mr Eastwood respond at once to his son's cry this time?'

Alice blushed. 'Not that second time. He let him cry. It woke Kate up as well.'

'Did you hear him say anything?'

'He swore. He said something like "that bloody bitch upstairs" . . .'

'Which you took to refer to his wife?'

Alice agreed.

'Did he leave the kitchen quietly?'

'No. He flung the door back like he wanted to wake up the whole house. Then he charged up the stairs.'

'He was angry?'

'Yes, I'd say he was angry.'

Hugh had not returned to the kitchen, Alice went on. She presumed he had gone back to bed after dealing with Charley. She had fallen asleep once more until the third cry.

Alice frowned. 'There was something about that cry,' she murmured.

'Please explain.'

'Well, it really alarmed me. I don't know, its tone or something. I couldn't believe Roz hadn't heard it.'

Mady looked over at Roz. Two tears like stones were falling from her eyes.

'Then he stopped,' said Alice.

'Just like that?'

'Yes. Very quickly, which wasn't like him. I mean, usually once he got going, he kept at it.'

'But not that morning?'

'No.'

'He stopped crying abruptly?'

'Yes.'

The lawyer let the mystery hang in the air. Had Hugh, up drinking half the night, shaken Charley? Or had the baby suffered some kind of spontaneous brain damage that had caused him to cry out in terrible pain?

It won't work, Mady told herself; the jury would see through the poor attempt at deception. There had never been a third cry.

Alice went back to sleep until seven, her normal waking time. At eight o'clock she left Kate in her room and went into the kitchen to take Charley from Roz. Hugh had already left.

'I presume Ms Clayton – Mrs Eastwood's professional name, members of the jury – was also rushing out to work?' the lawyer suggested.

'Yes. She had an important meeting that morning.'

'So you were left in charge. Was there anything markedly different about Charley on that morning that you can remember?'

There was a beat.

'I thought he seemed a bit floppy,' said Alice.

A little moan escaped Roz's lips. Mady pressed her hand. 'Floppy?'

How many times had they rehearsed that, Mady wondered? The hesitation in Alice's voice, the curiosity in the lawyer's?

'Yes,' said Alice. 'Just a bit . . . I don't know, not himself. Not how he was normally. He was alert for his age. He was already sitting, babbling, vocal. That morning . . .' again the distant expression came over Alice's face, as if she was truly reliving that moment '. . . he just sort of lay there in my arms, not really looking at me.'

'He might have been tired?'

'Not at eight o'clock in the morning,' Alice countered.

'No, I suppose not. Did Ms Clayton make any observation to you about her baby's condition?'

'No.'

'And you didn't mention your observation to her?'

Alice reddened again. 'No, I didn't. Ms Clayton . . . Roz was late. She was supposed to go at eight. It was ten past. Her driver was outside, waiting, and it wasn't really until after she'd gone that I noticed anyway.'

'You didn't think to call her at work?'

'No. I didn't think there was anything seriously wrong. Maybe a little cold coming. It was only afterwards when the doctors asked me if there had been any change in his behaviour that I remembered he'd been not quite himself.'

How convenient, Mady thought.

After Roz had left for work, Kate emerged. Apparently she too had thought Charley seemed sleepy. They had put him in his buggy in the corridor next to the kitchen while they had breakfast. He had fallen asleep almost immediately, Alice said.

Mady saw that Hugh was making notes. A lawyer himself, it was the way he was coping with the trial.

She had never particularly liked Hugh, although she made an effort for Roz's sake. Mady considered him cold, and capable of emotional cruelty. He hadn't wanted a child although Roz had been desperate. When she had failed to conceive, he had steadfastly refused to seek infertility treatment even after five years. When Roz had finally become pregnant, he had been cool about it, in private as well as public, Roz had confided. Neither had he been very supportive throughout a miserable pregnancy.

Once Charley had been born, however, Mady had to acknowledge that he had changed. He had been besotted with his baby and had expected everyone else to be too. When Charley died, Hugh had closed down, apart from at the terrible funeral. Mady had never seen a man cry like that.

In the witness box, Alice's account continued. She had checked on Charley twice. He had been 'out for the count'.

At half past nine, Kate prepared to leave. For her stay to remain secret, it was important that she be gone from the house before ten o'clock, when the Filipino maid arrived to clean. Alice escorted her upstairs to the front door, where Kate remembered she had left her make-up bag on Alice's dressing table in the basement. She ran down to fetch it.

'Past where Charley was sleeping?' asked the lawyer.

'Yes.'

'She'd only be gone moments, I presume?'

Alice looked flustered. 'A few minutes.'

'Why so long? A quick dash down to fetch her bag, knowing that the maid was coming . . .'

'I don't know . . . I don't know why she took longer.'

'But it was definitely minutes?'

'Yes. I got worried. I was just going down to get her when she came up.'

'I see. So for those minutes – three? four? – your friend was out of your sight on the same floor where Charley was sleeping?'

Alice stared. 'I think maybe she went to the loo.'

'But you don't know that?'

'No. Kate wouldn't . . .'

'Kate wouldn't what?'

'Nothing.'

'Wouldn't harm Charley?'

'No,' Alice whispered. 'No, she wouldn't."

In the New Zealand case, although Alice had been the baby's nanny, it had been Kate who had discovered the six month-old boy motionless in his cot. Was Alice suggesting, even by denial, that Kate was Charley's killer? If so, why didn't she say so? Why seek only to cast doubt? Because doubt, Mady suspected, was the only weapon Alice possessed.

There was silence in the courtroom.

'Let us move on,' said the lawyer quietly. 'How long was it after Kate left that you went to check on Charley again?'

Alice took a breath. 'About five minutes later.'

'How was he?'

'He was . . .' Alice's voice constricted, 'he was fitting, rigid, his eyes rolled right back in his head, the whites showing. When I picked him up, he was stiff . . .'

Mady saw the emotion working in her face; it was evident that tears were not far off. Her distress seemed so genuine that it was hard to believe she was acting. Perhaps she wasn't, Mady wondered? Perhaps she truly believed what she was saying. If so, she needed to be locked away so that she could never again damage another child.

'He was rigid and jerking in my arms. I got really frightened. I screamed, "Charley?". I . . . I gave him a little shake, not very hard . . .'

Roz whimpered.

The lawyer said: 'You gave Charley a little shake, is that right, Alice?'

'Yes. I . . . I was only trying to see if I could bring him out of it . . .'

'A little shake not much harder than one might shake a baby's rattle?' suggested her lawyer.

'Yes,' Alice nodded gratefully. 'Yes, that's right.'

'You didn't fling him against the wall?'

'No,' she whispered.

'Or wham his head on the carpet?'

Tears coursed down Alice's thin cheeks. 'No I didn't.'

'So, being unable to rouse the baby, you ran with him to the hospital?'

'Yes.'

'Calling Ms Clayton on your way?'

'Yes.'

Her lawyer thanked her gravely. The court had already heard the medical evidence: how in cases of Shaken Baby Syndrome, the fatal injury could have been inflicted hours, days or even months prior to death. However, in Charley's case, the injuries were so severe that they probably occurred not more than twenty-four hours before he convulsed.

'Kate Armstrong was alone with Charley just before he fitted—'

'She didn't do it,' interrupted Alice.

'Let me finish please. Your reluctance to name your friend ensured that there was no evidence of her left in that house by the time the forensic experts arrived to search for her. Let me explain, members of the jury: the maid cleaned the house meticulously on a daily basis. Once Miss Bishop was charged, apparently the maid took especial care to wipe every trace of her from the house. No fingerprints, hairs, bits of DNA etcetera were left to be found. The evidence had been destroyed. A great pity, don't you think?'

Alice mumbled a response.

He looked down at his notes. 'Tell us, did you leave Charley alone with anyone else during the twenty-four hours before he became unwell?'

Again, Alice muttered something indistinct.

'I'm sorry?'

'No. Well, hardly.'

'Please explain yourself.'

'It was at the playground the afternoon before . . . There was a little girl there, about eight years old.'

The woman juror whom Mady had grown to like most raised her eyebrows.

'She was really sweet with Charley,' Alice went on. 'She asked if she could push him.'

'You let her?' intoned the lawyer with just the right degree of incredulity in his voice.

'Yes.' Alice's face crumpled. 'Just around the playground. I was there watching, and her mother was too.'

'Watching her all the time?' dug the lawyer.

Alice looked pleadingly at him but he reiterated his question.

'I, er, I took my eyes off her,' she admitted.

'For how long?'

'Not long. Really not long. Her mother wanted to know where "Eggy Breads" was – that's the name of a children's café near the park. I turned round to show her and when I looked back her little girl was over at the other end of the playground, bouncing Charley's buggy up and down.'

'Hard enough to make him move?' asked the barrister.

'Well, yes, a bit. I'd put him in the semi-recline position . . .'

'Meaning he was seated almost upright?'

'Yes, so he could look at everything.'

'So that when the child bounced him, he went forward and back, did he?' He smacked one open-handed palm against the other. 'Like this?'

Roz winced. 'I should never have left him with her,' she whispered.

'Ssh.' Mady felt her own eyes stinging. She fumbled for a tissue in her pocket and with it pulled out a round object, a teething ring, Archie's. She grabbed it too late. Roz had already seen, and the little colour that remained in her face drained away.

In the witness box, Alice said earnestly: 'He wasn't crying or anything. When I ran over to him, he seemed fine.'

'Not dazed?'

'No. Not at all.'

'As far as you could tell,' the lawyer said heavily. 'How long do you think the girl might have been shaking him in the pram?'

Alice stared. 'Not long. Seconds.'

'How many seconds?'

'I don't know. Ten?'

'And as we have heard, the fatal injury can be inflicted in less than that.'

'But it wasn't that hard,' cried Alice. 'She was only a little girl—'

'Thank you,' the lawyer cut her off. 'This incident occurred at around four-fifteen in the afternoon, I understand?'

'Yes,' whispered Alice.

'Was anyone else alone with Charley in the remaining hours?'

Alice shook her head exhaustedly. 'Only Hugh and Roz.'

The lawyer said nothing.

A chill shimmied down Mady's back. He wouldn't dare say it, she thought, and he did not. After a moment, he asked: 'Did you know about the hidden cameras in the house?'

'No.'

'The prosecution allege that you did know, and we have seen footage showing you staring straight into the lens of the camera hidden in the shoebox on top of Charley's cupboard.'

An obstinate look came over Alice's face. 'I didn't know it was there. I don't even remember that box.'

'Did you remove and dispose of the tape from that camera?'

'No.'

'Were you aware of the other camera, in the kitchen-cum-family room?'

'No.'

'What would have been your attitude if you had known about them?'

'I'd have left. I couldn't have stayed in an atmosphere of distrust.'

Fine words, Mady thought furiously, for someone who had been warned by the police in her native country never to apply again for a nannying job.

Alice's lawyer turned over his papers. 'Let us pause briefly on the subject of your good friend, Kate Armstrong. You would describe her as such, would you?'

'Yes.'

'Probably your best friend?'

'Yes.'

The man nodded. 'I think it is fair to say that this case has received global publicity. Your friend therefore must be aware of it?'

'I would have thought so,' Alice faltered.

'She must know therefore how critical her evidence is. She was there with you when the row took place between Hugh and Roz. She woke up when Hugh came down to the kitchen, she heard Charley cry, she heard Mr Eastwood go to attend to him. She could attest to the fact that you did not harm Charley, and, more, that she too noticed his floppiness before she left?'

'Yes,' whispered Alice.

'She is in fact crucial to your defence. And yet, in spite of almost superhuman efforts to trace her, she has failed to come forward. Can you suggest why?'

Alice shook her head. 'I don't know. I really don't.'

'Come now, Miss Bishop . . .'

'I'm scared something might have happened to her.'

'You fear she might be ill? Or dead?'

Alice swallowed. 'Yes.'

The barrister nodded gravely. 'Certainly no one has heard from her in the past five months. The last communication her mother had was a card last Christmas, posted from these shores.

'We know that she left England, by Eurostar, at noon on the day that Charley was taken to hospital. Where she went after that, why she has failed to appear here today to vouchsafe that

Alice Bishop did not harm Charley Eastwood, remains a mystery.'

The lawyer bowed to the judge, signalling that his examination was complete.

The cross-examination lasted a day and a half. During it, Alice wept but clung to her story. At the end of the week, the prosecution lawyer rose to sum up. The defendant's evidence, he told the jury in his velvety voice, was a pack of lies from start to finish.

There had been no row between Charley's parents. There had been no drinking by Mr Eastwood in the middle of the night; no loss of temper occasioning him to storm upstairs to tend to his infant son.

Charley had only cried twice that night. There had been no third cry, 'peculiarly cut off'.

'The videotape would have proved that, but of course we have no videotape. Not any more. We allege that the defendant destroyed it. Having done so, she believed she had free rein.

'A child of eight had flung Charley about in his pushchair. Incidentally one cannot help but compare the failure of this child's mother to come forward as a witness with the failure of the other vital witness, Kate Armstrong, to appear.'

He paused, leaning forward and then up on his toes, the better to ensure he had everyone's attention. 'On the subject of Miss Armstrong. According to her mother, she is something of a "free spirit", given to disappearing off without a word, for long periods. Five months is by no means unusual for her. Her family certainly do not believe she is ill or dead, merely being herself.

'It is possible, just, that she has not heard of this case, that she is in the jungle of Borneo, or in an ashram in India. But I would suggest that she is fully aware of it, and that knowing the defendant's claims are entirely fictitious, she feels that the best help she can offer her friend is to stay far away from this courtroom.

'Members of the jury, Kate Armstrong did not stay at the Eastwood house. She did not meet Charley; she witnessed nothing.

'Alice Bishop was aware that Kate was due to leave England on the day that Charley was injured. She therefore invented Kate's presence, in the reasonable hope that Kate would not come forward.

'She could not have known how extensive the police hunt for Kate would have been. What anxious moments Alice Bishop must have had, wondering whether her friend would be found, and made to tell the truth.

'But all went well. No trace was found. The defendant entered the witness box last week confident that she could tell us what she liked. And she gave a good performance, did she not? Possibly as good as the one she gave six months ago when she convinced Roz and Hugh Eastwood that their infant son would be safe in her hands.

'Probably no one, bar Alice Bishop, will ever know what brought about the fatal outburst of temper that killed this baby boy. Did his crying infuriate her? Did she harbour a grudge against her employers that erupted in a dreadful rage against him? Or was it much more premeditated than that? Did she take the job planning to murder him all the while? We can only speculate, and that is not our job.

'Our job, members of the jury – your job – is to look at the facts. Charley was shaken to death. Alice Bishop was in sole charge of him when he became unconscious. Not one jot of her alibi has stood up in this courtroom. Vital evidence was deliberately removed.

'I ask you to put pity for the parents of Charley Eastwood out of your minds. I ask you to be dispassionate, to decide this case on the evidence, and nothing else.'

After the defence counsel had made his final speech, the judge summed up. Alice Bishop had been charged with murder. To find her guilty, they would have to believe that she had intended to kill Charley or cause him serious harm.

On the evidence placed before them, they might very well arrive at that verdict.

On the other hand, if they felt that she had shaken him without meaning to cause him death or serious harm, then they could still find her guilty, but of a lesser charge, that of manslaughter.

The judge inhaled deeply. 'Of course you may find her not guilty altogether. It is time for you to consider your verdict.'

The jurors retired at eleven o'clock on that Tuesday morning. The Eastwoods knew that their deliberations could take days; that their solicitor would call them at once if a verdict or even a question from the jury looked imminent, but they could not bring themselves to leave the court building.

The hours of the first day ticked slowly by. At five o'clock, the jury were called back and sent to a hotel for the night.

The Eastwoods returned to the house where they were staying; Mady went home also to her husband Ben and baby son who crowed delightedly when he saw her and raised his arms to be picked up, which she did gladly, then broke down, hugging him fiercely to her as if she would never let him go.

*

The next day at two minutes before noon, the clerk of the court announced that a verdict had been reached.

In the press room, the journalists scrambled. Mady was with Roz and Hugh in their barrister's chambers.

'Thank God,' said Hugh with feeling. He got up.

Roz sat staring into space, as if she hadn't heard.

'Come on,' he said shortly. 'Let's get it over with.'

Still Roz didn't seem able to move. Mady waited awkwardly for Hugh to help his wife up, and when he didn't, she touched Roz's arm herself. 'There's only one verdict they can reach,' she promised.

'Is there?'

In the courtroom, the jury entered single-file to take their seats. The forewoman stood. The clerk read out the murder charge, and asked for the verdict.

'Not guilty,' said the spokeswoman.

The words boomed in Mady's head. Please God, no, she prayed desperately, don't let them do this . . . Beside her, Roz gave a dry sob.

'Regarding the charge of manslaughter . . .' continued the clerk.

Mady closed her eyes. 'Guilty,' she heard the forewoman say quietly.

'Thank you,' whispered Mady.

From the dock, Alice screamed, 'I didn't do it! I didn't do anything! Please, believe me . . .'

Everyone turned. Alice was up on her feet, grasping the handrail, red-faced. 'I loved Charley! I wouldn't ever have hurt him!'

'The defendant will be quiet,' ordered the judge.

'No!' yelled Alice, clinging on. 'Why should I listen to any of you?'

'One more outburst and you will be removed from the court,' warned the judge.

Alice subsided into murmuring.

Sombrely the judge thanked the jury for their verdict. The prosecuting counsel rose to put before the court, as he said, 'certain facts' about the defendant's history.

'Four years ago, in her native New Zealand, Alice Bishop was arrested and questioned about the death of a baby boy . . .'

As the story unfolded, the jury looked less tentative, more sure that they had made the right decision.

The judge had already received and read full medical and psychiatric reports on Alice. He told her to stand.

She was trembling now so badly that it was quite visible from the front of court but, watching, Mady felt not an iota of sympathy, rather nasty anticipation that Alice was about to get what she deserved.

'In failing to reveal your past, you lied in order to gain entry into the home of one of our most respected politicians. There you were responsible for the death of his child—'

'I didn't do it,' howled Alice again.

'Silence!' thundered the judge. 'Having caused the death of this infant you then destroyed evidence and weaved a tissue of lies to hide what you had done.

'I sentence you to six years' imprisonment.'

A cry burst forth from the public gallery where Alice's parents sat. Alice herself looked ashen.

'Take her down,' said the judge.

'It's not fair,' howled Alice. 'I love babies! Please believe me!' She looked wildly round. 'Please, Mady!'

Mady shuddered at the use of her name.

'I didn't do it, Mady! Tell Roz . . .'

'Remove her,' commanded the judge.

Guards unclamped Alice's hands from the rail of the dock and she was dragged down the stairs. Her cries echoed back up into the courtroom before at last there was silence. Mady's heart was still pounding. She felt almost as if she had been physically assaulted.

The court began to clear.

'It's all over,' Mady said to Roz.

'It is?' Roz said dully.

Of course it would never be over for Roz, Mady thought. For Roz there would only ever be grief and sadness, and Mady tiptoeing around her, careful to say the right thing, to keep Archie out of the conversation, out of sight when Roz was there, trying always not to cause more sorrow. Abruptly Mady didn't want it any more. She didn't want a killer shrieking her name in court or the mother of a murdered child for a best friend. She wanted to get home, hold her baby, be able to rejoice at the verdict, to be herself.

Outside the court, Hugh was giving a brief statement to the cameras. He delivered it dead-eyed. Justice had been done. Nothing would ever bring back Charley but at least the person responsible was behind bars.

He helped Roz into their car and it shot off, horn blaring to clear its path of photographers.

Mady made her way through the throng. If there were no hold-ups on the Tube, she could be home in half an hour. On the pavement another press conference was in progress, blocking her way.

'Alice is innocent,' declared a young woman tearfully but with defiance. 'We're going to clear her name.' She waved a banner for the cameras.

The family's campaign had received considerable media attention both before the trial and during it. Now, however, as the losers, they had lost their importance. After a couple of minutes most of the cameras, bar the two from New Zealand, switched off and the journalists started to depart.

'All right, Mady?' asked a colleague concernedly.

She nodded briefly. She had not written about the trial and, for the most part, knowing that she didn't want to discuss the case, fellow journalists had kept out of her way.

'Mady? Mady O'Neil?' queried a boy's voice.

Mady turned. She was being addressed by Alice's seventeen-year-old brother.

'Alice wants to see you. She said if . . . if it went this way, she had to see you. She's got something she must tell you.'

Mady stared at him. 'Why me?'

'She knows you. She trusts you. She's frightened about telling anyone else. Will you see her?'

He looked so like his sister. 'No I won't,' she said curtly.

'Please,' he begged her. 'You're her last chance.'

Her anger flashed. 'What chance did she give Charley?'

'She didn't—'

'Or Roz, or Hugh?'

The boy looked appalled but Mady didn't care. 'Tell your sister she can rot in hell,' she hissed and turned away.

CHAPTER THREE

All television news programmes were extended that night and the story received at least a mention across most of Europe and the English-speaking world, barring much being made of it in America where a childminder was on trial for killing twins.

The following day, the coverage continued with the mother of the New Zealand baby declaring that Alice Bishop should be repatriated to stand trial for the murder of her son too.

In Kensington, the Prime Nanny Agency, which had introduced Alice to the Eastwoods and had always insisted that it had checked her references most thoroughly, abruptly closed down.

The next day, there was a smattering of newspaper stories about Antipodean nannies being summarily fired by their employers; of some nannies being abused in the streets.

By the weekend, just as the story was beginning to run out of steam, one of the Sunday tabloids published a 'snatch' picture of Alice in prison. She was sitting on a bed in a single cell, cradling a telephone against her ear and smiling. The smile made her look both evil and calculating.

'LIFE INSIDE FOR CHARLEY'S KILLER,' screamed the headline.

The article described special treatment for Alice, who was being held temporarily in a men's prison while awaiting transfer. Her vegetarian diet was being catered for; she had a television set in her cell, use of the gym, a counsellor if she needed it . . .

'Where have we gone wrong?' wailed the editorial. 'Isn't prison about punishment? Why then is Bishop being accorded the privileges of a movie star?'

The newspaper cutting was on top of a stack on Mady's desk when she returned to work on Monday morning, her first time back in the office for four weeks, the period of the trial. Throughout it, she had deliberately not read any coverage in the press and now as she glanced through the Alice Bishop cuttings, she was pleased that no violent emotions were aroused at all. Ben was right. That awful chapter of her life was over. Normality would return. Of course she would always support Roz, but her own deep emotional connection, which at times had threatened to overwhelm her, would wane.

She picked up another paper. It was early and the office was still quiet. She had missed the place, missed being a journalist, although the previous night, contemplating her return, she and Ben had talked wistfully of a holiday abroad. They couldn't afford it. Getting back into their old routine of ten-and-twelve-hour days would have to be enough, they had agreed drily.

'Good morning, Mady.'

She had not seen Jack Simpson, the Editor, approach. They had worked together, on and off, for seven years. They liked and respected each other. Jack pulled up a chair alongside her. 'Good to have you back.'

He hesitated. 'Seen your post yet?'

'No.' There were four piles of mail neatly stacked beside her newspapers.

'You've got a letter there from Bishop's father.'

'I have?' she repeated, taken aback.

'Yes. I've had one too, that's how I know.' He picked up a stack and handed her an envelope. 'Read it.'

She raised an eyebrow. 'Right now?'

'Please.'

She shrugged. The envelope bore her name in stiff black lettering. There was no address, so she realised it must have been hand-delivered. She slit it open and extracted a single piece of notepaper, headed with the name of a London hotel. It was dated four days earlier.

'Dear Ms O'Neil,

'My wife and I have just returned from visiting Alice. She "begs" you to see her. Her words not mine. She says it will be to your advantage, as well as hers. I have no idea what she means; she will not discuss this matter with me. I personally would prefer to bring an official complaint against you concerning your abusive behaviour to our young son yesterday, on the most terrible day of his and all our lives. However, Alice is adamant and therefore I look forward to hearing from you shortly.' It was signed, 'Mike Bishop.'

'Bloody nerve,' said Mady lightly.

Jack wasn't smiling. 'I'm afraid it's not as easy as that.'

She frowned. 'Yes it is. She killed my godson, remember? She's in prison. End of story. Who cares what she or her father have got to say?'

'Let's go into my office.'

Wondering what more there could be to say, Mady followed

him in. He closed the door behind her and sat down. 'It would be a great exclusive,' he started.

She looked at him incredulously. 'Maybe. But not for me. Get somebody else to do it.'

'I can't.'

'Why not?'

'Mike Bishop won't have it.'

She couldn't believe what she was hearing. 'You've spoken to him?' she exclaimed.

'I had to.' Jack took a deep breath. 'He's got Collins on his side.'

'Collins?' she repeated dumbly.

Peter Collins owned *The Register* newspaper. A New Zealand tycoon with over fifty media companies across the world, he prided himself on a policy of 'no interference' in his titles. To date, at least publicly, he had kept that promise. There had been no bias shown towards Bishop in *The Register* during the trial. Why would Collins now insist Mady interview Bishop?

Jack said: 'You know you were filmed telling that Bishop kid to piss off?'

'I didn't say that,' she protested.

'Words to that effect. It got a lot of airtime over there. It didn't look or sound pretty . . .'

'It wasn't meant to,' she flashed.

He sighed. 'I know. But Bishop's supporters have milked it for all it's worth. They're powerful over there. Claim it wasn't a fair trial. No one listened to Alice . . .'

'My heart bleeds.'

'They've lobbied their parliament and got some heavyweight politicians on their side, including one who is very important to Collins.'

She felt sick. 'I don't believe this. Alice and her friend killed that New Zealand baby too.'

'There was never any proof of that. Anyway, Collins is being accused of turning against one of his own, of denying one of his countrywomen the right of free speech in favour of, and I quote, one of his "foul-mouthed foreign journalists". He doesn't like it.'

'So he's going to force me to do the interview, that's what you're saying?'

Jack looked down at his desk. 'I'm sorry, but effectively, yes.'

'What happened to our independence?'

'Temporarily misplaced. Mady,' he appealed to her, 'try not to make this a big deal . . .'

She snorted. 'Are you crazy?'

'You've got to do it.'

'I don't.'

He studied her. 'Oh yes you do.'

He didn't need to say more. He knew the state of their finances. Ben had lost his City job a year before. With his redundancy, he had set up an investor relations company, working from home. It would be another twelve months before they knew if he was going to make it.

Moreover, Jack allowed Mady, his chief investigative reporter, outstanding flexibility. He didn't mind if she worked from home, as long as she brought in the stories. That meant that it was possible to juggle Archie's care between herself, Ben and, reluctantly, her mother. After what had happened to Charley, Mady knew she could never leave Archie with a stranger.

'Isn't Collins aware of my relationship to Roz?' she pleaded.

'I've told him. I've done my best for you, Mady, believe me. You don't have an option.'

'You should have let me know sooner.'

'I was trying to give you as long a break as I could. I know what this business has put you through.'

He was a good man, she reminded herself unwillingly.

'You'll do it?' he prompted.

'As you say, I don't have an option.'

'No, but thanks anyway. The deal is, you agree to interview her. That's what I told Collins. You can write what you like.'

'Don't worry, I will.'

'It's being arranged for tomorrow morning. She's being transferred down to the West Country in the afternoon.'

Her pulse quickened. There could be no putting it off. 'Okay,' she said quietly.

She went back to her desk and called Mike Bishop's hotel. There was no reply from his room and she fervently hoped it meant he and his family were gone for good back to New Zealand, but then he answered. When he heard who it was, his voice turned bitter. 'You've left it to the last minute, haven't you? I was just going to put through a call to my friend, Mr Collins.'

She said nothing.

Curtly Bishop informed her that she was to meet Alice's solicitor outside the prison at nine o'clock in the morning. The lawyer would have documentation proving she was in his employ. She would have a half-hour consultation with Alice on her own. No guards would be present, it being ostensibly a legal visit. He gave her the solicitor's name. It was unfamiliar and she said so.

There was a snort from Bishop. 'I fired the old lot first thing this morning, after I found out they took that photograph of Alice and sold it to the Sunday paper.'

'Ah.'

'The British legal system,' Bishop sneered.

When she had hung up, she wondered what Roz's reaction would be to the interview. Would she understand that Mady had been coerced, or would she feel betrayed? Mady didn't want to call her, especially with such news; she and Hugh were still recuperating from the trauma of the trial; they hadn't even returned home yet, as far as she knew, but were still staying in the house they had rented to escape the media's attention. But if Mady didn't forewarn Roz, the first that her friend would know about the interview would be when it appeared in print. Although perhaps, like herself, Roz was avoiding the media?

The burden of caring for Roz descended once more. The day dragged. When she got home, Ben was fraught, having spent the entire day with Archie who he claimed had screamed for most of it. Normally the baby was pleased to see her after an absence, but that evening he pushed her away when she picked him up and continued to scream until Ben took him. Increasingly, Archie was showing a preference for Ben. She felt so jealous and rejected that she went into the bathroom and cried, aware that she was overreacting but unable to do anything about it.

They went to bed early but she lay awake, watching the time flick away on her clock, trying not to think about the morning.

For Hugh, sleep had been drug-induced for months. Before Charley had died, alcohol had helped. Now he did what the doctor ordered and took the little white tablets, one, sometimes two, a night.

He actually preferred them to the whisky; they blotted out everything, gave him six hours of mainly dreamless sleep. There was so much he didn't want to think about. Only when he was particularly stressed would a dream penetrate.

He was asleep now in the house they had rented in a quiet Surrey village. Roz said she felt safe there. Safe, he smiled sardonically in his sleep. No one was ever 'safe' no matter where they were; thoughts could always slip through gates into the unconscious mind, there to provoke and terrorise, to remind one of what the waking mind chose to forget.

Awake, he could not remember what had happened on the night that Charley died. It was a blank. Amnesia, according to the doctor. Asleep, a version of events had played themselves out to him in such terrifying detail that he feared they must be true. He had the dream twice before and now it was coming back. He moaned and moved about on the bed, trying to wake himself up, but the drug pinned him down.

Charley was still alive. He, Hugh, was a father. A tear trickled down his face as he remembered how good that had felt, better than anything else.

He was back at home in Chelsea. Upstairs in the nursery, Charley was crying. Drunk and dead asleep at the kitchen table two floors below, Hugh heard him, and woke up.

His head throbbed most painfully and Charley's screaming was making it so much worse. Didn't he have enough to cope with, without a screaming brat? Why didn't somebody shut him up?

Roz had said it was his turn that night. They had rowed about it. First in the restaurant over dinner, and afterwards down in the kitchen where he sat now. Roz hissing that she wasn't a dull little housewife any more. She was back at work; Hugh had to share night-duty. And Hugh himself, most unlike himself, mewling that Alice would have to do it for once, other nannies did nights; it was crazy Alice didn't . . . He was too tired, he was frightened, he was slipping off the edge; wouldn't Roz please help him? Wouldn't she listen to his problems?

But Roz wasn't interested. She was exhausted too; she had her own problems. He knew the score: turn and turn about. Parenthood was about sacrifices. She had gone to bed and determinedly to sleep, not waking – or seeming not to – when Charley had cried, leaving Hugh to get up and go in to comfort him and by then too wide awake for sleep, to seek refuge down in the kitchen with the bottle, as he had so often that week.

In his dream Charley was yelling again for a third time.

'Shut up,' he swore viciously. He lurched to his feet. He saw his own hands, enormous and red, angry. He leaped for the stairs and was on the first floor before he knew it. It was such a real dream. Their bedroom door was ajar. Roz was in there, in bed but awake, waiting for him, watching to see when he arrived. She smiled when she saw him, and with an elaborate yawn, turned her back.

Blood thundered in his head. But he knew how to get his own back. He charged into Charley's room.

'Hugh, wake up.'

Was he dreaming still? He heard the voice pulling him out and clung to it as to a lifeline. He surfaced at last, awake.

'You're having a nightmare, that's all.'

He looked up into his wife's concerned face. She had saved him again. The memory of what he had done, or not done, was already retreating. He could not grasp it any more.

'Are you all right?' she asked anxiously.

She looked as if she loved him still. Had she lied for him? Could he trust her?

'I'm fine,' he snapped.

Her expression faltered.

'Go back to sleep,' he urged her more gently, more in keeping with the man he had been before his world fell apart, before he had been dealt more than any man could cope with. He felt tears close by and shut his eyes. He had a live radio interview in the morning, his first since the trial. That would explain the stress that had caused the dream. He turned on his side so Roz couldn't see and pretended to fall asleep.

CHAPTER FOUR

The prison was in south London, grim red-brick Victorian, set back from a busy dual carriageway and overlooking some of the most expensive family homes in the capital.

At 08.25 that morning, Mady circled the area trying to find a parking space. Vicious mothers in Jeeps deliberately jammed each other in roads outside school entrances.

On the car radio, the sports news ended; the headlines followed and then the programme's next guest was announced: Hugh Eastwood, who would be discussing the Government's latest proposals to improve family life.

So Hugh was back in public life so soon after the trial? Perhaps that was no bad thing, Mady thought. Going back to work part-time, a month after Charley's death, had saved Roz, in Mady's opinion. She hoped she would return to work full-time very soon.

On the radio, the interviewer did not refer to Charley or the trial before Hugh came on the air:

'Our teenage pregnancy record is the highest in Europe. Children born to young single mothers perform less well at school, enjoy poorer health and, figures suggest, are more likely to be unemployed than their counterparts.'

He sounded like his old self, Mady thought. Firm, authoritative, and yet compassionate. But the subject matter must surely be painful for him?

'Young people about to embark on parenthood must be made aware of the difficulties they face as well as the joys. The strain and demands on relationships. The sleepless nights . . .'

Mady shuddered. He was talking about people getting desperate, to the point of breaking, of harming their children . . . how could he after what had happened?

'Are you urging young girls to get abortions, Minister?' queried the interviewer mildly.

'Abortion is an option, and for many the best,' declared Hugh.

That should grab the headlines, Mady judged, which was no doubt his intention.

Abortion should be made easier for young women, Hugh went on, and the 'morning-after' pill available over the counter for anyone who needed it, irrespective of their age.

He was in full flow but Mady found a parking space and gladly switched him off. She needed to get him, and Roz, out of her mind. She needed to prepare herself for Alice.

A homeopath had once advised her to zip herself mentally into a plastic bubble before conducting interviews. Ben had mocked, but Mady found the device useful when she was feeling particularly apprehensive. She walked down the tree-lined street, imagining herself cocooned in that bubble, cotton-woolled against Alice.

She found the road she was looking for and the solicitor's Saab double-parked, waiting for her. She got in, and they exchanged brief introductions. He handed her a file of Alice's police statements – for camouflage purposes, he explained, not that she ought to need it. And there was her false identification tag as well.

She stared at it. Under the laminated plastic was a head-and-shoulders snapshot of her.

'Your office sent it over yesterday,' the lawyer explained.

'Yes.' But she felt manoeuvred and she hated to feel like that. 'Aren't you taking an awful risk, smuggling me in?' she asked of the lawyer.

'No choice,' he said flatly.

'What do you mean?'

He drove off towards the prison. 'Our client insists.'

'You could tell her it couldn't be done.'

'Then she wouldn't co-operate with us.'

'Powerful, isn't she, considering she's a convicted killer?'

He paused at a junction.

'Who's paying your fees?' she asked.

'You wouldn't be able to write it even if I told you.'

Peter Collins, she guessed. Alice Bishop's family – Mike, a garage mechanic and Heidi, a secretary – had managed to attach themselves to power, in its most despicable form, all because their daughter had killed a baby.

She could stop it, Mady reminded herself. She could refuse to do the interview and walk out on her job. Write the story of corruption on *The Register* for another paper – which would earn her a fat one-off fee, if she was lucky, and then what? Freelancing, living from day to day, having to accept any and all commissions because she needed to pay the mortgage. She wasn't brave enough. She couldn't do it to Ben or Archie.

The car turned into the prison entrance. A barrier lay across their path and a guard emerged from a booth. He checked their names on his clipboard, stared at their identification tags for a long time, hers in particular or so it seemed, and then the barrier rose and they proceeded gingerly to a designated parking bay.

Part of the prison was being extended and the lawyer led her up the ramp of a Portakabin. He pressed a door buzzer and again gave their names. A swivelling CCTV camera watched them, recording her presence, Mady thought, creating the evidence that she was there, breaking half a dozen codes of practice. To be in violation not to expose a terrible wrong, but simply to do her master's bidding . . . It flew in the face of everything she believed in.

The entry door clicked open and a guard motioned them through a metal detector. They were shown into a small side room and told to wait. Neither spoke. From outside came the monotonous hammer of a pneumatic drill. Mady glanced at her watch. 09.03. Her mother would have arrived to look after Archie. Ben had a meeting he had to attend in the City. Mady hoped Archie would look pleased to see his grandmother – often he didn't, frequently he howled at the sight of her. After the interview Mady intended to get home as quickly as she could.

A prison official appeared and asked them to follow him. They went down dark corridors of red linoleum and pale green walls, through innumerable doors, then up stone steps and into a newer section of the prison. There the floor was carpeted dismal brown. The official came to a halt at last before a steel door with a spyhole. A warden stood on guard, waiting for them.

'She's all yours,' the official addressed the lawyer.

'Actually my colleague is going to conduct the interview.'

'Fine.' He pressed a code into the key pad on the wall, and the door clicked open. Mady's stomach was jumping as she went in.

She saw Alice at once, sitting at a table in the middle of the room. Alice looked round nervously, and when she saw Mady, she started but said nothing. She followed Mady's progress across the floor to the chair opposite her own.

The door closed with a click.

'Oh Mady,' she breathed. 'I'm so pleased you got in.'

She did look genuinely delighted, Mady saw. She remembered when she had really liked Alice. On the second of the three occasions Mady had met her, she had talked to the New Zealander for some time and felt that they had clicked. Alice had a wry sense of humour, and she was, Mady had thought, a genuinely nice girl. How wrong she had been, and how wrong Alice was now to suppose that any of that liking remained.

'I was worried maybe they wouldn't—' Alice stopped, scanning Mady's face. 'I'm glad you're here,' she finished more soberly.

She was wearing her own clothes and looked better, Mady thought, than she had in court. More rested, less tense. To her annoyance she saw that she herself was shaking and bent to unclip her briefcase, hoping to calm down.

'I know you didn't want to come,' Alice faltered.

Mady took out her notepad. Her mouth felt dry and she didn't quite trust herself to speak.

Alice bit her lip. It went white and then pink as the blood surged back. 'All I ask is that you listen.' She glanced at the door and back again. 'None of this must be published,' she said softly.

Mady found her voice at last. She said sarcastically, 'I thought that was the whole idea.'

'No. Please don't even talk about what I'm going to say. In case they hurt me, or my family.'

Mady stared at her.

'You know how important Hugh is. I don't know how far they'd go to protect him.'

'What exactly do you want to tell me?' Mady asked crisply.

'I didn't kill Charley.'

'Of course not.'

'Please. Just pretend to believe me for one second. Ask yourself: if I didn't, who did? I don't think it was that little girl in the playground.'

'At least we're agreed on that.'

'And no way was it Kate.' Alice looked her straight in the eye. 'That leaves Roz or Hugh, I'm afraid.'

Mady felt anger burn inside her. She had been wrong to come.

'Please,' Alice begged. 'I know how close you are to Roz. I know what a shock this must be, but you see, Hugh was under terrible pressure that week. I don't think Roz knew.'

Mady had meant to say nothing but she couldn't help herself. 'He confided in you, did he?'

Alice shook her head. She spoke fast as if she knew Mady was about to walk out. 'I overheard him on the phone the week before Charley died. It was the Tuesday afternoon. He didn't realise I was in the house. I'd popped back to get Charley's blanket and Hugh had left his study door open. I didn't know he was in there, but then he made a sound, like a . . . well, like he was crying. He said, "This is going to ruin me. I won't have anything left. Please don't do this to me . . ." He was begging; I'd never heard him sound like that.'

It sounded authentic. For a brief moment, Mady entertained the notion, as she had in court, that perhaps Hugh had been in trouble? But Roz would have known; Roz would have told her – wouldn't she?

Alice was still talking earnestly: 'Hugh said, "I'll pay you. Anything you like. Everyone's got their price." Then he said, "Why don't you lose the film?" He'd something Trump Card wouldn't be able to refuse . . .'

'Trump Card?' Mady queried aloud. The name was distantly familiar.

'Yes. Then he said, "How about the inside track on the Grey Team?" '

Mady caught her breath. The Grey Team did not officially exist. They were the dirty tricks brigade that Number Ten had supposedly used to smear their opponents in the last General Election. There had been rumours of Watergate-style break-ins at party headquarters, illegal telephone taps and suggestions that a prostitute had been paid to ensnare a politician.

Mady knew that the Grey Team did exist because at a drunken dinner party, Hugh had admitted it to her. Even drunk, however, he had refused to do more than confirm the Team's existence. 'One day, my little friend, you shall have it all,' he had teased, attempting a slobbery, winy kiss, 'and what a story that would make, eh?'

Mady's heart thumped. Was Alice telling the truth? What sort of trouble could Hugh possibly be in that he had tried bartering with such dirt? And who had he been talking to? 'Trump Card' . . . she thought furiously. It was media-related. She got it: it was a production company, one of the small ones that had done terribly well with a scoop two or three years before . . . something to do with the Royals, if she remembered correctly.

What could they have on Hugh? In his youth he had been notoriously wild, but all that had been documented, and nobody cared about it now. Now he was viewed as an out-spoken but clean politician, his public ratings at an all-time high because of Charley. He was being talked of as a potential candidate for leadership of his party.

Across the table, Alice was watching her closely. 'Do you believe me?'

Mady felt chilled. She hated Alice. She was a killer, a cal-culating liar who would say anything to free herself, and what better recruit for her cause than Mady, investigative journalist, best friend of Roz? And yet, how could she know about the Grey Team?

She could have overheard Hugh talking unwisely to a colleague. She could have remembered the name 'Trump Card' from the documentary, and meshed them together for Mady's benefit . . . Mady knew she was clutching at straws. As a non-journalist, as well as a foreigner, Alice could not know the significance of the Grey Team. Was it possible she had come across the name in a paper Hugh had been foolish enough to leave lying about the house?

'What else did Hugh say?' she demanded.

Alice looked startled. 'Nothing. I mean nothing special. I think he was listening. He said, "You do that," then he put down the phone.'

She could find out what Trump Card was working on, Mady thought, gauge for herself its significance, whether its exposure would have been enough to make Hugh so desperate that he could have harmed Charley. She tried to imagine that picture and could not. She remembered instead visiting Roz not long after Charley had been brought home from hospital, and going downstairs into the kitchen to find Hugh cradling his tiny newborn son, and the look of utter adoration on the man's face which had brought her quick tears.

Hugh had been at his softest, most likeable with Charley. He couldn't have hurt him . . . But if he had been in trouble? He had a terrible temper. Mady had seen it, and heard about it too from Roz. He had never been violent, to the best of her knowledge, preferring cruel words rather than blows, but if he had wanted to hurt Charley? A baby couldn't be hurt by words.

She teetered.

Hugh, more than anyone else she knew, knew how to conduct cover-ups, how to lie, and convince others of what he believed in. Mady remembered the political editor at the paper saying that if Eastwood announced black was white, a sizeable proportion of the population would believe it. Hugh could hide behind his public persona, confident that everyone, including Roz, would assume it had been the nanny.

She looked over at Alice, trying to see her in a different light, but she had spent so long believing in her guilt that it was difficult to switch.

At the door, the cover on the spyhole swung up. Someone was checking on them.

Mady leant forward until her face was inches from Alice's. 'What I don't understand, Alice, is why you didn't mention this crucial piece of evidence before? Like at your trial? Or to your solicitor? Or the police? It's a bit like how you forgot to mention Kate being around until two weeks after your arrest. Don't you think?'

'I was scared . . .'

'Why tell me? Is it for sheer dramatic purposes?'

Tears welled in Alice's eyes. 'You hate me, don't you?'

'My feelings don't come into it.'

'I did try to tell someone. Not at first, I admit. I was in such a state of shock, I couldn't remember anything. But later on, I told my solicitor. He thought I shouldn't say anything because of Hugh being a minister. He said it would only look as if I was making up stories.'

'Great advice,' said Mady.

Alice shrugged. When she spoke again there was a harshness in her voice that Mady hadn't heard before. 'I didn't know any better then, did I? I didn't know the system. When I was on remand, I tried telling a policeman about it, a detective who used to come to see me. He said we didn't need a solicitor present.'

Mady looked disbelieving.

'I've said, haven't I, that I didn't know the system? I didn't know I was being screwed.'

There was more anger in her than Mady had seen before. She wondered what another year in prison would do to Alice, another six years?

'I started to tell the detective about Hugh . . .' Alice went on.

'And?'

'. . . he told me the same thing, near enough, as the solicitor. That if he was in my position, he wouldn't go around "casting aspersions about good men". It wouldn't go down well with the jury.'

Had there been a cover-up, Mady found herself wondering? The powers-that-be protecting the elite? Hugh was popular with the police force. He had got them a payrise. But no. To an officer convinced of Alice's guilt, her story would sound pathetic. He would have heard it a thousand times before from a thousand suspects. He would have dismissed it, as Mady would have, had she cut Alice off before she had mentioned the Grey Team.

Alice continued: 'When we got to court, I thought, "they're going to believe me. They're going to know I'm telling the truth." But no one listened to me.'

'Have you told your new solicitor?' Mady asked.

Alice shook her head.

'Why ever not?'

She looked mulish. 'I only met him yesterday. Why should I trust him? The last one sold me down the river to get that picture into the newspapers.'

That much was true. 'You have really told nobody else? Peter Collins, for instance?'

'What?'

Mady studied her. 'You don't know?'

'Know what? What's he got to do with it?'

'It doesn't matter.' But Mady wondered what Collins would say if he knew the wildness of Alice's allegations. What Roz would say?

'What's the good of just telling people, anyway?' Alice continued. 'It would only be my word against Hugh's. That's what my old solicitor said. We'd no proof, and who would believe a nanny against a minister?'

A nanny, all of whose witnesses had failed to materialise. A nanny whose previous charge had died mysteriously. If Hugh was guilty – she suspended her disbelief – how delighted he must have been when Alice's history came to light.

'Hugh was right,' said Alice bitterly. 'Everyone thinks I did it. No one believes a word I say. Take that tape! I never knew I was being filmed. I never knew there were cameras in the house. I didn't destroy the tape. I didn't replace it with an old one. I reckon Hugh did.'

Was she right? Or was Mady only willing to toy with her accusation because she didn't like Hugh? 'What do you expect me to do with this?' she asked.

'Get the proof.'

'Oh sure.' It was only what she had thought of herself, but she rebelled at being told what to do by Alice. 'And if I refuse?'

Alice sagged. 'I suppose I'll have to tell my solicitor in the end.'

Mady thought quickly. If she did that, Hugh and Roz would be questioned and she doubted whether Roz could bear that. Whereas if she, Mady, put out a few feelers, cleared Hugh – as she surely would – no one need know. If she found evidence to suggest Hugh might be guilty . . . the chasm yawned again.

Alice said quietly: 'I'm not guilty, Mady. I don't know if Hugh is. All I'm saying is, he had more reason to lose his rag and kill Charley than I did. And I don't see why I should pay the price because I was just the nanny.'

A silence fell between them. In it, Mady remembered arriving at Roz's house with Archie screaming. Alice had offered to take him, and he had settled at once. Alice had entertained him and Charley in the family room for the rest of the afternoon, while their mothers had sat out on the patio, watching through the window. After a while, so excellent had Alice seemed with both babies, that had stopped watching.

Mady had thought Alice quite wonderful. She remembered how deeply she had envied Roz when she had left that afternoon.

'Will you do it?' begged Alice from across the table.

There came a tap at the door. Time was up.

'Please? You're the one person I could think of . . .' Her eyes met Mady's.

'I'll see what I can do,' Mady promised. The door opened and, before she could be called, Mady left the room.

During the high season, the resort on the tiny Greek island of Laros was swamped by German holiday-makers. In November, owing to its warm climate and unspoilt terrain, it was still popular with the Swedes and the British.

Kate Armstrong's job remained the same as it had been all summer: to supervise the maids who cleaned the villas.

At noon that Tuesday, she let herself into Jasmine Villa on the far side of the island. She saw at once that the maid hadn't been. The kitchen was a mess, the beds unmade; the guests, already noted as difficult, would be furious.

Swearing softly to herself, Kate set to work. She stripped the beds, thanking God for clean sheets in the cupboard, then moved into the sitting room. Books, magazines and beer cans lay strewn about the place. On her knees, Kate painfully extracted some of the debris from beneath the sofa.

She pulled out a newspaper, an English tabloid. She saw the headline, 'Killer Nanny Jailed', and the photograph. A wave of disbelief, and then of nausea, swept over her.

With blinding clarity, she remembered that morning in Chelsea. Alice's mild concern about the baby; her own suggestion that they put him down early for his nap, and how sweet he'd looked lying there zonked out in his buggy when she had gone past to get her forgotten make-up bag. So sweet, so like Baby Simon in Auckland. She hadn't held a baby since Simon . . .

That memory led into another: the grey, windowless room in

the police station in Auckland, the endless questions, the suspicion in the policeman's face, her own transformation from a nice girl into a monster. And she hadn't done anything! Neither, she knew, or thought she did, had Alice. But here, it had happened again.

Had Alice done it?

Of course not! She had to go back and save her friend, both of them backing each other up, the way they had before.

But if she went back, they'd question her like they had that other time. Her trembling increased. If the best happened, if they believed her and released Alice, what then? Someone must have killed that baby. She, Kate, had been alone with that baby. They would be looking for a scapegoat; the same way they had with Simon.

Sweat broke out on her forehead.

No one had found her yet, and how likely now were they to do so? She cast her mind back. She hadn't had to show her passport at either Waterloo or Paris. From Marseilles she had got the ferry to Corsica, and then crewed on yacht charters, winding up at Piraeus. She had shown her papers several times, but to border guards who clearly hadn't bothered to enter her details on computer. At Piraeus, she had gone island-hopping, as so many travellers did, arriving at Laros in June, where she had then stayed. Her movements had escaped official notice.

She had not looked at a newspaper or watched television in months. Kate glanced again at the headline. She made a little moaning sound. They were blaming Alice for that baby's death, just as they had tried blaming her for Simon in Auckland.

Kate turned the pages and saw her own name, the reference to worldwide appeals for her to come forward and stand up for her friend.

She couldn't. She had made a new, wonderful life for herself there in Laros. She had met Dimitris, a kind, gentle man, who was in love with her, and treated her well. To give him up, all she had made for herself, to return to England and the police . . .

If Alice knew the truth, Alice wouldn't want her to go. Alice knew what an awful life she'd had. Alice would want her to stay there with Dimitris, where she was safe and happy at last.

Kate stuffed the newspaper into the black rubbish sack and tipped the beer cans on top of it. She wouldn't think about it any more; she would take care not to read any more papers, or watch television, which was easy because she didn't own a set.

She dragged the sack into the kitchen, and set to work there with a will.

Although Sally Winter claimed to dislike watching daytime television, she usually switched on the set when she was at home on her own. It kept her company, she excused herself, while she did her dull household tasks.

She saw that a chat show was coming on and went to fetch the ironing. When she returned, the audience was clapping the arrival of their host who in turn was holding out his arm in welcome to that morning's guests. The sound was too low; Sally increased the volume.

' . . . the family of Alice Bishop, the young New Zealand woman found guilty last week of . . .'

Sally knew what she had been found guilty of, as she guessed most of the country did. She stared at the girl's parents. Nice-looking people, she thought distractedly. She hadn't seen them for any length of time before, having previously only caught glimpses on the news. They looked exhausted, desperate, but in their place, she asked herself, who wouldn't be?

'. . . Now campaigning to have their daughter sent home so that at least they can visit her . . .'

Sally had thought that after the court case the matter would be finished and she could forget about it. She didn't have to watch the parents, she reminded herself, staring transfixed at the screen.

The father was talking. The mother sat working her hands together. 'We're poor people,' the father was saying. 'We can't visit her here every year for six years . . .'

'Are you saying the sentence should be reduced?'

'Of course it should. To nothing. Alice is innocent. They had no evidence against her . . .'

The presenter reminded him that her alibi had not stood up in court.

Sally's mouth went dry. There it was again. Somebody else talking about the witness, or lack of.

Sally had never imagined for one moment that they would find that lovely girl guilty. She had been so good with children. That was why, after recognising her from the picture in the paper after her arrest, Sally had kept quiet. They'd realise their mistake, she told herself, they'd release her. When months of silence had followed, Sally had almost convinced herself that it hadn't happened, that poor baby was still alive; she, Sally, didn't have to do anything.

Camilla had not hurt that baby. But the incident had occurred more or less exactly as the nanny had described at the trial.

Camilla loved babies. When reproved, she'd told Sally tearfully that she had only been jiggling the baby to make him look up at a kite in the sky, she hadn't know her own strength. The fault lay with Sally herself and the nanny, if it lay anywhere, in letting Camilla take the baby in the first place.

A minor fault, a minor piece of evidence that would have made no difference to the outcome of the trial, Sally had reassured herself time and time again.

And yet. If the nanny was telling the truth about that, which Sally knew her to be doing, what else was she telling the truth about? Sally believed her when she said she hadn't done it. That was what she imagined the jury doing, but then, she acknowledged, the jury didn't know what she did.

She ought to have spoken up at the very beginning. But she hadn't wanted her little girl interrogated by the police, photographed, made out to be some sort of criminal.

Sally closed her eyes. Camilla had not hurt that baby.

'We don't know why Kate Armstrong hasn't come forward . . .' the father was saying thickly to the TV host.

'Or the mother of the little girl?'

Sally's eyes snapped open. That was too much. Her hand moved to the remote control to switch it off.

'I don't know . . .' the father choked. 'Imagine how you'd feel if you were us.'

Sally tasted salt tears and saw that on the screen both parents were crying too. In a heartfelt voice, the host asked the audience, both in the studio and at home, if anyone had anything to say?

CHAPTER FIVE

Within the confines of the prison, Alice's lawyer remained tight-lipped. As soon as they reached the safety of his car, however, he asked how the interview had gone. Mady had been expecting the question and awkwardly she told him she could say nothing.

'Oh come on, we're in this together. I got you in there . . .'

'Sorry.'

Without speaking again, he dropped her at her car. She set off for the office knowing she had to see Jack in person. On her way, she called home to ask her mother to stay on with Archie and, with bad grace, her mother agreed to.

As soon as Mady entered the newsroom, she saw by the level of activity and the number of telephones ringing that a major story had broken.

'Mady! Good,' cried the news editor. 'Been trying to get hold of you. Jack said you've got a wing-ding exclusive on Bishop?'

'I, er . . .' Damn Jack, she thought.

'We need it now, fast.'

'What's happened?' she asked uneasily.

'The mother of the kid in the playground has come forward. Phoned a TV show half an hour ago, owned up it had happened just like Bishop said.'

A coldness like velvet crept down Mady's back. Alice had been telling the truth about that, as well as the Grey Team. What else had she accurately reported? Had the row in the kitchen between Hugh and Roz taken place? A row that Roz as well as Hugh had denied, on oath? Mady had never doubted her friend before, but now she thought: did Roz know what Hugh had done? Was she covering up for him? She felt her mind spinning. It was too horrible, she was going too fast. She needed definitive proof before she switched sides and believed Alice over her friend. She saw Jack was talking hard to the picture editor. She approached them.

'Mady! How did it go? Terrific timing, huh? D'you think you can do us a thousand words?'

She asked if she could talk to him in private.

'What? Sure, okay.'

They went into his office. 'Well?' he asked, still hyper.

She summoned her strength. 'I can't write it.'

'Ha ha.' He frowned. 'Why the hell not?'

She had thought about it carefully in the car. If she wrote anything about her visit, it would alert Hugh to the fact that she had been talking to Alice. If he was guilty, he would know she was on his trail. He would muddy the waters, or disappear, or even harm Roz.

'I need to check out what Alice told me first,' she said.

'What is it?' Jack demanded instantly, as she had known he would.

'I can't tell you.'

His brow buckled. 'Stop fucking me around.'

She took a deep breath. 'I think just maybe she didn't do it.'

That shook him. He asked softly, 'What the hell's she's been saying to make you change sides?'

She said nothing.

'Who's she saying did it? The kid? She's a skinny little eight-year-old . . .'

'No . . .'

He sneered. 'Not "Have-it-out" Hugh Eastwood?'

Mady had forgotten about Hugh's abortion speech. She felt herself change colour but Jack moved on: 'Or Roz Clayton, society journalist of the year?'

She looked up at him.

'Sorry. Forget I said that.' He sighed. 'I hope this is worth it. You'll need to go off-rota?'

She nodded.

'You'll be quick.'

'As quick as I can be.'

'Okay.' Suddenly wistful, he added, 'You couldn't write me a colour piece, could you? It's such great timing with this other story breaking, and you could keep off the meaty stuff. Just say what she looked like, how she seemed, you know?'

'I know, but then I'd be flagging I'd been there.'

Jack's face sagged. 'Okay, okay.'

Mady went to her desk. On her way, two colleagues asked her how the Bishop interview had gone. It was like being in sniper valley, she thought; she had to get out of there. She gathered her things together, and her telephone rang. 'Yup?'

'Oh God, Mady? Is that you?' It was Roz, sounding desperately upset. 'They've found that little girl. They're saying we did it!'

'No, they're not,' Mady soothed automatically, as she had been doing for months, but even as she did so, she acknowledged how differently she felt now. The possibility was there that Roz was lying. If only she could ask the direct question, but then Hugh would be warned. She had become a spy. 'Of course you didn't do it,' she murmured, hating herself, but Roz didn't appear to have heard her. She was speaking too fast:

'We've had the most terrible row. The first time since Charley . . .'

'I'm not surprised. The relief of the trial being over, and now this . . .'

'No,' said Roz firmly, 'you don't understand.'

Didn't she? Mady heard her own heartbeat. Was it going to be that easy? Roz confessing to her right now? A nasty thought occurred that she should get her tape recorder going.

'We rowed this morning before he went to work, before the mother of this child came forward. Hugh said—' She broke off. 'My head hurts, Mady.'

'Poor love.'

'Can I see you?'

Mady didn't know if she could do it, if she was ready. 'But, er, aren't you miles away?'

'I can be in London in less than an hour. Please?'

Her best friend was pleading for her help. What option did she have? Reluctantly, she agreed to meet her at home.

The first Hugh knew that the child had surfaced was on the midday news on the vast television set in his office. It disoriented him. It made him think, perhaps Alice hadn't done it, perhaps an innocent child was his son's killer? Then they'd flashed up Camilla Winter's photograph on the screen and he had dismissed that notion.

The child merely proved that Alice Bishop had been telling the truth in one small part. It didn't let her off the hook. Even a liar had to tell the truth sometimes, Hugh told himself rapidly, as rapidly as he was breathing. Nothing had changed. He wasn't culpable in any way. He started. What was he thinking of? The killer was behind bars.

'Minister? Are you all right?'

He had forgotten about the presence on the sofa of Alan Hardy, his Special Political Advisor and currently the most important man in his life. Alan, the best in the business, had been brought in to groom Hugh for stardom. 'Quite all right,' Hugh managed gruffly.

Alan's eyes lingered. 'It would help if they bloody well left it alone, wouldn't it?' he asked gently.

Hugh gave a quick nod. That morning he and Roz had rowed. They had both said some things that would have been better left unsaid, dreadful, hurtful things . . .

'Here you are now,' interposed Alan, still looking at him concernedly.

Again, Hugh brought himself back to the present. He couldn't afford to drift off in front of Alan. They were there to monitor the coverage Hugh was receiving as 'Have-it-out' Hugh Eastwood. The cameras has been there in his office.

On air, the newsreader described him as the father of a dead child and now Family Minister, advocate of abortion.

Dead babies. What a thing to be known for. Hugh suppressed a shudder and concentrated on his screen image. He looked good, he had to admit: handsome, mature as he sat squarely behind his desk, prepared to do battle for his beliefs, no matter how unpopular.

'We cannot shy away from the truth. Abortion has become

an almost taboo subject, giving birth to unwanted children, the norm. Why? Only due to a powerful anti-abortion lobby whose views, I suggest, are specious, but which have been taken up by a wide cross-section of the medical professions, people who should know better.'

After Hugh came an angry proponent of the pro-life lobby.

Alan killed the sound. 'Coming along nicely,' he commented and Hugh nodded. The abortion idea had been Alan's: startling, emotive, headline-grabbing, and yet, viewed in a few months' time, not such an outrageous idea that it would put off the party faithful.

Wasn't the criticism of the present government that it was dull? Afraid of its own shadow? That the prime minister, in seeking to be everyone's friend, had become too weak to rule, and that in turn he had weakened his party, perhaps irretrievably?

A general election was due to be held the following summer and internally the putsch to oust the Prime Minster had already begun. It was a campaign orchestrated by the Home Secretary herself, Rebecca Moynihan, a woman whom the PM regarded not only as his ablest minister, but close friend and confidante.

It was she who had suggested to the PM the previous spring (a month before Charley's death) that Hugh be brought down from the back benches. He was an arrogant, still youngish man, Rebecca opined, just the type they were looking for, who could be persuaded to put his head above the parapet, say firm, bold things – the sort of things the Opposition mocked them for not saying – boost the party's standing, and then got rid of well before the race for the election began.

The Prime Minister had been doubtful. He had spent seven years in power, and during the last term had deliberately surrounded himself by men and women who were unlikely to challenge him. Hugh on the other hand had a history. He was flamboyant and boisterous. His wife was sharp and independent and, worst of all, a journalist.

But the Home Secretary had been at her most persuasive. Government needed a firework or two. She and Alan Hardy could handle Eastwood and Roz Clayton. Hugh would be dancing to their tune and when the music stopped, he would be gone. To Hugh they had told a different story.

He had gratefully accepted his new appointment. Following Charley's death, the Abortion Debate, initially planned for June, had gone on hold until now. After it, there would come a call for a curfew on all twelve- to sixteen-year-olds, with the sweetener of a hand-out for good exam results, and in the New Year a substantial increase in family support was planned for the most needy. Then, the Prime Minister had been told, Hugh would bow out, on the promise – never to be realised, naturally – of a Cabinet position.

'And if he doesn't?' the PM had worried, already concerned by the scale of Hugh's post-trial popularity.

'Trust me,' Rebecca had sworn.

Of Hugh, the morning after the trial, she had demanded to know if he was still up to it, or if his baby's death had knocked the stuffing out of him? Hugh had taken only a moment to consider. He knew it was now or never. He was an outsider, too junior for such high office, but now how the public loved him. Past problems, once so enormous, had slipped back into abeyance, hopefully never to resurface. And as Rebecca had told him repeatedly, the power was there for those best able to seize it.

He had told her he was ready, he could do it, and he knew he could, as long as he kept his head focused, the lid screwed tightly down on errant thoughts, and Alan and Rebecca pleased with his performances. They were a dazzling pair: Rebecca with the vision and the clout, Alan with the ideas and the flair to carry them out. Hugh knew one thing for certain already: he didn't trust them an inch. Once he was PM, he would fire them both.

Alan took a call on his mobile. Still listening, he got to his feet, slipped on his jacket, and motioned Hugh to do likewise. It was a producer from *The World at One*. They would devote the lion's share of the programme to Hugh, but they wanted him in the studio, now.

Dutifully, Hugh followed Alan to the door.

CHAPTER SIX

As Mady was driving up her street, she saw Roz emerging from a taxi outside her front door. Give me time to get home, she thought irritably, let me breathe, and then she recalled what she was about to do to her best friend. Pump her. Hope that she might be in such a state she would make a slip about Hugh. The least she could do, Mady admonished herself, was to be kind.

The taxi moved off and Mady tooted. Roz swung round as if she'd been shot and then, seeing Mady, stood there stuck to the ground outside the house until Mady parked and caught up with her. Her face was swollen with crying. She appeared to have lost weight even in the last week, Mady thought, kissing her, and she also looked as if she hadn't slept. She couldn't interrogate her in that state: what had she been thinking of?

Roz clung to her arm. 'I just needed to see you, I'm sorry.' More tears were not far off and Mady hurried her up to the front door.

Roz hadn't been there since Charley died. Mady fervently hoped that Archie wouldn't be screeching, or her mother strident, but the house was absolutely quiet. She called out and Ben answered from the basement where he worked.

With an apology and a promise not to be a moment – not that Roz seemed to be listening – Mady put her in the sitting room and went down the cellar steps. Ben was seated at his desk, the low room lit by uplighters.

'Where's Archie?' she demanded hoarsely. She knew how voices carried in their house and she didn't want Roz to overhear her.

'In his cot. Asleep. Your mother put him there the moment I came in. Great to see you, by the way,' he grinned up at her, his spiky grey hair on end from a too short haircut and looking, she suddenly thought, vulnerable, his best look, or so she had always thought.

'Good to see you too.' She bent and kissed him. 'I'm afraid I've got—'

'An overwhelming desire for your husband.' He pulled her down on to his knee and nuzzled her neck. It was nice.

'Um, Roz is upstairs.'

His expression went flat.

'She's in a bit of a state.'

He sighed. 'When isn't she?'

'Ben . . .'

He could not have been more shocked at Charley's death or more understanding initially of Roz's desperate dependency and Mady's desire to be of help, but as the months had dragged on, his patience had worn thin. He and Mady had argued, which they rarely did, him accusing her of forever putting Roz first, Archie second, himself a poor third. No one had been happier than he when the trial ended, when Roz and her tragedy had withdrawn finally from their lives. He'd likened it to a prison door opening.

Keeping her voice quiet, Mady quickly told him a little of
Alice's allegations and Roz's desperate call to her at work. It
didn't occur to her to keep any of it a secret from him, they told
each other everything. She saw that in spite of himself Ben was
intrigued. 'Hugh did it?' he breathed.

'I don't know . . .' Hearing Ben say it, it sounded as ludicrous
as when she'd first thought it.

'He was nuts about Charley!'

'I know . . .'

'What did she say the row had been about?'

'She didn't.'

'Well, go and find out.' He pushed her off his knee.

'I can't. She's in an awful state.'

'Don't be wet.'

'I'm not wet,' she protested, ducking to avoid a beam in the
cellar ceiling. 'She's my friend. I can't pump her for dirt when
she's like this.'

Ben rolled his eyes. 'Has it not dawned on you that she wants
to unburden herself? And who else would she do that to? I'll
manage Archie if he yowls.'

He had the baby monitor on his desk. She bent to give him
a quick kiss. 'You're an angel.'

'M-m-m.'

She left him. In the sitting room, Roz was exactly where she
had left her, square in the middle of the sofa, and staring
straight ahead at nothing. She hadn't even taken off her coat.
Mady asked her if she wanted anything to eat or drink, but it
was as if Roz hadn't heard.

Where did she begin, Mady wondered? Or even, disregard-
ing what Ben had just said, should she?

Roz spoke suddenly. 'He said I was a bad mother.'

'That's ridiculous.' Mady sat down beside her.

'He said it was me who had wanted Charley in the first place.' Roz was talking in a faraway voice, remembering everything word for word. 'If I was so bloody keen to be a mother, I should have looked after him myself. But my precious career came first, didn't it? It always did. So he got sacrificed, him and Charley.'

'He was upset . . .'

'He said I shouldn't have made him look after Charley that night. He was too tired.'

Mady was conscious of holding her breath, of hanging on to every word her friend uttered. But then Roz paused, and for the first time seemed to come fully to her senses. Her eyes locked on to Mady's. 'He told me at the time he couldn't cope.'

Mady felt her heart thunder. Roz had never told her that before. She had never mentioned anything about the events of that night, and Mady had always shied away from asking. The only version she knew had been Roz's account in court, when she had been corroborating Hugh's evidence. Lying for him, she wondered now?

'Hugh told me that night that he needed to sleep and then Charley kept waking up . . .'

Mady couldn't help herself. 'Only twice, surely?' she murmured.

Roz avoided her gaze. 'No. Three times.'

Mady went hot and cold. Roz had lied to the court. First Hugh, then Roz.

'Today before he went to work, Hugh said to me . . .' Roz seemed about to drift off again . . . "Charley kept crying. On and on. I never meant . . ." ' She shuddered to a halt.

Mady's own lips were dry. 'He never meant what?' she managed to ask.

More tears flowed. 'I love him.'

'Yes, I know but . . .'

'And he loved Charley so much. So very much.'

Mady had to ask the question but she didn't know how she could. It came in a rush: 'Do you think he hurt Charley?'

'No! Oh God, I don't know,' Roz wailed.

'Did you see anything? Hear anything?'

Roz gave her a look of pure misery. 'No, I didn't see . . . You know Charley was always crying at night? When Hugh said it had been twice that night, I believed him – why shouldn't I? I thought I'd imagined that third cry . . .'

Mady's throat felt tight. 'You heard him cry three times? You're sure?'

Roz nodded miserably. 'Yes. The second time Charley woke up, he . . . he seemed to go on crying for ever. I couldn't understand it because Hugh wasn't in bed, so I assumed he was in the nursery, and normally Charley quietened pretty quickly once he was picked up. I was just going to go in myself, when I . . . I heard Hugh running up the stairs. He must have been down in the kitchen all along . . .'

Precisely as Alice had described.

'Hugh slammed the nursery door shut. After that I . . .' Roz closed her eyes.

'Yes?' Mady couldn't bear it.

Roz spoke in a faraway voice. 'Charley cried again about an hour later.'

'And?' Mady croaked.

'Not for long. Really, not for very long at all.'

But he had cried. 'Did Hugh get up to him that time too?' Mady asked.

'I don't remember. I don't even know if Hugh was in bed. I was only half-awake.'

'So, what happened?'

Roz turned blank eyes upon her. 'Charley stopped crying.'

Was that it, every detail? Or was Roz still covering up? She looked badly in need of comfort now, rocking herself back and forth on the sofa, but Mady didn't move. She needed to know everything. 'You saw Charley,' she reminded her gently, 'before you went to work?'

Roz said nothing.

'And he was fine?'

Roz spoke into the quiet air. 'He was a bit floppy.'

Mady's stomach twisted. Once more, Alice had been telling the truth. She felt dizzy with the speed of change she was expected to absorb in one day. That morning she had been convinced of Alice's guilt. Now she had to get her mind around it being Hugh. It was too much. She found herself snatching at theories. Perhaps everything had happened as Alice and Roz were now saying but it still didn't make Hugh the killer . . .

The little girl? No, impossible. Or Kate Armstrong? That was better, she thought weakly, turning the idea around, afraid to put it down. But it all depended on whether Kate had ever been there. And something else was troubling her. 'Roz,' she appealed, 'why're you only saying this about Hugh now?'

Roz gazed at her. 'Well, I . . . I thought it was all going to be all right. I mean, I couldn't believe Hugh . . . I literally could not believe . . . And there was that other baby that Alice killed in New Zealand . . .'

'That was supposed to be a cot death, remember, Roz. Charley was shaken.'

Roz shuddered and too late Mady realised what she had said. Roz would never need to be reminded of how her baby had died.

Roz went on in a small voice, 'Yes, but everyone thought it was her, it all fitted in . . .'

'It could still be her,' Mady found herself saying.

'Yes! Yes, of course you're right. No one ever even thought that Hugh . . . Hugh couldn't . . .' A tremor shook her, and Mady put an arm around her shoulders.

'It's all right, darling.'

'I don't know what I'm saying,' Roz sobbed against her. 'I don't know if Hugh did anything. But if it wasn't Alice, then who . . .?'

'Kate Armstrong.'

'But Alice just made her up,' Roz wailed. 'It's all my fault.'

'You know it isn't.' Although her evidence had sent an innocent woman to prison . . . Mady let go of that train of thought. Alice could still be guilty. She could have harmed Charley while she'd been babysitting, the night before, the damage to his brain only reaching the critical stage the next morning . . . that had been one of the theories put forward by the prosecution.

'You don't understand. Hugh was so tired, so stressed out: I should have listened to him.'

Mady saw her opportunity. 'What was he so worried about?' she asked as casually as she could.

Roz sighed. 'I don't know. That's what I mean. I didn't listen to him when he needed me so much. I was so wrapped up in my own work those first few weeks . . . It was to do with Hugh's work,' she added vaguely.

'Nothing more specific that you can remember? A particular crisis?'

'No.'

In her distress, Roz didn't seem to realise that Mady was

interrogating her. 'Did he mention a film to you?' she probed.

Roz frowned. 'A film?'

'Or a film company?'

Roz shook her head. 'No. Why do you ask?'

She didn't want to tell her about her visit to Alice, at least not yet. Roz might tell Hugh. Mady lied as little as she could, saying there was a rumour at the newspaper that Hugh had been in trouble around the time of Charley's death.

'What sort of trouble?' Roz asked dazedly.

'I don't know.'

Roz's eyes snapped open. 'Financial? A prostitute? What?'

Mady had forgotten Roz was a journalist too. 'I don't know . . .'

'Well, can't you find out? You say a film was being made about it? For God's sake,' Roz gave a high, false laugh, 'why hasn't this come out before? Did you know before?' she demanded, taking Mady aback.

'No, I . . . I swear. I only heard the vaguest rumour today.'

Roz was studying her narrowly. It felt most uncomfortable. Not for nothing, Mady reminded herself, was Roz known for her determined interviewing technique. Then she dropped her head and Mady realised what she must be thinking – her nightmare was true then: Hugh had killed their baby and now Mady was suggesting a motive.

'He was terribly on edge that week, I do remember that . . .' Roz's voice faded away. 'D'you think he was being black-mailed?' she asked pitifully.

'I'd be guessing . . .' Mady stammered.

'Can you find out? I'll do anything I can to help you.'

Did Roz realise what she was saying? Where it might lead? 'You mustn't let Hugh know,' she hedged.

'No, of course not.'

As a team at the news agency she and Roz had been formidable: Roz the tough nut, Mady the gentler questioner. Now they were conspiring against Roz's husband. She didn't think Roz was aware of that. It was all very well now, when Mady was right before her, but that would Roz be like that night with Hugh? She adored him. She'd already covered up for him. Would she cave in? Tell him what she had confessed to Mady?

'What are you going to do next?' asked Roz.

'Find out about this film.'

'And then?'

'And then tell you, and together we'll decide what to do.' She sounded sure of herself, but what if she found evidence against Hugh that was overwhelming? Where would her allegiance lie then?

Roz nodded slowly. 'Where's Archie?' she asked suddenly.

Mady flushed. 'Er, upstairs, asleep.'

'I'd love to see him sometime.' Roz smiled. 'Don't be afraid, Mady, I can take it. I miss him.'

Tears came to Mady's eyes. How easily Roz could read her, she always had been able to. She embraced her clumsily.

'You'll tell me as soon as you find out anything,' Roz murmured into her shoulder.

'Sure.'

'I'll be on my way then.' Roz stood up.

'You'll be all right? I mean, with Hugh . . .'

'He's not going to hurt me if that's what you mean.'

Mady felt herself redden. 'I didn't really . . .' But she had meant that.

'Call me,' said Roz, going to the door.

'I will.'

As soon as she had gone, Ben came up from the cellar. 'Well? Did she tell all?'

Mady nodded.

'Did he do it?'

'I don't know.' She told him what had been said.

'Jesus! So he did do it. What a bastard.'

'How come you're so sure?' she asked, wondering what she had missed.

'Why else would he have said, "I never meant . . ."? "To give Charley a goodnight kiss"? "I never meant to shake him to death" is what he meant.'

'Yes, you're right.' She pondered. But it was hearsay and Hugh would deny saying it; moreover, she doubted Roz would give evidence against him. Even if she could be persuaded, what sort of witness would she make? She had lied to the court already; it would be said she was lying again. 'I need independent proof,' Mady concluded aloud.

'You're right. Had any lunch yet?'

She smiled at him. 'I've got to get on. I'll grab some crisps.'

'Have a sandwich,' he pleaded, 'with me.'

'Ben . . .'

'I'm lonely. Take ten minutes out.'

She followed him down the narrow hall into the kitchen. It was forty years out of date: turquoise wallpaper, yellow Formica work surfaces, chipped tiles. They had been about to rip it out and get a new one when Ben had lost his job. Now they told each other that they liked it, it was almost fashionable again.

Ben presented her with a glass of wine. She took one sip and from the floor above came a thin wail.

Ben's mouth set in a hard line. 'Little bastard.'

She winced. 'I'll get him.'

He sighed. 'No, I'll do it. You go off and nail Hugh.'

They followed each other up the flight of stairs, Mady peeling off into the tiny boxroom where she worked, Ben going up another flight to Archie's room.

She closed her door, switched on her laptop and requested all information on Hugh Antony Eastwood.

The pavement was dirty with cigarette stubs, discarded wrappings and dog excrement. Stepping over it, an expression of revulsion on her face, Roz wondered, not for the first time, how Mady could bear to live in such an area. Because she had to, came back the clinical response. Because she was poor. She had married a loser like Ben, not a winner like Hugh.

That Hugh came from wealth was written on his face, in her opinion. Well-groomed, an air of relaxed self-confidence because he came from the class that ruled and always would. He had been married when she had first met him fifteen years before at a PR party in Belgravia. He had been far more desirable in the flesh than on the television screen. It had quite shocked her, a girl not used to being overwhelmed by such feelings, how much she had wanted him. She had desired most dreadfully to touch his hair for some reason; the very thought of doing it had sent little electric shocks sparking all over her. He had been part of a small group laughing and he had looked up and seen her watching him. His response had been a slow, wonderful smile and a long look inviting her closer. But she had been a prude, had known his reputation as a playboy MP, and had left the party without talking to him.

She had thought about him, though. Eight years later, she

had met him again at another party, a political affair that time, and he had asked her out, then and there, to dinner at a restaurant in Bloomsbury. She remembered how deliriously happy she had felt, how excited to be seen with him, and yet afterwards, on their honeymoon two months later, he claimed she had been so cool that night, so poised that he hadn't been sure she even liked him.

But I love you, she told him nakedly. I love you so much it hurts. She had been like that with him then – completely, painfully honest – until a year into their marriage, she had confided how desperately she wanted a baby and he had stopped in the middle of their lovemaking, and said in that case, she had married the wrong man. He didn't like children. They got in the way and they irritated him. Then he had carried on, or tried to, and when she hadn't responded, he had grown angry and sarcastic, and finally left her crying in bed and taken the car and gone out.

She had been so frightened of losing him that she hadn't mentioned the baby subject for another year, which was a full year after she had stopped taking the contraceptive pill. They were in Venice for the weekend when she suggested they saw an infertility specialist. Hugh erupted. He had seized her by the wrist so hard in making his point, that he did not want a baby, she had carried the bruise for days. She remembered Mady remarking upon it, and how she had had to think fast, blaming it eventually on bashing into a doorway.

She had nursed her infertility to herself, telling herself it didn't matter, Hugh was right, babies did get in the way, she saw that repeatedly in her own profession, but it had hurt deeply as all around her friends got pregnant. She had closed herself off more or less successfully most of the time, and then, like a miracle, it had happened. She had been dumbstruck, and quite terrified to tell Hugh, but when at three months pregnant, she had had to – 'You're getting fat' he'd drawled – his response had been so much better than she had dared hope.

Silence. Absorbing the shock, she supposed. He'd stared at her, hard, and then one corner of his mouth twisted up. 'You got what you wanted in the end then,' he'd said and gone to work without another word.

She feared he would never bond with the baby, but when he fell so utterly in love with Charley, it made her love him completely again. In becoming a family, it seemed their marriage healed. For those brief months, she had never been so happy.

And then that terrible night, so terrible, the grief counsellor said, that her mind wouldn't let her recall most of it, only fragments that hardly made sense. Charley crying on and on.

'Three times in one night, you poor man!' That was what she had said to Hugh in the morning – what a dreadful night for him, but, never mind, it would be her turn the next night.

But he had frowned and told her it had been only twice, she must have dreamed the third time. Lucky her, to be able to dream, he had snapped. He had been in a terrible mood, she remembered, but so clear on that that she accepted at once she had been mistaken. It was what she told the hospital had happened: two bouts of crying only.

She had been shaken on hearing Alice's evidence – her description of the third cry had been what Roz herself recalled – but she knew by then she had to stick to Hugh's account, included in which was: they hadn't rowed. They must present a united front against Alice, let no cracks show.

Alice had slotted right in to the role of killer, with her

dreadful history and her alibi full of holes. It had been easy for
Roz to convince herself.

But now they had found the missing child. A bit of Alice's
jigsaw had been found. What would happen if they found Kate
Armstrong? Roz felt weak. She would like very much to believe
that Kate would be made to confess to harming Charley, but
she couldn't. Now the memory of that third cry was clear in her
head again, as was the awful memory of Hugh stamping
upstairs to deal with Charley the second time. That must have
been when he . . . when he hurt him. And the third, strange cry
an hour later must have been when the brain had first registered
the extent of the damage done to it.

She whimpered. No wonder she had blotted it all out, not
wanting it to be true. But it was, she had to face it. She recalled
Hugh writhing in his nightmares that morning. His mind was
remembering too, the memories coming back to accuse him.
His façade was crumbling. 'I never meant . . .' – that dreadful
hanging sentence for which there could be only one ending.

Her eyes filled. She still loved him, whatever he'd done. Who
did she love better? Her dead child or her living husband? Her
clever, ambitious husband on his way to greatness?

She had heard him on the radio that morning and, in spite of
the bitterness of their recent row, had thought him marvellous.

Her mind felt fuzzy like a TV station losing its signal. She
had to think fast. She had failed as a mother, she knew she
would not be a mother again. But she could be a successful wife
again, couldn't she? She could rise with Hugh once more? To
dazzling heights this time.

She felt an inrush of happiness, the first since Charley had
died. She could see a future for herself and Hugh! Her work was
terribly important to her, naturally, but since Charley had died,

it had lost its sparkle. She didn't want to be a hack all her life, and work would never fill the hole that Charley had left. She needed more, much more: power and status as the Prime Minister's wife, experiences she could now only dream of! And she would be good at it. She would serve her husband and her country well. The only fly in the ointment, her thinking slowed, was the trouble Hugh had been in. The trouble that she hadn't listened to at the time, but about which a film was being made, a film that perhaps could ruin him still?

She frowned. She had promised Mady she would do all that she could to find out what Hugh had done, but where would that lead?

To Hugh going to prison? Herself as a creature of pity? A social outcast because of what he had done? She thought not.

If she warned Hugh that she had confided in Mady, he would leave her, she had no doubt about that. He might even hurt her. If she asked Mady to stop investigating, it would merely whet her friend's appetite further.

There was only one thing for it: to play them both, two kites in the sky at once. Let Mady investigate while keeping Hugh in darkness. Once she knew what the evidence was, she would know what to do with it. Whether to let Hugh know that she knew, or not? Prevaricating would also give her time, she told herself dreamily. The notion slipped into her mind that she was being duplicitous, a little crazy even, but she nudged it gently aside. Nothing was her fault, for wasn't she a bereaved mother? She saw herself as others might see her, a lonely, elegantly dressed woman picking her way along that dirty street, shouldering her unspeakable grief and fear bravely.

She arrived at the mouth of an Underground station. She had taken a taxi to Mady's but now she thought, how droll to travel on the Underground again! She hadn't done so in years and once Hugh was voted into power, she never would again. As for now, she bought a ticket and descended the escalator smiling. If she was careful, and she was, no one need ever know what she was thinking. Humming to herself, she boarded a Tube train and vanished at speed into a tunnel.

CHAPTER SEVEN

The database supplied Mady with little information about Hugh that she did not already know.

He was forty-six years old, had been married twice and had one son, Charley. In his youth, both before and during his first marriage, he had been a notorious womaniser, indulging in a series of well-publicised affairs, most memorably with the wife of the then Shadow Home Secretary. However, Hugh appeared to have settled down upon marrying Roz.

His father had been a Conservative MP, knighted in the eighties by Margaret Thatcher. His mother held the purse strings. Hugh was the youngest of three sons and the most flamboyant; he had done well at school, had excelled at sport and been a Cambridge blue as well as obtaining a good degree in law. He had taken a postgraduate course in America, returned home to sit his bar exams and join a successful set of barristers specialising in intellectual property law. At twenty-four, and to the consternation of his parents, he had stood as a Labour MP for an inner-London borough, and won.

He had obtained early notoriety within the party for his

outspoken and, some claimed, frankly Tory views on trades unions and education. On the other hand, he was extremely popular with his constituents, with whom he had a deserved reputation for fighting their corner. He was also an excellent public speaker, and cameras loved him. However, after one spell as a Shadow Foreign Office minister in the early nineties, he had been relegated to the back benches, and left to languish. Many believed he had been kept there until recently because the current Prime Minister, and leader of the party for ten years, was afraid of him, possibly with good reason.

But such was politics, Mady acknowledged, and to give Hugh his due, he had been patient. He had played the long game, and professionally had kept his nose clean. There was nothing, either on the databases or garnered from Roz over the years, that hinted at a political or financial scandal. Yet there must be a reason why Hugh had been so stressed out, why he had been bartering with the Grey Team data, why he had done whatever he had to Charley. If he had.

She still wasn't convinced. She flicked open her notebook and dialled a number in New Zealand that the crime editor at *The Register* had given her. The call was answered promptly, and she asked for the name on her page.

'He's not in right now,' came the response.

She asked when he would be, and was told later in the morning; it was four o'clock in Auckland.

'Four AM? I'm so sorry . . .' She left a message. How not to make a good impression, she told herself.

Her thoughts returned to Hugh. No one had actually seen him attack Charley. The videotape had been destroyed, and Hugh had loved his baby. So what if he'd lost his temper and stormed into his bedroom? No matter how angry or exhausted you were, you didn't hurt your own child. Most of the time. Something stopped you. And yet, and yet . . . Roz had said Charley had seemed floppy in the morning. Roz was tearing herself apart trying not to believe it, and Mady was beginning to do the same thing.

What had Trump Card got on him? Proof of another woman? More children somewhere? But Hugh lived too much in the media limelight, especially since Charley's death, for such a secret to have remained buried. Besides, in his own way, Hugh seemed pretty besotted with Roz. That was the main reason that Mady had persevered in trying to like him. In an out-of-character moment, he had once confided in Ben that he'd met his match in Roz. He'd waited for her for years and, having got her, he vowed he'd never look elsewhere again. Ben and Mady had been sceptical at first but there had been no more affairs, either reported in the media or by Roz.

It was no good, Mady thought, she wasn't going to find anything obvious in cuttings. If she wanted to know what Trump Card had on Hugh, she was going to have to ask them, and she knew how unlikely it was they were going to tell her.

She put in some calls to friends in film. She heard the front door slam: Ben taking Archie out for a walk. Her contacts were away from their desks, or still at lunch, or couldn't help her. Trump Card, one contact told her, prided themselves on keeping a tight ship; there were no rumours, no helpful hints about current or future documentaries. Mady reached the end of her list and crashed the telephone back into its cradle, glaring at it. It was four o'clock in the afternoon and she was getting nowhere.

On her screen, she initiated a search for Trump Card. There weren't many entries, the company had only been in existence for five years. They hadn't done very much, except for a notable success two years before: a documentary on life below stairs at Buckingham Palace. In May, a fire had broken out at their premises, killing a security guard and destroying their office, along with several other floors in the building. In July one of the directors had left the company.

What had she been expecting? A potted version of the scandal on Hugh? Reasons why, neatly set out? Her telephone shrilled and she snapped into it.

'You're in a nice mood,' commented a male voice mildly.

She apologised. Her caller was an old friend from news-agency days who now worked as a freelance producer. With little hope, she explained to him what she was after.

'Haven't a clue what they're up to,' he volunteered cheerfully.

She ground her teeth. 'No. Well, thanks anyway . . .'

'You could try asking Christine Evans,' he suggested.

'Who's she?'

'Scary lady Trump Card hired last year. Christine's a big name in the business, very tough, lots of big ideas, great success rate in getting them on air, which is where Trump Card's been having problems of late. They paid Christine a fortune for a five-year contract, made her a director, the works. Then she goes and walks out within twelve months.'

'Why?'

'Nobody knows. She won't say, neither will they. They're suing, she's counter-suing.'

Mady closed her eyes in prayer. 'D'you know where she's gone?'

He gave her the number and she thanked him profusely, anxious now for him to go.

'What's your interest in Trump Card anyway?' he asked curiously.

'Oh, er, just following up a lead. You know.'

'Uh-huh. Dumb question. You're not doing the MI5 angle then?'

'MI5?' she repeated as casually as she could.

'Yes, you know. Funny little people in blue suits who follow you round town and bug your phone.'

'They're interested in Trump Card?' Her voice caught.

'That was the talk. That it was they who fired the premises to destroy Trump Card's archive.'

Fanatically she scrolled back to the item on the fire and saw what she had missed before: the date, May 13. She went cold. The fire had broken out the night before Charley had been rushed to hospital. That date didn't have the same significance to her as the date of his death, but of course it fitted in. Hugh had ordered the torching of the premises, and then, plagued by guilt at the guard's death, had lashed out at Charley, fatally shaking him . . . 'Was it definitely arson?' she asked.

'Don't know. The inquiry's still under way. But if that's the line you are following, beware, because others have gone down the same route and it's a time-waster. Looks like Trump Card started the MI5 rumour to give themselves publicity.'

Maybe, but maybe Hugh had been so desperate to save himself that he would have done anything. As soon as her caller had gone, Mady ran a search on Christine Evans.

The woman had joined Trump Card the previous September when a post had been especially created for her as 'Developmental Director'. Both she and the other Trump Card directors declared themselves delighted. There was a head-and-shoulders photograph showing a woman in her late forties with short, dark hair and a professional smile. Mady found a second article, no more than a news filler, which stated blandly that Evans had left the company in July.

There was nothing else Mady could do to prepare herself. She dialled Evans' new number at the London Bureau of an American satellite station. She was put through to a voicemail where a clipped female voice told her to leave a message. Mady did so, mentioning the name of her paper. It was five o'clock in the afternoon. Evans had probably gone home for the day, or was too busy to return calls from journalists who didn't state their business. If that happened, she would doorstep her, Mady decided. She was her one lead.

She stared at her telephone for a minute but it was silent.

Outside, it was already dark. Someone was kicking a can up the street, hitting it against cars. Probably hers, Mady thought gloomily, not wanting to look. The door slammed.

'Mady!' yelled up Ben and in an echoing crow came Archie's voice. Her stomach turned over as it still did sometimes when she realised afresh that she was a mother. She abandoned her office and ran downstairs. Archie was strapped into his pushchair in the hall, his cheeks apple-red from the cold, but when he saw her he grinned hugely and waved his arms about.

'He ate the bread for the ducks,' complained Ben.

'Were you hungry, my darling?' Mady unbuckled the harness and lifted the baby out. His snowsuit felt icy but inside he was deliciously warm. He nestled his cheek against hers and she thought how adorable he was. He wasn't rejecting her now.

'What news on Hugh?' Ben asked.

She told him briefly, speaking softly because the accusation seemed too terrible for Archie to hear.

Ben stood stock-still. 'I was thinking when we were out, there's no way Hugh could've done it but . . .'

'I know.'

Ben smiled at her bliss. 'D'you want some quality time with HRH?'

'Could I?'

'Be my guest. I've had him all afternoon.'

She carried Archie like treasure into the sitting room and presented him with his favourite toy, a bright yellow Beetle car that sang discordant plastic music. Archie was entranced and ran it back and forth in his fat hands, exactly as a little boy should, thought Mady, misty-eyed. Sometimes she found it difficult to switch from worker-mode to mother, but not that day.

'I love you,' she whispered and Archie turned from his playing for an instant and looked at her. She heard the phone ring and hoped Ben would answer it.

Archie had crawled with his car to the other end of the room. He knelt and put a hand on its roof, then shakily rose to his feet.

'Ben! Ben! He's standing!' Mady shrieked and Archie instantly toppled.

'You're kidding.' Ben appeared in the doorway. 'Who's a clever boy, then?' Ben scooped him up and Archie's legs went around him like a koala bear. 'Who's my little genius? And not yet ten months old. That call was for you,' he added over his shoulder. 'A Christine Evans.'

Mady was on her feet. 'Is she still on the line?'

'No, I told her you'd finished work for the day.'

'Ben!'

'What?'

'I've got to talk to her!'

She dashed into the kitchen to use the phone there, but when she dialled ring-back, she was told the caller had withheld their number. She galloped upstairs, found the number and rang. The switchboard answered and put her through as before.

'Hi, I can't come to the phone right now . . .'

The voicemail message again. She had missed her by moments, Mady swore to herself and tried not to be angry with Ben.

'Hullo?' demanded a woman, interrupting the message.

'Is that Christine Evans?'

'Who's speaking?' The tone was suspicious.

Mady introduced herself.

'Oh, yes. I just spoke to hubby, didn't I? I thought you were playing with Baby?'

Mady's hackles rose but she needed Evans on her side. 'I was, but I'm not any more.'

Evans grunted. 'What d'you want?'

'I need to speak to you in person.'

'What about?'

'I really don't want to say over the phone.'

'Oh God,' Evans drawled, 'another conspiracy theorist. What did you say your name was?'

Mady told her, although she guessed Evans knew her by reputation perfectly well.

The woman sighed heavily. 'Can't you give me some indication as to what it's about?'

Mady apologised.

'Well, you're going to have to wait a week . . .'

'Oh but—'

'I'm off to Rotterdam first thing in the morning.'

She would be, Mady thought grimly. Aloud, she supposed that that evening, for half an hour, would be out of the question?

'My, you are desperate, aren't you?'

But Mady could tell she was hooked. She offered to meet her wherever she liked.

'You won't feel the need to bring the screaming brat?'

Equably, Mady promised she would not.

Evans mentioned the name of a wine bar in Knightsbridge, at seven o'clock, which gave Mady scarcely enough time to get there, but she didn't argue. She grabbed her bag and her jacket and dashed down to Ben. He and Archie were playing as she had been; she felt supplanted and jealous, but she didn't have time to linger. 'Ben, I've got to go and meet this woman.'

'Oh, come on! Why can't it wait till tomorrow?'

'She's going away. Look, I'm sorry, it's vital, she's my only lead.'

His face took on a resigned expression. 'Go on then.'

'I'll be as quick as I can. Bye, darling.' She gave him a kiss, and tried to kiss Archie too but he pushed her away. It didn't mean a thing, she told herself, hurt.

She drove fast and against the traffic, but even so it was the rush hour, and by the time she parked, it was five minutes past seven. Evans was exactly the type who wouldn't wait.

The wine bar was in the basement of a hotel and reached down a metal staircase. Mady clattered down into a hubbub of noise. The place was extremely popular and gleaming with glass and chrome and smart people. She felt suddenly very aware of her own shabby appearance. Cotton trousers that she had been wearing all day and flat pumps. She zipped up her black leather jacket, her only vaguely trendy item, and wished she'd had time to apply fresh make-up. She moved between the clusters of customers, muttering, 'Sorry.'

She could see no one who looked like Evans and no single

woman was looking for her. She's gone, Mady thought in despair. She could think of no other avenue to explore; she couldn't do anything with Roz's suspicions alone. She turned to go and it was then that she saw a woman watching her via a mirror on the wall. She was sitting on a barstool with her back to her. Mady approached tentatively. 'Christine Evans?'

She was stubbing out a cigarette in an ashtray. She took a long time about it, and longer still to turn around. She was thinner than in her photograph, tired around the eyes, and wearing a lot of make-up.

'Yes?' She stared at Mady unsmilingly.

Mady introduced herself and offered to get her a drink, but the other woman indicated a bottle of wine that was already halfway down. She poured Mady a glass.

'So,' she said, lighting another cigarette, 'what's all this about?'

On the way Mady had debated how best to start the conversation and had come to no firm conclusion. She had to expose herself in order to expect any assistance but she had no idea about the level of Evans' trustworthiness. She had to assume it was zero. She began asking questions about Trump Card but Evans shook her head.

'Look, if it's them you're interested in, you've come to the wrong person. I've left.'

'I know.' Mady took a sip of wine. She wished the bar was less crowded, so she didn't have to speak so loudly, but no one appeared to be interested in what they were saying. 'Why did you leave Trump Card?' she asked.

'Because I wanted to.'

'You signed a five-year contract . . .?'

Evans glared. 'About which I've got nothing to say. This is a waste of my time. If you'd told me this is what you wanted to talk about—'

'It isn't,' Mady broke in quickly. 'I'm here about Hugh Eastwood.'

Evans turned sharply. 'What about him?'

'Was Trump Card making a documentary about him?'

Evans inhaled her cigarette smoke but didn't answer.

Having gone so far, Mady could not retreat. 'They believe he was responsible for firing their premises. Don't they?'

'Do they?'

'So I understand.'

Evans gave her a long look. 'When I left Trump Card, I undertook not to talk of projects I had brought to the company during my time with them. I have no intention of exposing myself to more litigation and bad will to help you out. I take it your paper's investigating Eastwood?'

'Beginning to.'

'Well, good luck to you.' She drained her glass and stood up to leave.

'Please . . .' Mady started.

'Goodbye.'

'Did he give you the dirt on the Grey Team? Is that why the film wasn't made?'

Evans glared. 'Who've you been talking to?'

'I can't say.'

'And yet you expect me to.' She sat down heavily and reached for another cigarette. Her hand shook as she lit it, tapping off the ash too soon, so the end glowed fiery red like an undressed wound.

'My film was made, all right, or most of it. I wanted to go ahead with it badly but the decision was taken out of my hands.

That's why I left the company.' She took a deep drag. 'My film would have been the end of Eastwood. He knew that. Six hours after we told him we weren't interested in his bribes, our premise got burned to the ground. Most of our films got burned too, but we'd a copy of some of his, enough to cobble together something. We took a decision the day after the fire, that we'd go ahead with the film, including TV footage of the fire, hang the bastard out to dry, and then what happens? His baby gets shaken to death.'

'And?'

Christine shrugged. 'My two fellow directors ruled that it would be bad taste to go ahead. They were convinced that given the wave of public sympathy for Eastwood, no television station would touch the film for at least a year, possibly not even then. There were one or two legal issues with it. I thought they were wrong; they thought I was; I left.' She tilted her head back to blow out her smoke. She smiled tightly. 'And now what I warned them would happen, is happening. Someone else will get the story.'

'I don't suppose you've got a copy of that film?'

'You don't suppose right.'

Mady tried again. 'Bishop is bound to appeal. A TV station might take it . . .' How much time did she have, she wondered suddenly, to find out what they had? To run the story before they did? However deeply involved she was personally in the case she was also a journalist, she wanted to be there first with the story.

Evans shook her head. 'Believe me, Trump Card won't put it forward. They'd say it was on legal grounds but my partners were more frightened by that fire than they care to admit. They won't budge. Not unless Eastwood owns up to killing that baby.'

Mady's insides tightened. How many more people believed that? She said as lightly as she could: 'D'you think he did it?'

'Hardly. It was the nanny. You only have to look at her to know.'

Mady remembered when she had thought that.

'How much have you got on him?' Evans asked.

'Just starting.'

'Been to Orangeboro yet?'

Mady's heart skipped a beat. 'Er, no. What's . . .?'

Evans stamped out her cigarette. 'If anyone asks, you didn't get that from me. Okay?'

'Okay. Thanks.'

'Understand this. That film was my baby. What Eastwood did really got to me. Now it looks as if he's going to get away with it. If Trump Card aren't going to use it, I guess someone ought to.'

'Can I call you again?'

'No.' Evans smiled briefly. 'You won't need to.' She slid off her stool and was gone, the crowd at the bottom of the staircase swallowing her up.

CHAPTER EIGHT

The first radio station on which Hugh had spoken that morning had been delighted to get him and had readily agreed to his request not to make any reference to his son's death. There was still awe for the politician who had lost his son so tragically. As the day wore on, however, and Hugh appeared dry-eyed and increasingly confident on nearly every major news programme, the media's mood changed. By the evening it was felt Hugh had milked them for all they were worth and now he was considered fair game.

The presenter on the live television news programme would afterwards claim he decided on the spur of the moment to breach Hugh's terms. In fact he had plotted since lunchtime to do it: live, on air, to turn to Hugh seated at the table beside him, frown down at his papers and then ask, 'Minister, does the emergence of the child who shook your baby's pushchair make you reassess Alice Bishop's guilt?'

Hugh froze. 'I'm not here to answer questions on that. As I was saying, the latest abortion figures show . . .'

'It is true, is it not, that the evidence against Alice Bishop is entirely circumstantial? The spy-camera tape having disappeared?'

Hugh mouthed an obscenity which the microphone failed to pick up because at that moment, he was engaged in ripping it out of his shirt. He exited the studio, the camera following him for as long as it could offstage.

'Well,' said the presenter smugly into the viewfinder, 'it seems that the Minister declines to answer that question.'

In the VIP Welcome studio to which Hugh had stumbled, Alan Hardy rose to meet him. His face was set. Only someone who knew him very well could tell how angry he was. Hugh felt sick inside, but he had had no option. Those questions were strangling him.

The producer rushed in. 'I'm terribly sorry, Minister, Alan, that was completely unscheduled. God knows what got into Derek . . .'

Alan didn't attempt to smile. 'The Minister will never appear on this programme again,' he said.

'No, I quite understand. All I can say is—'

'Hugh,' Alan cut in, 'shall we go?'

In the back of the car, having ensured the intercom to the driver was switched off, Alan said, 'You never walk out on an interview.'

'No, I know, but—'

'There is no excuse. It makes you look weak.'

Hugh nodded. He was tempted to babble an explanation but he knew there was no point. Alan's mobile rang. He said, 'Yes, yes. No, the Minister has no comment to make.'

The same call, or a variation of it, was received more than a dozen times in the short distance between the TV studio and Earl's Court. After that, Hugh stopped counting and stopped listening. He watched the sleety rain.

Alan broke in abruptly on his thoughts. 'That was Rebecca.'

Hugh blinked. 'Does she want to talk to me?'

'No. Not tonight. She wants to see you in the morning. You're to make no comment to any media contact or organisation until then. Okay?'

Hugh could imagine what Rebecca might have to say to him. That he was out. That he had blown it. He could kiss his career goodbye. He knew he wouldn't get any sleep that night, white pills or no. Then an idea occurred to him, and grew with such rapidity that he had to find out if it could be true. He spoke up. 'I'd like to go home please.'

'That's where we are going,' said Alan, as one suffering fools and not gladly.

'No, to Chelsea.'

Alan frowned. 'Why?'

'There's something I've got to do.'

'We'll wait outside for you.'

'No, it might take me some time.'

Alan looked a bit awkward. 'You're okay? These things happen, you know.'

'I'm not going to top myself, Alan,' Hugh assured him, some of his old confidence returning.

They dropped him outside the house. As they left, he saw Alan was on his mobile again. The man never stopped. Hugh extracted his set of house keys, and stood under the street light searching for the Chelsea one.

The house had been cold when Roz had first arrived but she had put on the heating and retreated to the kitchen, always the warmest room in the house due to the Aga, which hadn't been switched off in their absence.

No one had lived there for six weeks now, and in spite of the ministrations of the maid coming in on a regular basis, the place felt damp and musty.

She hadn't set off to go there, but when the Tube train had pulled into South Kensington station, she had acted on instinct. Now she was glad she had. She felt more at peace there than anywhere, in spite of everything. When darkness came, she put on a lamp in the kitchen, closed the door and dozed off in an easy chair by the window. Unlike Hugh, she found it easy to sleep. She didn't remember her dreams.

She woke now to the sound of a telephone ringing, not the house phone but her mobile. She rummaged in her bag, praying it wouldn't stop before she located it.

'Roz?' said a voice eagerly. It was Mady. Roz's heart thumped loudly; she had feared it would be Hugh. That was one reason she had come home, to get away from him.

'Are you all right?'

'Yes, I'm fine.'

'You sound a bit distant.'

She must make more effort, Roz told herself. It wouldn't do for people, even Mady, perhaps especially Mady, to consider her mad. She explained she had been asleep, but she didn't say where she was.

'I need to ask you something about Hugh.'

Roz frowned. Mady was investigating her husband, that was right. To see if he had killed their baby. Her heart thundered again and it was with effort that she calmed herself. Compartmentalisation was all. That was how she had survived the last few months. She was simply helping Mady with her story. 'Fire away,' she urged quite cheerfully.

'Does the name "Orangeboro" mean anything to you?'

Roz thought hard. 'It's a place?'

'Yes, I think so.'

She racked her brain. 'I've got a feeling it might be where Hugh went to college in the States. To do his American Law degree. "Orangeboro County"? Somewhere in the south.'

'Brilliant!'

'Check it out,' Roz warned her.

'I will.'

'How's it going? Anything definite yet?'

Mady hesitated. Neither fully trusted each other, Roz realised, which was sad, but understandable given the circumstances.

'Nothing definite,' said Mady eventually, and there was a crackle on the line. She too was using her mobile. Roz wondered where she was.

Mady asked awkwardly, 'Did he do anything in particular at law school?'

'Studied law, I presume. D'you mean, anything wrong?' She considered. 'Nothing. That he's ever told me about anyway. Should I ask him?'

'No,' said Mady hastily, 'don't do that.'

What did she have on him? Roz wanted to know desperately. He was her husband. 'Is there anything I can do?' she inquired.

'No, you take care. Bye now.'

Getting rid of her before she could quiz her any more. Roz knew the score. What had she and her best friend become to each other? She stared into the dark garden where miserable, wintry rain was falling. She could hear it against the glass, scratching.

On such a night as this, she had sat in that same chair, writing Christmas cards. Charley had been not quite one week old, herself exhausted, but she had been determined to write those cards.

No one who had not waited for a child as long and desperately as she could understand the exhilaration of finally having a baby. Charley, born on the second of December, had looked so adorable wrapped in white, lying in her arms, with Hugh posed awkwardly beside them in the photograph she'd had made very quickly into a Christmas card. Corny, he'd groaned, but she'd loved it.

The 'family' at last, their perfect Christmas baby.

She had been so proud of that picture, she had wanted as many people to have it – to know – as possible. She had scoured old address books.

She started, fancying she heard a sound from above. A creak of a floorboard? She looked up. Someone in the house, coming to get her? A ghost? Charley? Then the sound came again. And she saw its source: the old olive tree, planted close to the house by a previous owner, scraped against the wall, creaking its age.

Hugh had let her go through his address book. A careless man in many ways, he was meticulous in other respects, like keeping addresses up to date. Why, she remembered where she had seen the name Orangeboro before. She had written it on an envelope only last year . . .

Air caught hard in her throat. She had promised to help Mady, hadn't she? And she too needed to know what Hugh had done, for her own sanity. She stood there, swaying slightly on the limestone floor, undecided what to do.

As a child, Hugh had been secretive. He'd kept treasures in boxes and he had always had a hiding place. Somewhere safe, away from the prying eyes and mean hands of his two older brothers. Sometimes those hiding places had been found quickly, sometimes it had taken them weeks, but one place had never been found in spite of their searchings.

A small space into which a cigar-box could fit in the slope of the roof in the gamekeeper's cottage. You had to know it was there to find it. His brothers had searched that loft but found nothing. Hugh could remember his seven-year-old terror, standing in the garden, knowing they were up there, and his relief when they came down empty-handed.

He had forgotten all about it until now, until the ride home with Alan. A hiding place that no one but he knew about. That no one else could find. Hadn't he had one at the house? A place that his amnesia had blocked out of his mind? Did that forgotten space contain the vital piece of missing evidence?

What would he do if he was right, if the thing was there?

He trembled. At least he would know the worst was true. Wouldn't that be a relief?

He inserted the key in the front door.

The house was warmer than he expected, and for that he was grateful, it being such a filthy night. But the place was far too still and too silent. He shivered. He mustn't linger long. He didn't turn on the hall light in case the house was being watched outside by journalists. He wouldn't put it past them; after his performance that night, they'd be after his blood. He grimaced. Hating journalists so much, it was amazing that he had married one.

He mounted the stairs to the first floor, quickly past Charley's nursery and their own door, up again to the guest suite on the second floor. On the narrow landing there, above his head was a trap door. He stood on his tiptoes, tugged the metal ring hard, and the door came away releasing the stepladder. He ascended gingerly into the darkness of the loft and grappled around on the right for the light switch. The roof was well-insulated and unlikely to show light.

He saw suitcases – the beautiful although impractical set that he'd bought for Roz as a wedding present, and the bulky plastic ones that he insisted they use for travel. To the right were cardboard boxes filled with Christmas decorations. Hugh remembered last Christmas, Roz holding Charley and weeping on Christmas morning because she was so happy. He choked up. He couldn't start thinking about that now.

On his hands and knees, he advanced cautiously across the crawlboards, trying to imagine where his hiding place might be. He tugged at the hardboard covering but it was nailed down tight. He considered going through the suitcases. Roz kept half her wardrobe in them; he might have slipped it in amongst her clothes. Or the Christmas boxes? Perhaps somewhere in the tinsel? Then he paused. The police had been up there searching and they were professional hunters. They would have found anything that was to be found. He was wasting his time. Jumping at shadows. He did one last sweep with his eyes. There was nothing. He began to crawl backwards, then he saw it. Right over by the edge of the hardboard, where the roof sloped down towards the street, there was a piece of insulating wadding that wasn't lying quite as it should, but raised, as if it concealed something.

A memory pulled at him again. He'd laid his collection of gulls' eggs in the cigar box, then taken it to the gamekeeper's cottage where in the loft he knew there was an old mattress with a slit in the seam. He'd pushed the box inside. It didn't show. Only by looking at it at eye-level did you see a very slight bump where the wadding was raised. The perfect hiding place.

Hugh narrowed his eyes at the wadding, and the slight bump was undeniable. A sheen of sweat broke out upon him. Why hadn't the police seen it? What a gross omission! But he more than most, having served on committees into police misconduct, knew what the police were capable of.

Did he really want to go over there now? Couldn't he too pretend he hadn't seen it? But it would haunt him, he knew it. It would draw him back to the house the next day or the next and by then certainly the ratpack would be waiting for him. It had to be now.

He edged towards the place. Better to know, better to confront it. He felt everything he was, everything he had worked to achieve fall away like dust, but it didn't matter. He reached the spot. He felt the wadding, and yes, there was something there, something hard. He yanked back the yellow stuffing and there it was. He couldn't bring himself actually to look, but he saw it clearly out of the corner of his eye, a shape about the size of a wooden box, the perfect container for a digital tape.

Had he viewed the missing tape? Had he seen who'd harmed his son? But if he had, why hadn't he handed it over to the police? He trembled. If the film showed the unimaginable – his mind veered away from any distinct image – why hadn't he destroyed it? There could be but one explanation: he hadn't looked at it, he had been afraid to look at it, because he had known what it would show . . .

He could destroy it now. He put his hand out then stopped. He couldn't destroy it without viewing it, and if he looked at it, he might go crazy.

He moaned. He was going to be sick, he was going to pass out. Ought he to kill himself now? Top himself, in spite of what he had promised Alan? He gave an ugly laugh. Who cared for Alan, or Rebecca, or any of them? What did they matter, compared to this horror?

Then it hit him. He alone knew where the missing tape was. The police had searched that house from top to bottom and failed to find it. The evidence had gone. End of story. He frowned. Could it be that easy? Yes, it could. All he had to do was continue to blank it out. Resist the urge to tell anyone, and really, who was he likely to tell? Roz? Scarcely!

He took a deep breath. He had nothing to be guilty of. He repeated the phrase softly to himself: he was innocent. That was how he had got through. It was the script and he was sticking to it. Already, he believed it again. Bishop had done it. She was the guilty one, or that friend of hers, Armstrong.

Below in the street, someone called out. He had to get out of there. It wasn't a safe place for him to be. Crawling backwards rapidly, he reached the top of the steps and descended once more to landing level. He nearly ran down the stairs to the family floor, catching a brief, unwelcome sight of Charley's mobile moving in the moonlight and the wind. He turned the corner sharply and was down in the entrance hall in another moment. He put his hand out for the front doorknob and it was then that he heard a sound, quite distinctly, the slam of a drawer below.

Someone was in the house. Someone who shouldn't be there, who was hunting for what he had found. Hugh kept a weapon in the house to deal with such intruders. Soundlessly he went to fetch it.

In the top drawer of Hugh's desk in the basement, Roz found his personal address book. She flicked through pages that were chock-a-block with names. She had no idea of the surname she was looking for, just that place name, Orangeboro.

She tore a page, turning it too fast, and told herself to slow down, she had plenty of time. She thumbed through the 'D's, the 'E's, then the 'F's. She hoped she was right, that she hadn't dreamed up that Christmas card because she was so anxious to help Mady, to supply her own lead. Always a journalist, she thought, always competitive.

From above, there came that sound again, like a floorboard creaking, but she ignored it now, knowing it was the olive tree.

Her eyes returned to the page, and she saw it, Orangeboro. She blinked: John Fitzgerald and family, 1126 Providence Road, Durlington, Orangeboro County, South Carolina 29107.

She had remembered rightly. She hadn't lost her mind. She copied down the address and telephone number on a yellow 'Post-it' and slipped it into her trouser pocket. She felt a surge of satisfaction: she'd got an exclusive. If Mady had done her homework properly she could have found out where Hugh had gone to law school from a database . . . but of course the fact that she hadn't meant that she'd got the name Orangeboro from elsewhere . . . so, it must have real significance? He had done something as a law student that merited a film being made about it twenty years later.

She wouldn't think about it now. She replaced the book in the drawer, slamming it without meaning to, hearing the noise echo in the empty house. She heard a sound right behind her, a 'click' of metal on metal.

Before she had time to whip round, she felt the gun in the nape of her neck. She whimpered, knowing she was going to die.

'I nearly killed you, my love,' said Hugh, but he didn't take the gun away.

How long had he been standing there, watching her? Did he know what she'd found? Would he kill her for that?

'What're you up to?' he asked, almost playfully, the gun's mouth still pressing into her soft flesh.

She could think of nothing to say. If he searched her, he would find the note. 'I was just . . . going through old photographs,' she exclaimed, inspired by the stacks of photograph albums before her on the shelves.

'Find anything interesting?'

'Photos of us . . . in Venice. Before Charley.'

'Oh.'

She felt him evaluate her lie. It surprised her he couldn't hear her heartbeat. Then: 'You'd finished, had you? Only, you've put the albums back exactly as they were.'

How could he possibly know that? The absurdity struck her. 'Have I?' she said with as much airiness as she could muster. 'How neat of me. Hugh,' she added, putting her hand on the gun, 'put that bloody thing away.'

For a fraction of a second, it seemed he pushed the nozzle harder and she fancied hearing him draw the trigger, but it was only a fancy, for a second more, he removed it. She rubbed her neck. 'Maniac,' she said, turning round.

He had cobwebs on his jacket, and there was a look in his eye that scared her. Perhaps he had really gone mad? She mustn't mess about. He had a gun. 'Wherever have you been?' she asked concernedly. 'Look at the state of you!'

'What?' He looked at the cobwebs, seeming to see them for the first time. 'I . . . I've been looking for something,' he muttered, and he was the one to look furtive now, like a little boy caught out in a naughty act.

What had he been doing? Cobwebs in that house? Never! He had been up in the loft! She'd never been up there, he always brought the cases down. What had he found? Papers? Documents, incriminating evidence about Orangeboro, that he hoped to destroy before the film company or she or Mady got hold of them . . .?

Should she tell him it didn't matter? That whatever he'd done she had decided to support him, conceal the truth from everybody else, even if that meant stopping Mady? She gazed at his gun. It was she and Hugh together from now on. Where he went, she would follow . . .

No, she pulled herself back, not yet. Not until she knew everything. It was her right. In the meantime, she must be careful, he was a clever man. The furtiveness had gone, now he was looking at her in that hunter's way he had. He put the gun on the desk, and pulled open the drawer she'd shut.

'What were you doing in here?' he asked mildly.

She thought fast. 'Looking for that photo of us at the Duomo.' It was a fantastic picture; they'd had copies made.

'You won't find any in here.' He stopped rummaging and looked up. He hadn't picked up the address book, so he could not have seen her with it. 'They're in that envelope by the albums. You're the one who put it there, remember? So we'd always know where to look?'

She swallowed. He always did that to her. Turned the tables, even if he was the one in the wrong. 'I forgot,' she said humbly. 'My mind . . .'

'Playing tricks on you, is it?'

She remembered his nightmare that morning. 'Did you find what you were looking for? In the loft?' she reminded him sweetly.

His face went white. What was up there, she wondered? She must have a look.

'No,' he said hoarsely. 'Roz?'

'Yes?'

He put out a hand and caught her wrist so suddenly that it took her breath away. His fingers entwined it to the point of hurting. 'Darling,' he said, and she recognised the venom in the word, 'we've got to help each other. That's how we've survived so far. Remember?'

She remembered all right. That according to him, Charley had only cried twice. To forget what he'd blurted out during the row that morning.

His grip tightened. 'If we don't look out for each other, who will?'

'You're right.'

'You haven't turned against me, have you?'

His eyes were grey with exhaustion and confusion. She felt a wave of pity. 'No,' she promised.

'Only I don't think I could take that.' He spoke softly into her ear.

'No.'

He brought her forward and kissed her hard on the mouth. Her body responded hotly. Her lips opened to receive him. He took her in his hands and tugged her to him. Gladly her legs parted.

On the night of Charley's death he had made fierce love to her. She'd felt nothing, like a doll being raped. He hadn't touched her since, and she hadn't wanted him. But now, she wanted him so much she ached.

He pushed her down on to the floor. His knee came up between her legs, and she groaned in anticipation. His hands sought out her nipples, squeezing hard, rubbing at her. She tried to feel for him, but he pushed her away. He pulled down her trousers.

'God,' he whispered delightedly, 'you want me, don't you?' He entered her, and she gasped, but kept his rhythm, feeling everything else fall away, wanting only him.

He cried out, and a shudder ran through him. She clung to him, loving the fact that she could do that to him. That she had that much power.

He said, 'You're mine now.'

'That's right.'

'Let me give you what you want.'

He made her come twice, quickly, and then slowly. She had never loved him so much. When they lay side by side, he asked: 'You'll always tell me if anything is troubling you, won't you, my love?'

'Mm,' she promised, smiling up at him, thinking how beautiful he was.

'If there are any questions you might like to ask me?'

What did he think she was, she thought with a smile, a journalist? 'Questions?' she echoed aloud.

His eyes bored into hers. He seemed on the verge of saying something else. 'I'm going to have to keep my eye on you, aren't I?' he murmured, fingering her again.

'That sounds nice,' she said lasciviously, loving it.

He kissed her on her lips which were bruised now.

CHAPTER NINE

By the time Mady reached home, Ben had put Archie to bed. She was desperate to follow up her Orangeboro lead but Ben had cooked her a meal and wanted her to eat it with him and not up in her study, he said, between telephone calls to the States.

'Evans said their film would have been the end of Hugh,' she tried to convince him.

'Good,' said Ben, handing her a knife and fork.

'And Roz has just confirmed that Hugh went to law school there . . .'

'Great. Call them in the morning.'

In the morning, she wanted to remind him, he was out so she would be on Archie-duty and anyway, with the time difference no one would be at the college until the afternoon. It would be another seventeen hours before she could make further headway, an agonising prospect. Whereas, if she put in those calls now . . .

But she held her tongue. Ben had been superb that day but he had his limits. They ate and talked about other things, and lolled on the sofa together watching an American sitcom they had seen before. She almost relaxed. The news came on and suddenly there was Hugh on the screen, red-faced and swearing, ripping off his microphone and storming out of a live TV interview.

'Not quite as cool and calm as he seems then,' she commented.

Ben said nothing.

'Ben?' Glancing round, she saw he was asleep. She considered her obvious duty: the kitchen, stacking the dishwasher, preparing Archie's night-feed. With the utmost care so as not to wake her husband, she eased off the sofa and slipped upstairs.

She checked her atlas first. There was only one 'Orangeboro' in the entire world, and that, most satisfyingly, was a county in South Carolina near Charleston. She called international directory enquiries but they had no listing for Orangeboro Law School.

She went on-line and asked for a list of all adult educational establishments in Orangeboro. Six names came up on the screen. She was able to dismiss two immediately: The Aviation Safety School and the School for The Business Image. Of the rest, the University of The Carolinas looked most promising, but it had no law department.

Another college turned out to be a school for separation counsellors. Muttering under her breath, she requested more information on the next name, Chesterfield University.

It had a law department. It had been founded in 1970. It also had a sizeable graduate program. It had to be the right place. She dialled the telephone number. There was a pause as the call connected and a prerecorded voice listed the departments available.

Mady asked to be put through to Administration. She was told she would have to wait. She did so impatiently. Ben wouldn't sleep for ever. Administration put her through to 'Student Affairs'.

'Hullo? How can I help you?' An unhurried female voice came over the line. She introduced herself as a Student Advisor.

Mady explained that she was looking for information on a student who had been at the college twenty years before.

'My! We just about go back that far! What's his name?'

Mady told her, and waited for the exclamation that a British film company had been enquiring about Hugh only recently . . . and wasn't he the British politician whose baby had been murdered?

But the woman merely said, 'Hugh Eastwood? No, I can't say that name rings any bells.'

Christine Evans had gone a different route, then. She had known what she was looking for and hadn't needed to expose herself by approaching the college authorities. Obviously the Eastwood trial, of such importance to Mady, had been entirely forgettable elsewhere.

The Student Advisor offered to check her records and Mady heard the tapping of keyboard keys. She also heard, from next door, a whimper from Archie. Please don't scream now, she begged.

'Here we are,' the Advisor announced triumphantly. 'Hugh Antony Eastwood from London, England. He was here from the fall of 1979 through 1980.'

Mady felt a fillip of excitement. 'Do you have anything else? Any, er, detail of what he did?'

'He graduated, if that's what you mean.'

'He did? That's great. Perfect.' For authenticity, Mady even wrote that down. 'Did he do anything else of particular note?'

'I've no idea. I wasn't here back then. It was just a little place in those days, about four hundred students, I guess. Now we number four thousand.'

Mady began to see why Hugh might have been forgotten.

'Are you a relative of his, ma'am?' the woman asked belatedly.

'I'm a researcher. From England.'

'Oh, that's all right. Only we have to be careful not to release personal data.'

'Sure. Um, might any of your tutors remember Hugh personally?'

'Well, I don't know. It's such a long time ago . . .'

'Please.' Mady let some of her desperation slip out. 'It's . . . it's just I've got to write about Hugh's life in great detail – his wife's commissioned me to do it as a wedding anniversary present . . .'

'Gracious, how sweet.'

'Yes . . .' Sometimes Mady surprised herself with her own inventiveness under fire. 'Er, I'm not doing too badly over here in England, but his wife loves America and is particularly keen to have as much detail as possible on his life as a student in the States . . .'

'Oh, I see.' The Advisor was completely won over. 'Would you like me to ask in the office if anyone remembers him, or can think of anyone who might?'

Mady accepted gratefully and was put on hold. Through the wall, Archie was cranking up. Jamming the walkabout phone between her shoulder and ear, Mady emerged on to the landing. It was Archie's hungry cry, and it would only get worse if she went in without a bottle. She made her way softly downstairs, past the sitting room and into the kitchen. There was still no sound from Ben. She opened the fridge and muttered a prayer of thanks to see a bottle in there, already made up. If she had been doing the thing properly, she told herself, she would have heated the bottle in a saucepan of water, or at least the microwave, but she wasn't doing anything properly that night.

She retraced her steps and nudged open Archie's door. He was sitting up in his cot, mouth open for a really full-bodied yell. He stopped, gazing at her hopefully.

'There's a good boy.' She proffered the cold bottle which he snatched greedily. 'Mummy's on the phone,' she explained but he didn't care. He was already gulping down the milk.

'Ma'am?' the American voice broke in. 'No one in the office here remembers your Hugh. No one's been here anything like twenty years, but I've got two names for you. The old chaplain, now he knew everyone . . .'

'Oh yes?' Excellent, Mady thought, returning to her office and picking up her pen.

'Unfortunately he died last year.'

Mady set her jaw.

'And then there's Dr McCloud. Amos McCloud.'

'He's alive?'

'Oh yes! Very much so. He's been with us right from the start. He's semi-retired now but still teaches part-time from home in Charleston. Would you like his address?'

Mady took it, and the telephone number. She asked what McCloud taught, preparing herself for physics, or PE, but it was Ethics. Wasn't Ethics connected to law? She thanked the woman sincerely and said goodbye.

She was about to call McCloud's number when the phone rang. It was quarter to eleven. No one rang at that time of night unless it was an emergency. She picked up the receiver.

'Can I speak to Mady O'Neil?' The caller was male, with a pronounced Antipodean accent.

'Speaking.' She wondered who on earth he was.

'Mike Lyons returning your call.'

Then she remembered. Mike Lyons was the New Zealand police inspector she had tried calling that afternoon. Lyons had been in charge of the 'Baby Simon' case, the cot-death baby, or, depending on one's viewpoint, Alice's first victim. That afternoon, Mady had wanted to speak to him desperately. Now he seemed an irrelevance but she could scarcely dismiss him. She explained who she was and that she was investigating Charley's death.

'Surely that's all over now,' he sighed.

'I've just got a couple of questions.' She flicked back in her notebook, trying to find them.

'Go on then,' Lyons prompted and she could tell he enjoyed media fuss, and was probably missing it. She couldn't find the page with the questions on it. She asked, 'Do you think Alice did it?'

'Yep. Either her or her chum.' There was no trace of doubt in his voice.

'The post mortem showed no signs that the baby was shaken,' she reminded him.

'She put a hand or a pillow over his face.'

'What was her motive?'

'I don't think these girls need a motive. Maybe they don't like baby boys? Maybe Simon had been crying earlier and annoyed them?'

She entertained his theory for a moment. 'Do you think they did it together?'

'Who knows? They're tough, they never cracked. They cried, sure, but they never admitted to what they had done.' He paused. 'Myself, I think Armstrong did it."

It was a distinct possibility, Mady thought. 'Why Armstrong?' she asked.

'Bad background. Divorced parents; she lived with her mum, got touched up by her stepdad; ran away from home at twelve. Maybe what had happened to her as a kid warped her, I don't know.'

'But if it was Kate who killed Simon,' she said more slowly, 'isn't it much more likely to have been her who also killed Charley?'

'That's what I told your British police but they didn't want to know. They'd got Alice, they hadn't got Kate.'

Mady had a sudden flash of Alice in the prison room that morning, flatly denying Kate's guilt. Too flatly? How could she be so certain? According to her own evidence, Kate had been alone with Charley for long enough to have harmed him . . . 'If Kate did it, why is Alice covering up for her?' she asked Lyons.

'Who knows? Maybe it was Kate this time, Alice the first. They made a deal not to talk.'

'Why couldn't your baby just have died of cot death?'

'He hadn't any of the predisposing factors: he wasn't premature; he didn't have a cold; his parents didn't smoke; he was a perfectly healthy baby boy.' Lyons broke off. 'Look, I've got another call coming in. If you want any more, you can call me back . . .'

'Sure. Thanks very much.'

Mady replaced the phone and sat thinking. On the face of it, Lyons' argument was convincing. Both girls had been present when the two babies had slipped into unconsciousness. Lightning never struck twice.

But it hadn't, she reminded herself. Whatever suspicions Lyons had, a postmortem had concluded that Simon had died of natural causes, whereas there had never been any doubt that Charley's injuries had been inflicted by a third party.

As for Lyons' theory that Kate was the guilty one, Alice the willing scapegoat, it simply didn't make sense. No one went to prison for six years for the sake of a friendship, no matter how strong.

Had she been too quick in suspecting Hugh? Might Alice actually be guilty? She felt her mind reeling. But Roz didn't think Alice was guilty, not any more. Roz suspected her own husband, and had come to Mady for help, and as ever Mady had promised to give it.

Uniquely Mady was in possession of two testimonies: those of Roz and Alice. Put together, they pointed at Hugh. Hugh, backed into a corner, terrified of Trump Card's film, driven to the point of insanity . . .

'I thought so.'

She jumped. Ben stood in the doorway. 'I'm sorry . . .' she babbled. 'I was just . . . There was a phone call . . .'

'I know, it woke me up.' He shook his head. 'You're incorrigible.'

'Yes,' she agreed humbly, 'I'll do the kitchen.'

'You bet you will. I'm going to bed.'

For the second time that night, Alice awoke to the bright light of a torch shining in her eyes.

'Get some sleep,' barked the male warder as if it was her fault she had woken. He withdrew and the door slammed.

It was one o'clock in the morning and Alice had been in the new prison in Dorset for less than ten hours. On her arrival, the governor had informed her that she would find conditions with him tough but fair. She hadn't asked what he meant, being fearful of the answer.

The two women warders who had strip-searched her at reception had chatted casually to each other, as if Alice wasn't there, about the recent suicide of an inmate who had swallowed bleach. In her single cell – she was segregated for her own protection – there had been a bottle of bleach beside the lavatory in her tiny bathroom. It stayed there for two hours until one of the warders, without comment, removed it.

They wanted her to go mad, they wanted her to take her own life. That was why they kept waking her up. Throughout the long evening, the spyhole in her door had been slid open for someone else to stare in at her, and then after varying degrees of time, shut again.

They must realise what it did to a prisoner, knowing they were being watched at all times, that they had no privacy whatsoever. It was a torture reserved for her alone.

She was a novelty, a baby-killer, segregated under prison Rule 43, from the other prisoners for her own safety. At the other prisons, there had always been someone worse than she. A Paediatric Intensive Care nurse who had killed nine children and brain-damaged a dozen more. Another woman who had tortured her own baby. But there, she outstripped them all. There were two other Rule 43s, the first a woman serving life for killing her husband, but he had beaten her for years, so she was seen sympathetically by all. The other Rule 43 was a terrorist who was due for deportation any day.

Alice was there for keeps, and hated, as far as she could tell, by everyone. She hadn't met the other prisoners yet and she dreaded to think what they had in store for her.

It was only the beginning. There were six more years to go. By the time she got out, she would be thirty-two. Her youth gone and the rest of her life marred by what she was supposed to have done. No one would want her. She would never have her own children, never hold her own baby.

An aeon ago, it seemed, she'd told Mady O'Neil the truth about Hugh Eastwood, and Mady had promised to do what she could. Alice had felt buoyed, had allowed herself to hope throughout the dismal transfer in the prison van, but now she wondered: what would Mady really do? She was Roz's best friend. Best friends told each other everything. So Mady would tell Roz what Alice had said, Roz would tell Hugh, and he being the sort of man he was, would order Alice silenced, once and for all.

It would be easy to make her death look like suicide in prison. Already she was being set up for it.

She didn't care. Better to be dead than endure more hatred. Her mind wandered wretchedly to Kate. Was she really dead, as Alice's barrister had suggested, echoing Alice's own fear? What other reason for her non-appearance could there be?

Alice had always protected Kate as best she could, giving her money to run away from her stepfather, helping her to find work as a nanny. Keeping quiet about Kate's behaviour on the day that little Simon Wilson had died.

There were parallels between the two cases. Alice had been Simon's nanny for only a short while, two months. She had put him down for his afternoon sleep in his cot just before Kate had arrived. They had sat on the porch for an hour and then Alice had said she was just popping up to check on the baby.

'I'll do it,' Kate had volunteered and Alice had let her.

Kate had been gone a little time, longer in retrospect than it ought to have taken to look at a sleeping baby. But when she had come back down it was to report that Simon had been fast asleep, and looking angelic. They had gone back to the porch and resumed their conversation. Time had run on, and suddenly it was five o'clock.

'Simon!' Alice exclaimed, leaping up. He had been asleep for three hours, not unheard of, but definitely he needed waking now, if he was going to sleep at night.

'I'll get him,' Kate offered again, and again, Alice had let her. Then, Kate's scream. Alice had run upstairs to see what was wrong. In his cot, Simon was lying on his back with his head turned to the side, his hand up by his mouth as if he had been sucking his thumb and had then let go to lose himself more deeply in sleep. Only he wasn't moving, he wasn't breathing, and the pillow that his mother had banned from the cot had been lying on the mattress just above Simon's head . . .

Kate had been hysterical.

Acting without conscious thought, Alice had replaced that pillow on the shelf where it was always kept. Out of harm's way. Only then, had she called the police . . .

She had never asked Kate, perhaps fearing the answer, why she had put the pillow inside the cot. Had Kate hurt him? Under interrogation, just once, when she had been utterly exhausted, Alice had thought of telling that Auckland policeman, but then she had realised what she was about to do: betray her best friend, and she would never do that. Kate's stepfather had put her in an institution. Alice knew Kate would not survive prison, and as it turned out, Alice had been right to say nothing: the inquest had judged that Simon had died of natural causes.

What did it matter that Kate had put the pillow inside the cot? Kate loved to arrange baby things. It was a game to her. The little girl she looked after three days a week was always immaculately turned out, and her room, since Kate had been there, looked like a filmset for the perfect nursery. Kate much preferred baby girls to boys, she'd told Alice, they had much prettier things to play with. In fact, she didn't terribly like boys.

Had she hurt Simon? Was that why she hadn't come forward to defend Alice? Why had she, Alice, allowed Kate any time at all alone with Charley? She hadn't meant to. If Alice was wrong about Hugh, was it Kate who had harmed Charley? If she had, it was her, Alice's fault. She was as bad as everyone judged her. As for Kate, poor Kate had probably taken her own life.

At the door, the spyhole slid open once more. Alice turned her head to the wall and wept.

A burst of sound woke Roz up. Her surroundings were fleetingly unfamiliar to her before she realised where she was: in her bedroom in Chelsea. Next door was Charley's room, intact, the mobile still hanging above his cot, his clothes still waiting to be unfolded, sorted, thrown out.

Roz shook herself. If she carried on thinking like that, she would go mad. She must think of other things. The previous night, for example, hot sex with Hugh. That was better. Tune into that, tune out of all else. She realised that the sound she heard was the television coming up from the floor below.

Hugh watching television at five past seven in the morning? She saw from the undented nature of his pillow that he had not come to bed all night. Poor Hugh. He must get his sleep. For a job as important as his, he needed rest, and all the support he could get. She would make him coffee, then pop out to the supermarket to get him a proper breakfast.

Clad in one of his old shirts, she went quietly downstairs. Through the door, she heard snatches of television news:

'. . . share prices in the US continue to rise . . .'

'In Bonn last night, the president of the Green Party . . .'

'Buckingham Palace refused to comment on the story that Prince Edward . . .'

She smiled. Ever restless, Hugh was channel-hopping. The floorboard creaked, and she pushed open the door.

Hugh didn't see her. He was sitting on the sofa, staring at the TV screen. On it was a picture of a woman with a hard red mouth, very Essex in Roz's opinion, and the newsreader was saying:

'Police say they are treating as suspicious the death of the documentary-maker Christine Evans, whose body was discovered outside her home in the early hours of this morning. It appears that she had fallen from a fourth-floor attic window into her garden below. Ms Evans, forty-seven, was most well-known for her series of award-winning screen exposés on "the great and the good". She had recently joined the American network TTUS . . .'

Hugh was staring at the screen as if petrified.

'Did you know her?' Roz asked diffidently, and Hugh whipped round.

'No! Never seen her before.'

Liar, thought Roz. She could always tell. He must think she was stupid.

'It is known that the dead woman had been in dispute with her former employer, the production company Trump Card. A spokesman for that company would make no comment this morning . . .'

Hugh couldn't take his eyes from the screen. Why such overwhelming interest? Then the truth hit her! Hugh had been having an affair with that person. Roz gave an involuntary shudder. That haggard crow. She was what he was being blackmailed over. She would be the subject of the film Mady had talked about.

She looked at her husband, pop-eyed on the sofa. He had reverted to type. But how could he have betrayed her, for *her*? How everyone would laugh when that story came out!

He switched off the set and turned round. 'Did you sleep well?' he asked with a pathetic attempt at jauntiness.

'Pretty well. You?'

His eyes slid away. 'Not too good.'

No, she thought viciously, but it was in a sweet voice that she told him she was going up to have a bath.

Coffee, a great deal of it, Hugh thought, would help bring him to his senses, knock the shock out of him.

He'd never met Christine Evans, although he felt he knew her intimately. She had changed his life for ever.

She had called him at home, out of the blue, the week before Charley had been hurt, to tell him what she proposed to do: ruin him. She had found out about what had happened at Chesterfield. She had located witnesses — a letter, for God's sake!

Did he have any comment to make? Would he like to do so on air, or would he prefer to issue a written statement?

There had been oil in her voice, sheer poison. She had been enjoying herself, she could smell and taste his fear, and he'd been so very frightened.

He'd begged her not to do it; he'd promised her anything, he'd racked his brain, and it had come to him. The juiciest morsel, which no journalist could refuse: the inside track on the Grey Team.

She'd paused and, in that second, he'd thanked God. He was bartering with treason but somehow he'd square it.

Then she'd drawled, 'My, but you are desperate, aren't you?'

Not a word on whether she would accept his offer or refuse it. She had left him dangling but she would call again, she promised. Or he could call her any time. She gave him her numbers. Only, he mustn't think she was going to go away.

She was a witch from hell, a demon sent to destroy him. No wonder he hadn't slept after that. He'd stumbled through the days in a fog of alcohol and fear. Roz had been no use. But when a full week had passed and Evans hadn't called, he'd dared hope, which had been foolish, he knew now, because on the Wednesday evening, just as he had been leaving the office to meet Roz for dinner, Evans had rung on his direct line.

She wanted to let him know Trump Card was not interested in his bribes: the film was going ahead with or without his comment.

Then dinner with Roz, a terrible affair with his mind at breaking point, and Roz nagging him to be a nursemaid, and then Charley crying all night. Blank hours until the next morning, himself at work in a stupor, and Roz calling him to tell him about Charley . . .

He remembered thinking that nothing could be as bad as what Evans proposed to do to him, and then Charley . . .

He'd known nothing of the Trump Card fire, nothing about anything. It hadn't been until weeks later, when he'd been back at work, after the funeral, that he'd seen a reference to Evans in one of the newspapers. A paragraph tucked away downpage, but her name had shone forth like a beacon to him. She was suing her company for damages amid extraordinary claims that fellow directors had deliberately fired their premises to destroy her film.

Hugh's old terror had returned but only for an instant, until he'd realised what it meant: he was in the clear! The film must have been destroyed in the fire! By Providence, he had been saved. Certainly, as the months had passed, there had been no further word from her. No more threats. She had gone from his life.

Now she had truly gone. He'd had nothing to do with it! 'Police said they were treating the death as suspicious . . .'

He'd been there, all night, in the house with his wife, although not sleeping beside her. How could he sleep in that bed when he knew what lay directly above his head, in the loft?

He'd sat up instead, watching news programmes to see how much coverage his walk-out had got – less as the night had worn on. Then films, then nothing, when he must have fallen asleep. Waking at dawn, exhausted, he'd mechanically checked the news again, and there she had been on the screen, and right behind him, watching his every move, his wife whom he loved and hated both, whom he knew he must not trust, although he longed to.

His hand shook as he spooned out coffee. He must get a grip. He took a deep breath, and the idea came to him: that actually he was safe now. Providence had again stepped in. Not only was the film destroyed but the viper too.

Of course he'd had nothing to do with her death. Of course he hadn't confided in his special advisors – Alan or Rebecca . . . It would have been Alan – it was men's work – who'd told him never to talk of it again. Such a conversation had never taken place!

Hugh shook his head, dispelling the notion once and for all. Now no one who could harm him knew anything about what had happened at Chesterfield. Those ghosts could remain buried.

He felt a surge of confidence. He could control Roz. Hadn't she become his again last night? As for the video, it would remain forever where it was. They would never sell the house, or rent it out. Upstairs, he heard his mobile telephone ringing. It would be Rebecca calling to chew his ear. He could handle her. He mounted the stairs two at a time.

CHAPTER TEN

Opening the door to the church hall, Mady was hit by a wall of sound. A high-level hum of female conversation, pierced by shrieks and bellows. The Wednesday morning session of the Hickory Dickory Dock Mothers and Babies Club was in progress. This was 'free-play' half-hour. Soon would come sitting on the hard floor singing nursery rhymes with actions.

Mady had been once before, when Archie had been smaller. The experience had not been one to make her rush back but the baby books and the health visitor said Archie was now at an age where 'socialisation' was important, as much for Mady's sake as his.

It was true she didn't know any other local mothers. The two friends she had made at her ante-natal classes had subsequently moved out of London and she hadn't put in a great effort elsewhere, blaming her timetable as a working mother, and because, frankly, there had always been Roz and Charley, the perfect combination, ready-made.

If Archie wasn't to go through life friendless, if she was to develop contact with other mothers, she was going to have to push herself. Also, waking that morning to grey, raining skies and the frustration of not being able to get on with her work, Mady knew she would have to get out of the house or go mad.

Archie was now struggling in her arms and she found a patch of floor on which to set him down. At once he crawled off towards a garish Wendy house in the corner, where several toddlers were slamming the door energetically and hurling themselves out of windows oblivious to smaller babies. Mady tried to follow but found her way barred by three women holding teacups and loudly discussing the merits of local pre-prep schools.

'Boy or girl?' one boomed at Mady.

'Um, boy. He's over there, actually. I'm just trying to make sure he doesn't—'

'St Dunstan's or Marleycombe House?'

The women paused, cups hovering on saucers as they awaited her response.

'I haven't given it a thought,' Mady stated boldly. 'He's not quite ten months old.'

They gasped and tutted. 'But you should have had him down at birth!'

'I had Oscar down at Marleycombe when I was five months pregnant.'

Mady smiled. Depending on her mood, she quite enjoyed such encounters. 'Actually we're thinking of sending Archie to Honneyfield,' she murmured.

'But that's state!'

'Huge classes!'

'Think of his accent!'

'He's not talking yet,' Mady assured them earnestly. 'Excuse me,' she added, seeing a hefty male child raise a toy above Archie's innocent head. She wasn't quick enough. The toy, a plastic microwave oven, crashed down with a resounding wallop. Archie screamed. Mady lunged forward to scoop him up and the other child fell to the ground.

'Oscar, darling!' One of the women swooped, glaring at Mady who could already feel a lump forming on Archie's head.

'I think it's better to let them fight their own battles,' said Oscar's mother, picking him up.

'Yes, but Archie's only a baby.'

The women pointedly turned her back. 'There, darling. It's all right. Did the big lady knock you down?'

Mady tried to calm Archie and herself. The singing began, without accompaniment or the aid of a songsheet. Mady mumbled along with the general dirge, keeping her eyes down, and thought: if anyone had fastforwarded her to that moment two years before, she just might not have bothered getting pregnant.

Then she looked at Archie, recovered, and cherubic, joining in enthusiastically with an action rhyme and being smiled at by another mother. Mady smiled back, reminded of first days at new schools. After the singing, she and the other mother chatted about their babies, of similar ages, and exchanged telephone numbers.

She wheeled Archie home in the rain, noting that cars stopped for her buggy and people on the pavement got out of her way. They assumed she was a full-time mother, she realised, and was half-wistful that she wasn't, but also, bearing in mind how she had passed that morning, relieved.

A few minutes from the house, Archie fell asleep, as she had been hoping he might. Uneasily she acknowledged that she

spent a sizeable chunk of her time engineering either Archie or
Ben into sleep so that she could get some work done. Archie
ought to sleep for at least an hour, and if she was lucky for two
or three.

She got him into the house and closed the door. Then the
telephone rang. She ran to get it before he woke up.

It was Roz. She tried to collect her thoughts. 'Hi! Er . . . how's
Hugh? I saw the news last night . . .'

'Oh, you mean his walk-out? He's fine.'

Roz sounded strained, but there was quite a lot of background noise, and Mady guessed she was in a public place. She
asked her if she was all right?

'Perfectly.'

There was an awkward pause. In the background, somebody
laughed. Mady wondered why Roz had called.

'Does the name "Christine Evans" mean anything to you?'
asked Roz coolly.

Mady went hot and cold. How had Roz found out? Hugh
must have told her. Had Roz also betrayed her, Mady, to him?
'Why d'you ask?'

'Only that she's dead.'

The news thumped home. 'What?' said Mady weakly.
'When?'

'She fell from a window in her house last night. Haven't you
seen the news?'

'No, I, er . . .' She felt short of breath. 'I've been out with
Archie.'

'Oh.'

Mady tried to absorb it. It could not be coincidence that
Evans had died – in a fall? – within hours of telling her to check
out what Hugh had done at Orangeboro. She remembered

Evans saying that six hours after she'd told Hugh the film was going ahead, Trump Card's premises got burned. Had Hugh been involved in Evans' death? Had he had her followed to the wine bar? Then home afterwards, where he had interrogated and killed her? It couldn't be, it was crazy, too far-fetched . . .

'She's what the film was about, wasn't she?' Roz broke in on her thoughts.

'What?'

'The film you told me about. That Hugh got so worked up about before he . . . before Charley got hurt?'

Mady gathered herself together. 'No. No, it wasn't about her.'

'You can tell me the truth, you know. I'm not a child.'

How bitter Roz sounded. 'It wasn't about her, Roz. Evans was the film's producer.'

'So you say.'

Mady was taken aback. 'I'm telling you the truth.'

'The whole truth?'

Mady felt herself redden. 'Roz, you're going to have to trust me,' she said earnestly. 'Evans wasn't the subject of the film.'

'Was Hugh having an affair with her?'

'I think Hugh's got more taste. She was the producer of the film, not its subject. I met her last night. She wouldn't tell me what it was about. All she would say was to hint that it was connected to Orangeboro.'

'That's why you called me?'

'That's right. Look, I'm sorry I didn't tell you more last night, but . . . I didn't know if I could rely on you not to mention it to Hugh.' She perhaps ought not to have told her now, Mady rationalised, but it was too late.

'Fat chance,' snapped Roz. 'You should have seen the way he was looking at her picture. I know that look.'

'Roz . . .' Mady appealed.

'Never mind. I haven't got time to chat. I take it you're still investigating him?'

'Yes.'

'So presumably you'd be interested in the name and address of a man he went to college with in Orangeboro?' Roz spoke so clinically. 'D'you want it or not?' she demanded.

'Yes.' Mady scrabbled for a piece of paper and a working pen. She wrote down the details.

'Remember Hugh's got important friends,' Roz said suddenly.

'Is that a warning?'

'Look after yourself,' Roz murmured and the line went dead.

For a full minute, Mady sat motionless. Had Hugh killed Christine Evans, or had her killed? Roz herself seemed to be hinting at it. Mady rose and went up to her office, cautiously treading past Archie who stirred but didn't wake, and put in a call to the press bureau at Scotland Yard. Evans' death was the second item on the tape.

Police were appealing for witnesses to the death, which at that stage was being treated as suspicious. Ms Evans appeared to have fallen from a fourth-floor window at her Putney home. She had been found early that morning by a passer-by who had summoned an ambulance. She had died from multiple injuries shortly after arriving at hospital. According to friends, she had not been depressed.

So the police were considering the possibility of suicide. Mady thought back to the woman she had met, admittedly for less than half an hour and not in the most relaxed circumstances – but she hadn't struck her as the suicidal type; she had been too bolshy and full of her own importance for that. On the other hand, people killed themselves for a host of reasons. Perhaps she thought Hugh would never be brought to justice? Had it mattered to her that much? It wasn't conceivable. But the timing was too close for comfort. There had to be a connection somewhere.

She hadn't liked the woman particularly, but the manner of her death was shocking and Mady felt partly responsible. She realised too that she might have been the last person to see her alive, and as such, she ought to inform the police, but she would have to invent a reason for their meeting. If she told the truth, they would start investigating Hugh too, rendering her own work impossible. She was a bad liar; they would be instantly suspicious.

She would tell them nothing for the moment. If they traced her, she probably wouldn't be in the country.

She was going to Orangeboro. In reality, she had known that since her meeting with Christine, but now the woman's death propelled her forward. She called Jack Simpson first to get his permission to go. When he sounded reluctant, as he always did about the cost of foreign travel, she told him about Evans.

'Eastwood did it?' he breathed. Jack loved conspiracy theories as much as she.

'I don't know.'

'But you need to go there to find out.' She heard him suck in his breath for effect but she knew he was sold. 'Okay,' he said reluctantly, 'only don't go mad.'

She promised she wouldn't. She asked if she could have a spare mobile phone, as she didn't want to be pestered by callers from the UK when she was in the States, and Jack agreed to bike one over.

She called the airlines, jotting down details on the same page of her notebook that bore the notes from her conversation with Mike Lyons. The Guilty Alice or Kate Armstrong theories. They seemed to belong to another time and place. She was glad she had wasted no proper time on them.

When she had done everything else, she telephoned Ben, catching him between meetings. He laughed at first, then he said incredulously, 'Are you serious? Nine o'clock tonight?'

'It's the best flight. Direct into Atlanta, and I can catch an internal flight to Charleston first thing in the morning. Orangeboro is about ten miles away from there.'

'How about Archie? Who's going to look after him?'

She paused.

'Me, I suppose?' he said angrily.

'It's only for a couple of days, then it's the weekend.'

'How am I supposed to get any work done?'

'He does sleep,' she reminded him. 'And you did say you had no more meetings this week after today's.'

He didn't respond.

'There's always my mother?' she suggested.

'I'd rather do it on my own, thanks.'

She told him about Evans' death, and Roz's call, but he refused to be impressed. 'I don't see why you have to go to the States,' he complained. 'Why can't you just call or e-mail?'

'It won't work. You can't tell if someone's lying on e-mail or even over the phone. I've got to be there in person. If I can get out there tonight, I could be back home by, say, Sunday night?'

'Terrific.'

She tried for the lighter touch. 'Think of all that lovely quality time together.'

'Archie and I don't need it,' Ben said viciously, then he asked, 'You're sure it's safe, you going over there?'

She smiled. 'Absolutely.'

'You really think Hugh had Evans topped?'

'I don't know. It's possible.'

'Does he know you're on to him?'

'No,' she shook her head definitely.

'God, four days of undiluted Archie.' Ben hung up.

She knew she ought to feel guilty, but she had too much to do. She must pack. She ran down the stairs to check what the washing machine held, and saw Archie was wide awake in his buggy, watching her.

He looked reproachful.

'Darling,' she smiled, but got no response other than that solemn stare. 'Let's get you out of there,' she crooned, and unbuckled him. He clung to her tightly, the way she had seen him do with Ben.

'Hey, sweet-pea, are you hungry? It is lunchtime.' She shifted his weight to one side, and he snuggled into her shoulder, something else she couldn't remember him doing before. 'How about some yummy chicken, tomato and potato?' She made his meals herself, trying to use only organic ingredients. Apparently working mothers tended to do that, she'd read, to alleviate their guilt.

She carried him into the kitchen and tried to slot him into his highchair, but he wouldn't let go. 'Archie,' she pleaded, delighted but also aggravated, 'are you doing this because I'm going away?'

He merely clung on tighter and she gave up trying to resist and held him close. She had never left him before, she realised, not even for a night. Tears came to her eyes. Suppose something happened to her? Who would look after him? Ben would hire a nanny. He would do his best to find the right person, but whoever it was couldn't love Archie the way that she did. She might lose her temper with him, harm him.

'I'll come back, my darling,' she promised.

Archie's hand wrapped loosely around her neck. 'Da-da,' he cooed lovingly in response.

It had been Hugh's idea to meet for lunch at The Red Dragon, an old favourite of theirs from before Charley, being convenient both for Hugh's office and Roz's.

She saw he was still in the extraordinary good spirits in which he'd departed that morning. Extraordinary, she considered, for a man whose girlfriend had just been pushed out of a window. Perhaps they had rowed? Hugh possessed such a nasty temper. Perhaps that's where he'd been the night before, shoving her out of the window? Roz smiled at the mental picture.

'What, sweetheart?' Hugh asked, mistily.

He'd had a bit too much to drink with the meal. It had made him amorous. That thought made her smile too.

'You're very mysterious today.' His eyes slid over her. She was wearing a soft grey dress that he liked and bright red lipstick. 'As well as lovely. What is it?'

'Nothing.'

Having tried to get hold of Mady all morning, and refusing to leave sensitive information on the answering machine, Roz had finally spoken to her there at the restaurant while she'd been waiting for Hugh to arrive. As soon as she'd finished the call, she had popped her mobile back into her handbag and burned the piece of paper with the address on it in the ashtray on the table.

'You haven't taken up smoking on the quiet, have you?'

She'd jumped at the sound of his voice, not expecting him to come up from behind, having irritatingly forgotten about the secondary, spiral staircase that led up from the bar below.

'I was clearing out my handbag. Old till receipts.'

'How very tidy of you. Interesting telephone call?'

How long had he been watching her? Had he heard anything?

But he hadn't asked any further questions. He'd been so full of himself throughout lunch, chatting away as if he hadn't a care in the world, clearly loving it when the waiter recognised him. Hugh loved to be noticed, assuming that every turned head in the restaurant was caused by admiration of his political prowess. Not about Charley and the court case. His self-importance was quite breathtaking at times.

'Did you catch them on the hop at the office?' he asked her now.

'I didn't go in.'

'Oh? You said you were going to.'

'Yes but I chickened out,' she said.

'Well, people will understand. It's not even a week after . . . What did you do, then? Bit of essential shopping?'

She looked at him. She could say, she had gone up to the attic where there were so many cobwebs, and crawled around, as he had done the night before, looking for something. 'I put away Charley's things,' she said.

'Oh.' He looked punched. Exactly as if she had landed her fist in his soft stomach, pow.

'I thought it was about time.'

'Yes.' He'd gone white.

In Charley's room, she had dismantled the mobile, emptied clothes out of drawers, swept toys into carrier bags, moving fast so as not to give herself time to dwell. Then from under the cot, she had pulled Charley's soft yellow duck. It had the sweetest expression and huge orange feet. Charley had loved that duck, it had always been in the cot with him, Roz allowing it because of its fabric, filling, everything about it, was absolutely safe.

That morning, she had pressed her face against it, inhaling deeply. Charley's soft baby smell was still there. She had doubled up on the floor, keening for him.

'Pudding?' Hugh asked, clearing his throat.

She focused. 'No thanks.' Her throat hurt choking down new tears.

'Did you see the coverage I got in *The Times*? "The Minister who isn't afraid to speak out"? Rebecca was pretty pleased with it.'

'Yes, you already said.' Suddenly she had to get away from him. She excused herself to the cloakroom.

Hugh watched her go. Clearly, all was not well with her. She was brittle, distant, moody. Of course cleaning out the baby's bedroom was bound to have been upsetting. Hugh himself hadn't been in there since the death. He didn't know if he ever could.

The warm booziness ebbed away quickly. He had felt so buoyed by the morning: Rebecca and Alan mollified by his calm charm and by the press coverage of his 'walk-out', which had been almost universally sympathetic.

But Roz's behaviour was disturbing him. Last night she had been so hot for him. She would have done anything he asked. Now she was ice. What was going on?

His eyes fell on her handbag. In her rush to depart, she had left it behind. Poking out of the top was her mobile phone on which she had been speaking when he'd arrived.

Who had she been calling? Keeping one eye on the door through which she had gone, he extracted the implement and pressed the redial code.

A familiar number appeared but he couldn't quite place it. He pressed the 'call' button. 'Come on,' he muttered as it rang out. Roz wouldn't stay away for ever.

'Hullo?' said a voice breathlessly. 'Hullo?'

He switched off Mady O'Neil and replaced the mobile. No great surprise it being Mady, she and Roz being umbilically tied, but why hadn't Roz told him? Was it simply her mood? Or was she being secretive about everything towards him because of her great big secret regarding him? Was secretiveness becoming her second nature, along with her violent mood swings? No one, being with her very long, could fail to notice it. Was her behaviour, even if she intended to be loyal to him, going to give him away?

'No more slip-ups,' Rebecca had warned that morning, and he knew it to be his final warning.

He saw that Roz was on her way back. She was wearing his favourite dress, soft and clingy. She still had a great body. He noticed the looks she was getting from some other men. 'All right?' he asked her concernedly.

'Fine.' She gave him a radiant smile from lips newly shiny with lipstick. She was sending him such confusing signals.

The waiter came and Roz agreed that she would like a coffee. She crossed her legs, and in so doing, brushed hers against his. Now she didn't move them away.

'Heard from Mady recently?' he asked, and felt her flinch.

'No,' she said.

Why lie, he thought, stirring his coffee? What was she concealing? What were the pair of them up to?

'Probably busy wrecking some poor bastard's career,' he suggested with a smile.

'Probably. Hugh, I . . .'

'Yes?'

Her hand was plucking at a minute hole in the tablecloth. He put his own hand over hers, and turned it palm up. Such pretty little hands. She was trembling. She said nervously, 'I need to get away, I think. I thought, maybe up to Suffolk, just for a few days . . .'

They had a house up there whose garden opened on to the beach. It would have been Charley's playground in the summer. 'Good idea,' he said. 'The beach will be wild at this time of year. Great for walks.'

She nodded, clearly relieved it had been so easy.

He called for the bill. 'I was going to work from home tomorrow anyway,' he said breezily. 'I can push that into Friday and we can make it a long weekend.'

'I . . . I meant, I sort of needed a bit of space to think . . .'

'You go for walks and think. I'll sit and work,' Hugh offered generously.

She stared at him. He lowered his gaze and traced a circle in her palm. She mustn't suppose he was letting her out of his sight. 'You go up there this afternoon,' he proposed. 'Get Keith to drive you. I'll bring the Discovery up later.'

She had no choice and she must understand that was how it must be. He took her arm as they left the restaurant, applying gentle pressure to ease her between the tables.

That late on in the season, the bar was beginning to become popular again with the locals, men who sat at the zinc counter all night, intimidating any remaining tourists. Strangers were immediately obvious.

When Kate Armstrong saw the man come in not long after they had opened that evening, she assumed he was a stray tourist. He was tall, pale, with short fair hair, neither young nor old. He asked in English for a beer and took it to one of the small tables at the back. He produced a paperback and pretended to read it, but actually, he was watching her.

Kate wasn't vain. She knew she wasn't attractive, and her stepfather had taught her to make herself as unobtrusive as possible. She told herself she was imagining the man's eyes upon her, but as she turned away to polish glasses, he was there in front of her. 'Where are you from?' he asked, smiling.

She instantly thought of the British police. They had traced her and sent this man – a British policeman? – to find her, beat her, drag her back.

She looked to Dimitris for help, but he was busy with his friends and the stranger was waiting for her answer.

'Australia,' she lied.

'What's your name?' he asked, still smiling.

'Mary.'

He studied her. 'Ever been to England?'

She felt herself blanch. 'No.'

'Okay, Kate?' asked Dimitris, appearing by her side.

The tourist raised his eyebrows.

Kate stuttered, 'Yes, I . . . I'm fine.'

'Trouble?' asked Dimitris, frowning.

'No. No, nothing like that.'

The man drained his glass, and slapped down coins on the counter. He winked at her. 'Be seeing you.'

When he'd gone, she excused herself and went upstairs to the flat she shared with Dimitris. She looked out of the window and saw the man in a doorway a little further down the street, talking furtively into a mobile telephone. He turned and she ducked down to the floor and stayed there, crouching. She was trembling from head to toe. Should she run? But wasn't it better to stay where she was, where at least she had Dimitris, and the other men's protection?

She glanced out again, and saw that the stranger had gone. It was possible he had been no more than an ordinary tourist. She would try very hard to make herself believe that. She heard Dimitris calling and ran back down to the bar.

CHAPTER ELEVEN

At the airport, the queues for the security scanners wound backward and forward like string between fingers, allowing passengers glimpses of the terminal they had just left behind, and their loved ones, if they were still there.

Ben had gone, walking away with Archie roaring in his arms. The parting had been much worse than she had anticipated, Archie clinging to her, and she doubting suddenly that she could leave him.

'Just go,' Ben ordered, and she had, closing her ears to Archie's cries and wiping away tears of her own. When she had turned to wave, they weren't there.

She felt pathetically abandoned, not at all like a tough, investigative journalist but more like a lost child. What was more important to her, she chided herself: her baby or her work? She saw Archie's face in her mind's eye and fought down tears. What sort of mother was she?

The queue inched forward dreadfully slowly, giving her plenty of time to berate herself. She counted the number of people in front of her, and divided it between the number of interrogators, and reckoned she would be there for at least another half-hour.

As a distraction, she read the address labels on the suitcases around her. Then she got out her book and read it.

Finally, her time came to be processed by security. She boarded the aircraft and immediately counted three babies in close proximity to her seat. As if the airline knew, she thought grimly. She predicted that as soon as the aeroplane took off they would scream, which they did. She put in her earplugs and took out her book which she read determinedly. She slept more than she thought she would and was dozing nine hours later when the intercom announced that they would shortly be landing in Atlanta.

It was nearly four o'clock in the morning when she checked into her hotel room at the airport. Her connecting flight was at seven o'clock, and it almost didn't seem worth falling asleep, she told herself, only to awake on the bed two hours later. She arrived in Charleston at eight-thirty.

As she emerged from the airport it was a bright, blue day, with a blustery little wind and the sun beating down hotly on her head. In England, she reminded herself, it had already snowed. She took possession of her hired car, which surprisingly turned out to be a convertible Ford. She guessed there had been a mistake. *The Register* normally didn't hire such luxurious cars, but she said nothing. Sitting in the parking lot, she opened the roof and took out her mobile.

She wanted to know how Ben and Archie were, particularly Archie. She had had vivid dreams of him, and at one point during the long night she had woken calling his name.

Ben sounded harassed. It was two o'clock in the afternoon in England. He had been unable to get any work done all morning, he complained. And he'd hardly slept the night before because of Archie.

Mady made sympathetic noises.

'Oh, b-lood-y hell. There he goes again. Can you hang on a minute?'

She did. She heard Archie wailing as Ben brought him closer to the phone. She felt a tug inside her, as if a piece of her was missing. 'Hullo, my darling,' she soothed and Archie stopped crying. She could hear him breathing heavily into the mouthpiece.

'Be a good boy for Daddy,' she told him and, like a dream, he made happy, gurgling noises.

'The mere sound of his mother's voice. You're a natural. You ought to try looking after him sometime.'

'Ben!'

'Only joking,' he lied.

She gave him her hotel details. 'I, er, don't suppose you've heard if there've been any developments on Evans or Hugh?'

'You don't suppose correctly. When d'you think I've had the chance to watch the bloody news?'

'All right, all right,' she said hastily. There was a pause but she was scared of saying the wrong thing.

'Good weather?' Ben asked.

'Not bad. Oh Ben . . .'

'Look, this isn't a good time. Archie's stinking. I'd better go and change him.'

'Okay,' she faltered. 'Look after yourself.'

'You too. Bye.'

She felt weepy. She had hoped for so much from that telephone call. She had meant to tell Ben she loved him. She thought of phoning him back to do so, but feared the conversation would go wrong again. She was only tired, she told herself, and the sooner she got on with things, the quicker she could get home.

She put on sunglasses against the glare of the sun. She studied her map and set out in search of the city and her hotel in the historic district. After leaving the highway, she passed cobbled streets and white clapboard houses, graceful old churches and magnolia trees. Ben would love it there, she thought.

At the hotel, a doorman in gold and green livery took her keys and parked her car. A bellboy in the same uniform carried her bag up to her room and showed her how the television, air-conditioning, blackout blinds, safe and telephone worked.

When he had left, she tried them all. Before Archie, when she had travelled fairly frequently for work, she had grown blasé about such luxuries. Now they were a treat. She crossed to the window, opened it as far as it would go – which was not far, to prevent suicides, she supposed – and thought of Christine Evans falling. Would she have lost consciousness in such a short drop? Would she have seen the ground coming for her?

The sound of jazz floated up from the street below. Opposite the hotel, at the base of broad stone steps, stood a saxophonist playing 'The Lady got the Blues'. He wore dark clothing that fluttered in the wind, he was thin and his music seemed ethereal, the sun glinting on the highly polished brass. Mady could have stood listening for hours, and watching people strolling by, each one looking so relaxed, or so it seemed to her, and enjoying themselves.

Instead, she closed the window. She must assume she had very little time: that Roz would break and tell Hugh what she, Mady, was doing, which was why, after debating it briefly, she hadn't told her she was going to the States.

Roz had sounded too odd on the phone the day before. Roz was at breaking point, Mady judged, and therefore no longer to be trusted. In the past, pity might have persuaded her otherwise, but she could help her friend more now, by finding out the truth about Hugh quickly.

She had brought her laptop with her and checked on the Internet: there was nothing new on Evans or Hugh. She called Jack Simpson who told her Hugh had turned his walk-out to advantage and was being written up everywhere as the hero; the interviewer had been suspended after pressure, it was alleged, from Number Ten's chief spin doctor.

She was on her own, with her two leads: Amos McCloud and the contact Roz had given her. It wasn't much.

She dialled McCloud's home number. He had to be there, he had to be helpful.

'Dr McCloud's residence.' A quavery yet haughty female answered the phone.

Mady wondered politely if she might speak to the Doctor? She gave her name, adding that she was a journalist from England.

There was a definite pause. 'Wait, please.'

The phone was put down with a rap. Doddery footsteps faded away on a hard floor. Very remotely, Mady heard voices then a heavier tread returned.

'Hullo? Amos McCloud speaking.' The voice was pure treacle, straight out of *Gone with the Wind*.

'I wonder if you might be able to help me?' she started.

'I'll do my very best.'

Mady imagined him smiling, twiddling the pointy ends of his moustache. Concentrate, she told herself. 'I wonder if I might come to see you?'

'Well! By all means, but . . . from England?'

She smiled. 'I'm already here actually. In Charleston.'

'Oh! In that case . . . May I ask why you wish to see me?'

She asked if it would be all right if she explained when she met him?

'How intriguing!' But then he paused.

Please, she begged him silently.

'I have no known enemies who would send young women to assassinate me. I take it you're not one of those?'

She liked him. She assured him she was not.

'I believe you. Let me see . . .' She heard a page being turned. 'How about tomorrow morning, say around ten o'clock?'

Far too long to wait. 'Would it be at all possible to see me today?'

'Today!' He seemed to be the sort of man who spoke in exclamations, or perhaps it was the manner of her questions. 'I'm not at all sure I've got any free time today,' he said doubtfully.

'It wouldn't take long.'

'I really don't know.' He sounded more dubious still.

'I've got very little time.'

'Dear me. You say you're in the city?'

She told him the name of her hotel.

'My, we're almost neighbours! Look, I've got a twelve-thirty luncheon engagement today. If you could come now . . .?'

It was eleven-thirty. She accepted with alacrity and left the hotel a few minutes later, following the directions he had given her. She passed the saxophone player who bowed elaborately but didn't stop playing, and turned into a series of side streets, heading roughly south. She seemed to step back in time. The houses were Victorian, the streets cobbled, wide and almost empty, and very quiet, with hardly any cars. A horse and carriage clipped by, its passengers – tourists, she presumed – hidden under a black hood. She walked hurriedly, hearing the hiss of sprinklers as she went by neat front gardens, but not a voice anywhere. She came to McCloud's street. The fourth house on the left was his, pink-faced with white shutters and white lace-like woodwork bordering the roof. She opened the black wrought-iron gate and nodded at a Vietnamese man tending the tiny front garden with a hand-trowel. She mounted a short flight to the front door and rang the bell. An elderly lady answered.

Mady put on her best smile. 'Mrs McCloud, I'm Mady O'Neil.'

'I'm the housekeeper.' No ghost of a smile. 'Come in.'

Mady stepped into a wide hall. The floor was highly polished and a grandfather clock ticked away in one corner. The air was filled with the scent of flowers. Magnolias, she saw. A door clicked open to one side.

'Mady?' A man emerged. Her first thought was, he wasn't old enough to be McCloud. From the voice, she had imagined someone in their seventies. McCloud looked to be in his early fifties, grey-haired with a white goatee beard. When he smiled, he showed perfect white teeth. 'You must have shot round here like a bat out of hell,' he said disarmingly. His handshake was warm and dry and his eyes crinkled attractively but yet there was something about him that didn't quite gel for her.

He ushered her into his study, a light, book-lined room. A leather globe stood on its axis in the window overlooking a monkey puzzle tree in the back garden.

'Please.' He indicated one of two battered leather armchairs and took the other himself. He crossed one long leg over another and steepled his fingers. He smiled at her. 'So, how can I help you?'

She wanted to lie as little as she could. She told him she was researching the background of a British politician.

'I see,' he said encouragingly.

'Hugh Eastwood.'

If she had expected a flash of recognition, she was disappointed. But McCloud did nod.

'Do you remember him?' she asked, full of hope.

He looked surprised. 'No. Should I?'

Perhaps he had a bad memory? 'He was at Chesterfield, twenty-three years ago. Studying law. As a postgraduate.'

McCloud continued to look blank. 'Hugh Eastwood?'

Please God, let it ring a bell. 'You were teaching at Chesterfield at that time?' she prompted.

'Yes, I was, but I really have no recollection . . .' McCloud shook his head. 'I'm so sorry. Nineteen-eighty to eighty-one?'

'No, seventy-nine to eighty.'

Relief passed over his features. 'That explains it! I didn't join the staff there until the fall of 'eighty! Your politician would have left by then.'

Mady felt her stomach drop. She'd been sure that the Registrar had said McCloud had been at Chesterfield when Hugh had . . . Or had it been herself, pushing, and the Registrar, wanting to be helpful, had not been exact with her dates, not realising how important it was?

How could she, Mady, have been so careless? It was a fault of hers, being so keen to get the story that she sometimes failed to listen to what was being said. Now she had no more leads, except for the address Roz had given her, which probably wasn't a lead at all.

'I'm very sorry to disappoint you,' McCloud was commiserating. 'Is he a particularly famous politician? I'm afraid I haven't heard of him.'

'His baby was killed earlier this year. There's just been a big court case about it in London.'

McCloud wrinkled his nose. 'I really don't care for such things.'

It wasn't a soap opera, Mady wanted to point out.

'I'm afraid I've got that luncheon,' he reminded her.

'Of course. Thank you so much for your time.'

He escorted her courteously to his front door, wished her good luck, and shook her hand farewell.

Back out in the street, she kept walking, although her impulse was to sit down on the kerb and weep. She had flown from one continent to another, abandoned her baby, made her husband's life hell, pushed Jack's foreign budget deep into the red, and for what?

Two minutes' conversation that she could as easily have had over the telephone. Ben had been right. Now Jack was going to kill her. Fire her first. She, Ben and Archie were going to be out on the street. At least Roz would never know where she had been, she thought disjointedly.

She bought a fat sandwich from a deli-bar, collected her car from the hotel and headed out of the city.

For a full minute after his guest's departure, McCloud stood at the spyhole of his front door, not staring after her – she had already gone off, tip-tapping down the street – but deeply remembering.

If it had been left up to himself, he concluded, he would have done nothing further, but he had made a promise. He returned to his study, closed the door and looked up a telephone number which he dialled, and then replaced the receiver. Ten minutes later when it rang, he snatched it before his housekeeper could.

'Amos?'

'Yes. I thought I ought to let you know . . .' McCloud informed Hugh of Mady's visit.

Hugh felt his heart flutter in his chest like a small, trapped bird. So that was what Roz's call to Mady had been about in the restaurant. They had been plotting, conspiring against him, as he had surmised at the time. But . . . Roz knew nothing about Chesterfield! He'd never uttered a word! Unless – mad thought – he'd been talking in his sleep? He gave a little laugh. Was there to be no end to it? How many more need die? All who were in contact with him, like a virus?

Get a grip, he told himself. Trump Card must be her source, that Evans woman, who had only ever stumbled on it by chance, by sheer, bloody bad luck. But that didn't fit either! Trump Card had never approached Amos McCloud; they had been unaware of his involvement. Hugh felt dizzy at the deceptions going on around him. He felt whirled about like a spinning top.

'How did she get your name?' he rasped of Amos.

'I don't know, dear boy. But don't worry too much. She didn't know anything, you could tell.'

Hugh was not convinced. Mady's reputation was formidable and Amos, he knew, could be gullible in his arrogance. When Amos had gone, he walked to the back of the house where the wide deck, American-style, gave way to the Suffolk beach and then to the thundering waves. It was a desolate place, and at five o'clock on that autumn evening, beginning to get dark.

Far down on the sand, walking slowly towards him, was the small figure of his wife. His faithless wife who even now was planning his downfall. How completely the ocean would cover her, reach out a finger, snatch and she would be gone as if she had never existed. He would mourn her, oh yes. He would remember the good times, how she'd been with Charley. But she'd also been very bad.

He descended to the beach. The wind flung rain at him, the waves slapped and spat. He bent his head against it, jamming his hands into the deep pockets of the Barbour he always left at the house, finding a torch there. A metal torch with a dull, round end, useful.

He neared his wife. She too had her head down and didn't see him until he was just a few feet away. Then how she jumped!

'Hugh!'

Who else had she been expecting? Her lover? He laughed and the wind tore the mirthless sound from his mouth.

'Are you okay?' she asked worriedly.

Look who was calling the kettle black! Look who'd been sitting in the dark when he'd arrived the night before. Who'd wanted him so badly, then just when he'd got going, pushed him off? He wasn't the crazy one there, or if he was, then it was she who had made him mad. 'Where's Mady?' he barked.

'I don't know.'

A gust of wind pushed her back, and automatically he put out his hand to steady her. She was as thin and fragile as a sparrow. 'Don't you really know where she is?' he breathed, drawing her close.

'No. Hugh, that hurts.'

'Does it?' He expected it did. He tightened his grip on her arm. Not a soul in sight. Not a boat on that storm-tossed sea. No pairs of eyes but their own. He could see the fear in hers. It wouldn't hurt much, he promised. He took a step towards the sea and she, attached, necessarily came too.

'Hugh! Please, what're you doing?'

He waded into the angry water. The politician who lost his baby, now loses his wife. If the public had sympathised before, what would they do now? Line the streets. At the next election, by popular demand, he would be carried into Number Ten shoulder-high.

Then he considered. Might it not be thought: two suspicious deaths in one family? Was two too many? If the likes of Mady O'Neil were worming into his past now, what might others do to him if Roz got drowned? He glanced down at her, dragging against him, her heels digging into the sea-bed in an effort to save herself. She wasn't worth it. He let her go and she fell backwards into the sea, and stayed there, mewling.

'What's the matter with you?' he said harshly. 'Get up!'

'Oh, Hugh!' she whimpered.

He felt like stamping on her. He left the water and, without looking back, returned to the house. Mady O'Neil would not have gone to Charleston without knowing something. Her penny-pinching newspaper would never have allowed it. She probably knew the lot.

So had Christine Evans, and look what had happened to her. His mind fogged, but he cleared it. There was still one person who could help him. Taking his keys, Hugh slammed out of the house.

That Hugh had lost his wits must now be beyond doubt. He

had tried to kill her, Roz acknowledged dazedly. Soaked, still tearful from shock, she made her way unsteadily back to the house. She heard him drive off, and thought, thank God: she hoped he would never come back.

She stripped off her cold, wet things and stepped into a hot shower. She had thought she could control him; she had been wrong. She had seen the look in his eye. He was a dangerous man. If she had harboured any doubts before about him being capable of killing, those thoughts were banished now.

Hugh's future career, her own dreamed-for place in it, were not worth dying for. That was obvious. She saw too, with awful clarity, that she had betrayed her baby. She owed Charley a duty: to bring his killer to justice.

In the end they would find that Alice hadn't done it. She ought to go to the police now, and tell them her suspicions. But they were only that. She needed evidence. She needed to know what Mady had got, what was driving Hugh, once more, to the edge of violence.

Hugh knew where Mady was, she realised. Or at least he suspected. Was that where Hugh had gone now? To get Mady? Could she be in danger?

She stepped out of the shower, dried herself quickly and dialled Mady's mobile, but it was switched off, so she couldn't leave a message. She called *The Register*, but the newsdesk secretary told her importantly that Mady was 'off on assignment', and could she help?

Roz however had no intention of leaving a trail with a third party. She dialled yet another number. 'Come on, come on,' she muttered.

'Hullo?' snapped a voice.

'Ben?' Ben would know where Mady was. 'It's Roz.'

'Oh, hi.'

She knew he had never particularly liked her, and she felt the same way about him. Mady could have done so much better for herself. 'I was wondering,' she began diffidently, 'if Mady was around?'

'No. Not at the moment.'

'Will she be in later?'

'Nope.'

Unhelpful, boorish bastard, but now was not the time to quarrel. 'She's not at home, I take it?' she pushed gently.

'No. Look, Roz, I really can't say anything . . .'

'No, no, I see that. Only, she asked me about Hugh's time in America yesterday . . .?'

He remained silent; Mady had trained him well.

'Is that where she's gone?'

'You're making it very difficult for me,' sighed Ben.

Poor dear, thought Roz viciously. 'I'm worried about her,' she explained.

'What? What d'you mean?'

That got his attention, as one might have hoped. 'Is she in this country?'

Ben said huskily, 'Are you saying Mady is in danger, because if you are . . .'

'No. Not in danger.' Not if she was in America, out of Hugh's reach. She must placate Ben. She couldn't have him shooting his mouth off to the police, or muddying any crucial waters Mady was paddling in. 'Of course she's not in danger.' She spoke briskly. 'It's just . . . I'm concerned to know that she's on the right track. I need to talk to her. Share ideas.'

'You're sure that's all it is?' He sounded suspicious.

'Quite sure. Have you got a number for her?'

'I'll tell her that you dialled,' Ben promised in a final sort of a way.

How dare he shun her? As if she was an irksome punter? She heard a thin wail.

'I'm sorry, I'm going to have to go now,' he said tersely.

'Wait!' An awful thought had occurred.

'What?'

She felt a rush of panic. 'Who? I mean, if . . . if Mady's away, who's looking after Archie?'

'Who d'you think?'

'Her . . . her mother?'

'Guess again.'

'You?' she asked tremblingly.

'Correct.'

Dizziness threatened her. What was Mady thinking of? How could she have left Archie with Ben? Didn't she realise what men were like?'

'If . . .' Her voice was a squeak. With an effort, she spoke more normally: 'If there's anything I can do to help out? Any babysitting, or, um . . . anything?'

'Gosh, Roz.' He sounded stunned. 'Are you sure?'

'Of course. I'd love to.' It would also be much easier to spy if she was in situ.

'Maybe over the weekend?' he suggested eagerly.

'Or tomorrow? I wasn't intending to go to work.'

'Um, I'm probably okay tomorrow.'

There was a sudden hesitancy in his voice. She mustn't be too pushy or he wouldn't let her go there. 'Whatever,' she spoke airily. 'Call me. I'll give you my mobile number.'

She gazed out of the dark window at the sea in which Hugh had tried to drown her. She wondered where he had gone, and if and when he'd be back. She must go. She called a cab, and while she was waiting, scribbled a note for Hugh:

'Gone to stay with a friend.'

Then she packed the few things she had brought with her so that when the headlights of the car appeared at the top of the track, she was ready.

By the time that Hugh reached the outskirts of London it was after seven o'clock and when he called the number, it was to be told that the man he wanted had already left for the night.

Undeterred, he called the man's home, and got his wife. A sweet-sounding woman whose voice came to attention when he mentioned his own name. He wished he had a wife like that, someone who respected him.

Alan wasn't home yet, she explained timidly.

'I'll come round and wait.'

'Oh! Well, er, yes. O-of course.'

He drove there, to a leafy street in suburbia where all the houses had front gardens, and fences. As he parked, he wondered what the neighbours would say if they knew what the quiet-looking chap at number twenty-eight really did as part of his job.

Just then Hugh saw him approach, marching down the pavement, grey from the grimy Tube. He hurried after him, but too late, the front door slammed. He rang the bell.

The door opened at once. Alan stood there, frowning. 'What're you doing here?' he demanded, adding rather too late, 'Sir?'

Hugh didn't appreciate being spoken to like that. 'I need to talk to you.'

'Can't it wait till the morning?'

'No, it bloody well can't.'

Reluctantly, he was invited in. In the hallway, he edged around a tricycle and a doll's pram. He'd forgotten, if he'd ever known, that Alan was a family man. He was shown into the dining room, and asked to wait. Alan came back in.

'How can I help you?'

Neatly, Hugh outlined the nature of the problem. At first Alan interrupted with irritating questions, so Hugh asked him to shut up.

Alan's eyebrows shot up, but he kept quiet after that.

As Hugh continued, he observed the effect of his words: a flush on the other man's face, a look of shock. He supposed it was shocking to receive such orders, no matter how many times one had heard them before.

When Hugh had finished, there was dead silence, then Alan suggested quietly, 'Why don't you leave this matter with me, sir?'

'Excellent! I knew I could count on you.'

Much lighter of heart, Hugh left the house. Very shortly, if the departure of Christine Evans was anything to go by, Mady O'Neil would cease to be a thorn in his side.

He remembered her baby who would of course be orphaned. The child's own father was a pretty useless sort, as Hugh recalled: the baby would need a patron, a man in authority, with money and influence.

Perhaps Hugh could adopt it?

He didn't see why not. The child would have the best of everything. Schools, medical treatment, the lot. A sob escaped Hugh. Perhaps he could also change the baby's name to Charley? It was surely too young to mind? Hugh knew that if only he could be given a second chance, he could be the perfect father.

CHAPTER TWELVE

The signs for Chesterfield University began fourteen miles north of Charleston and two miles inside the boundary of Orangeboro County. Mady took the turn-off from the main highway and found herself in flat countryside, the road darkened by trees, the few glimpses of the land beyond being mainly depressing swamp.

She entered the small town of Little Corinne, which according to the map was the closest to the college. She had imagined a white clapboard town hall with the American flag flying. She saw a gas station and two run-down shops and drove on, still looking, before realising after a while that that had been it.

There was no other car on the road. The signs for the college stopped. She was about to pull in, thinking she had missed it, when she saw a white notice board up ahead: 'Chesterfield,' it announced, 'Home of Learning,' and there was a hand helpfully directing her to the left.

She drove down a long, gravelled drive lined with pine trees and white picket fencing. The land had been cleared and horses grazed on sparkling grass either side. The drive ended with a broad flourish before a series of clapboard buildings and a stone clock tower. A fountain played in the middle. It was very quiet.

It looked more like a health farm than a campus, Mady thought, conscious of her wheels on the gravel. She couldn't see any students. Maybe it was a front? Maybe it was really a drug rehabilitation centre, a human cloning farm, a Secret Service hideout? Steady, she told herself. Because desperation had brought her there didn't mean she had to get crazy.

She followed a sign to the car park and was relieved to see that it was packed, and that there were plenty of students about. They looked genuine enough. Lolling against cars, gossiping, eyeing each other up. They looked clean, very well-dressed, actually a bit suburban, she decided. As well as supercilious – or, horrible thought, was it merely her that made them look that way? She could easily imagine Hugh there as a twenty-three-year-old, charming, arrogant, clever, winning everyone over.

She asked directions from a girl with glasses and made her way to the building next to the clock tower. Inside, she found herself in a long corridor with names of people on the doors but no clue as to who they were. She tried one. It was the Admissions office; she was directed again.

The Student Affairs office was in a large, old-fashioned room with slowly whirring ceiling fans and at the front a wooden counter, against which was a queue of students. Two women were dealing with their enquiries, a proficient one with bright highlighted hair who handed out forms and took details swiftly, and an older, kinder-faced lady, who talked at length to each student, but who seemed perplexed by many of their questions.

Mady knew who she was going to get. When her turn came, she was passed by the sharper woman on to the nicer one,

Moira, who immediately exclaimed, 'You're the researcher from England!'

Everyone stared. So much for a quiet nose round, Mady thought.

'She's writing a book about one of our old students, isn't that right? As a wedding present!' Moira added further.

She hadn't actually said 'book', Mady told herself, but she didn't suppose it mattered.

'I didn't know you were going to come over here in person,' Moira gushed. 'Have you been to see that professor I told you about? Dr Mc—?'

'Yes,' Mady cut in quickly. 'I was wondering, would it be possible to get access to old student records? I'm looking for anything that might give me some more background material. Anything at all?'

Moira smiled. 'I don't see why not, but I'd better make sure. Sarah,' she called to the other woman, 'what do you think?'

'What?' frowned Sarah, who had been listening to every word. 'What's all this about?'

'This young lady here is writing a book about one of our old students . . .'

'Who?'

Mady yielded Hugh's name. She saw it failed to register any impact with Sarah. She couldn't tell by the students' expressions what they were thinking.

The frown still creased Sarah's brow. 'We need to get his permission,' she decreed and turned away to deal with the next student.

Terrific, Mady thought. Now what?

'But it's a secret,' pleaded Moira. 'He doesn't know the book's being written, does he?'

'No,' agreed Mady.

'She's come all this way—'

'Wait,' interrupted Sarah peremptorily.

They waited until she had finished, until the last student had departed and Sarah had typed something on her keyboard. Eventually she turned to face them again. 'What about his wife?' she demanded. 'She ought to give her permission.'

'She's travelling,' Mady lied sorrowfully.

'It can't hurt, surely?' urged Moira. 'Just what he was studying? It's really public information . . .'

Sarah silenced her with a look. 'ID?' she ordered of Mady.

Mady had several. She showed the card that described her simply as a researcher. Sarah stared at it for as long as she could. 'Very well, then,' she said reluctantly. 'As long as you make sure you're with her at all times, Moira.'

'Absolutely. Those records will be in the vault?'

'Where else?' Sarah sighed as one who was heavily tried, and lifting the lid on the counter, walked out of the room.

'Do come through,' enthused Moira. 'Sarah's so busy at the moment. Now, I've just got to find the right swipe card . . .'

It took some time for her to do so. Mady gazed around her at the framed portrait of the President, the enormous photograph of that year's students, the American flag draped against one wall. It looked so old-fashioned. There was even a row of filing cabinets.

Moira found the card and they left the building, going out through an archway at the back into a quadrangle. Two groups of students passed them and Moira greeted both but received only a single mumble in response.

'Is this a popular university?' Mady asked politely.

'Oh, it is. Particularly with Charleston families.'

'It's an academic place?'

'Well, yes.' Moira sounded less confident. 'We do keep an eye on the students, that's what the parents like. Of course, we've got an excellent graduate program, especially for law. It's the best in the country in some areas. It's had that reputation from the start.'

'Of course,' echoed Mady. Her unspoken question as to how Hugh had wound up there of all places – why not Harvard or Stanford – was answered. But at such an exclusive establishment, how had his crime, whatever it had been, failed to make impact? Wouldn't his name have been a siren for ever more?

Moira led the way through the green grounds, pointing out student halls of residence, the leisure centre, swimming pools, riding school, the cinema complex, and finally the lecture halls and the library which housed the vault.

It was a cavernous place in the basement of the building, made welcoming with warm furnishings, bright uplighters and a jug of coffee on a hotplate. There wasn't another person there. 'One of our best families donated it,' Moira explained. 'Now, you sit down and pour yourself a cup of coffee. Give me Hugh's dates and I'll see what I can find. You look exhausted.'

She was, Mady realised. It wasn't professional letting someone else look things up for her, but she could always double-check later. Just for that moment, she wanted desperately to sleep. She sat down on a fat leather sofa, closed her eyes and felt clouds of tiredness float in. She forced herself awake.

She focused blearily towards the other end of the room where Moira was working. There were double shelves of box files, and tables with computers, and masses of storage cabinets. Moira seemed very busy amongst them. Mady's eyes shut again. She saw Archie asleep or dead. Her eyelids shot open.

Moira was coming back, bearing a large, leather-bound volume in both hands, and smiling.

'The nineteen-eighty yearbook,' she declared and laid it down reverently on the coffee table.

Mady's heart speeded up. She wasn't the least tired any more.

'Let's see now.' Moira plumped down cosily beside her. 'Nineteen-eighty. Only three hundred and sixty students! Don't they look young! Younger than ours do today . . .'

Mady resisted the urge to snatch the book from the woman's hands and find Hugh herself.

'We've got her daughter with us now, isn't that amazing?' murmured Moira, staring at a photograph. 'Amy Grace. She looks so like her mother, the very image . . .'

Doing what was expected, Mady bent forward obligingly to look at the photograph. She saw a very innocent, plain-looking girl in a Peter Pan collar. The boy next to her was in a suit and had short hair.

'Now, let's find your Hugh.' Moira flicked over some pages. 'He should be in this section. The graduate students. Arbuthnot, Ayres . . . Look! Here's a Beauty Pageant picture! They don't do that any more . . .'

Come on, thought Mady.

'Duggan, Eastman, Eastwood. Ooh, wasn't he a handsome boy?'

Mady studied the face. He certainly was good-looking – gorgeous eyes, she noted, great bones – but was it Hugh? It looked nothing like him. For a moment she thought: Hugh was an impostor! That was the scandal; he had impersonated another boy . . . Then one feature caught her attention, the lips: they were quite fleshy, and curved girlishly. Hugh's were like that. She remembered Roz saying how sexy she found them and herself keeping quiet because personally she found them repulsive.

Eyes didn't change either. She gazed again at the boy's eyes, trying to superimpose Hugh's, which was hard because Hugh had a habit of not looking at people directly. The shape, she concluded, was the same. It was Hugh, before life had got to him.

'You can't take your eyes off him!' giggled Moira, giving her a girlish nudge. Mady smiled. In keeping with what she was supposed to be doing, she asked how she might get a copy of the picture?

Moira said she would get the details for her and hurried off.

Mady read the blurb under Hugh's name. He had enrolled to study American Law. His interests were English cricket, polo, film; he had joined the university's debating society, polo club and the American-Anglo League. She supposed that somewhere there lay a clue as to what he'd done, but where to start?

He was 'rooming' with another postgraduate, John Fitzgerald. Mady turned over the next page. John looked older than Hugh, solemn and thin-faced. She paused. The name, John Fitzgerald, was familiar.

She took out her notebook, flicking back through the pages to find the name Roz had given her: John Fitzgerald. Roz had struck gold. Roommates knew everything about each other.

'Here's the photographer's number.' Moira bore down upon her, beaming.

Mady switched gear. 'Great!'

'I'm sure he wouldn't mind selling you a copy . . . Now him, I do know,' Moira declared triumphantly.

'Sorry?'

Moira prodded the yearbook. 'John Fitzgerald.'

'Oh yes?' Mady said hopefully. The more information she had, the better.

'He became a minister.'

Excellent. Priests gossiped, and they liked to help people. The address was back in Charleston. She would find him; she could know everything by that evening.

'He did some great things out in the rural communities, especially with the poor. He's been back to talk to the students once or twice. Lovely man. I met him once. Still, he's not who you're interested in, is he?'

'Well, no . . .'

'I've called up Hugh's details on screen,' the woman went on. 'Would you like to come over to see?'

With alacrity, Mady accompanied her but she was disappointed. The information merely consisted of the courses Hugh had taken, and the grades he had achieved: straight As. He had graduated in July 1980 and left the university at the end of that semester.

'Doesn't give you very much, does it?' Moira looked worried.

Mady assured her that she had enough to make a start. She was anxious now to be gone, and Moira too said she had to get back to work. They returned to the administration building together. Beside the clock tower, Moira paused. 'I feel I haven't been of much help.'

'Oh, but you have.'

'It's been nice to do something different, anything to get away from the newsletter. "The Chesterfield Chronicle."' She rolled her eyes. 'One of the graduates is supposed to do it, but they never do and I end up writing it at the last minute . . .

'Now that's an idea! Would you like me to put a message in the newsletter asking anyone who remembers Hugh to call you?'

'Thank you,' enthused Mady genuinely.

'And I could pin a message on the Alumni website?' suggested Moira, warming to her theme.

'Wonderful,' Mady smiled upon her. She fished out a 'Researcher' card from her wallet, intending to write her new mobile number on it, and something else fell out.

'Oops . . .' Moira caught it.

Mady couldn't see what it was. Suppose it was one of her *Register* cards? How would she explain that?

'What a lovely baby.' Delight infused Moira's face and she handed back a picture of Archie.

'Yes,' Mady agreed weakly. 'Well, I think so anyway.'

'You don't look old enough to be his mother.'

'Thanks.'

'Take care now,' admonished Moira with a little wave.

Mady left her and returned to her car. She dialled Jack in London to give him a progress report but he had gone home; it was eight o'clock at night. She tried John Fitzgerald's number, but a tinny voice told her to leave a message, which she didn't. She drove off instead for Charleston.

Because of Alice's status, and also due to an outbreak of flu in the prison, it was nearly nine o'clock at night before she was finally called for the medical she ought to have had on her arrival.

Two guards escorted her from her cell, down two short flights of stairs to a landing where they paused.

As one unlocked the sliding iron gates that led into the main body of the prison, the other turned to Alice. 'Walk fast,' she ordered.

Alice prepared to obey. She was used to that now, obeying without question. She stepped cautiously on to the floor, and wondered dully what there was to avoid? The place was empty.

Then the noise began. From behind the doors spaced along the walls – cells, Alice realised – came the thumping sound of implements being bashed, and then the screams.

'Fucking whore!'

'Bitch!'

'We're going to get you, Bishop.'

The prisoners had known she was coming. They had been waiting for her.

The banging grew louder. From one cell came a blood-curdling scream.

'Move it,' roared a warder, propelling Alice forward so hard that she half fell through the door at the other end. She was trembling from head to foot, but no one cared. They merely hurried her on.

Inside the clinic, white and clean, quite a kind-looking doctor examined her, weighed her, took her medical history, and then, perching on the front of his desk, he asked how she was feeling?

She blinked at him. What did he care?

'Answer the doctor, Bishop,' snapped a warder behind her.

'Fine,' she mumbled.

The doctor frowned. 'Are you sleeping?'

Her mouth was dry.

'Bishop . . .' growled the warder.

'No,' she croaked, 'I don't sleep well.'

'Eating? You're very thin.'

'I'm not hungry.'

'You've got to eat, Alice.'

She flinched at the use of her Christian name. His kindness was in fact malign, reminding her how once she had been a human being too.

He was scribbling on a pad. 'I'm going to give you some tranquillisers, and sleeping tablets. I'd also like to see about scheduling you some counselling. Okay?'

She stared at him. 'Okay, yes, thank you.'

They took her away then, back the same route where the women still waited in their cells, only now the guards lingered, so Alice could hear in more detail precisely what the other prisoners intended to do to her. In spite of her best intentions, she found herself shivering again.

She sank back into the haven of her cell. Once the door was locked and the warders gone, she was fairly confident no one would disturb her for a while. They had stopped coming to stare; she guessed they had all had their turn by now, and enough of them had seen her break down that morning to have something to talk about.

A letter had come from her parents telling her they were going home, that their money had run out.

Her father had written. Her mother found it too upsetting. 'We're so sorry, love. Mum and I couldn't bear to tell you at our last visit, but we've got to leave this morning. We'll be back as soon as we can, I promise . . .'

They had promised to visit her there, in the new prison. Why should she believe any more of their promises? How could they do that to her? Didn't they know? Didn't they understand? That their presence in that hostile land was the only thing keeping her going, knowing that she would see them again at visiting times.

Now they had gone. She was on her own and she couldn't bear it.

On first reading it, she had started crying and hadn't been able to stop. When she had heard the spyhole swing open, and the warders laughing, she had dived down under her duvet to get away. She had stayed like that for a long time, and when she stopped crying, she had felt strange. Floating and hollow, and far away from herself.

She tested how she felt by imagining Christmas at home. It brought no tears, no feelings of homesickness, nothing. She forced herself to remember running with Charley that morning to the hospital, him convulsing in her arms. Normally that memory made her sick; not now though.

What had happened? She summoned up her mother's face, and then her father's. She saw them clearly, but felt no connection. It dawned on her like a mist clearing that she had come through to the other side. She was in a separate place from others, and therefore immune to them.

She felt curiously light-hearted and quite unafraid. She contemplated suicide, which had always seemed an utter horror to her, but wasn't any more. She was fascinated. If she was going to do it, how would she?

She looked around her cell. She remembered the bleach, but that wasn't there any more. Now, cruelly, the place was suicide-safe.

She could stop eating but they would only force-feed her. What other weapons did she have? Only her thoughts. She pondered: could she not turn her thoughts against herself? Didn't negative thoughts give you cancer? She was so strong now inside her head. She knew she could speed up the process. Would it take her a month to end herself? Could she do it before Christmas?

With such imaginings had she entertained herself that long day. Now, she saw that it needn't take that much time at all.

She knew about tranquillisers and sleeping pills. The killer nurse at Highmarsh had told her everything, even showing her how to do it; as she put each tablet in, let it fall to the bottom of the mouth and at the same time, swallow hard to divert attention away from what you were actually doing.

The other important factor was attitude: look glazed, accepting, dumb, grateful for the tablet, and start acting doped – but don't overdo it – around thirty minutes later. As a general rule, it went like this: ten tranquillisers for a cry for help; twenty for the real thing, taken at night. Coma first, and then death. You wouldn't feel a thing.

The detail had chilled Alice back then. Now she knew she had been told for a purpose. God, as well as Hugh, wanted her dead. She was only briefly sorry that the nice doctor should be innocently used but life was like that, he would learn.

He had prescribed her four tranquillisers a day, plus sleeping pills. Her mouth quite watered at the prospect. In five days' time, she would have enough. She could endure five more days. Deceiving them would give her something to do. It would be fun.

She heard footsteps coming down the corridor and quickly swung her legs up on to her bed. She stared straight ahead at the TV, as if she was watching it. When the spyhole clicked open, she pretended not to hear.

The door opened.

The grey-faced guard came in. Alice felt hatred radiate from her. 'Fooled the doctor, didn't you?'

Alice said nothing.

'Here you are, Bishop.'

She took the paper cone of water and the pill. The woman was watching her closely and she wondered if she ought to really swallow – if she had the nerve not to – but if she didn't do it now, when? She tucked it under her tongue and swallowed realistically.

The warder went out.

Alice resumed her TV staring until she heard the woman walk away, then quickly she spat out the tablet into her palm. It hadn't dissolved much. She had done it! Now, where to put it?

The cell and her own body were searched regularly. The carpet was too newly fitted to be of any use. The underside of a surface – the shelf, the table tops, too exposed. Could she loosen the heel of a shoe? She took one off. The sole was welded in one place. Where then?

She felt a flutter of panic but she told herself she must remain calm. There would be a way. She lay down on her bed and stared up at the ceiling which was smooth and flat, the light recessed. She felt along the edge of her bed, then worked her fingers down the side by the wall. The bed shifted and she whipped her hand away in case the noise had been noticed, but no one came. She slipped her hand back down, found the skirting board and then a whorl in the wood. She worked at it, tugging hard, and there was a splintering sound, deafening to her, but again drawing no outside attention.

Alice peered down. The skirting board now jutted out at an angle and behind it the wall was rough and pitted. She placed her precious tablet in there, and pushed the wood back into place. It looked flush with the wall. Of course, if they pulled out the bed and the wood fell off . . .

She must assume it wouldn't. That her course of action was the right one and that she would be protected. For her part, she must do nothing to arouse suspicion. She lay back on her pillow and let her mind go blank.

The train drew into London's Liverpool Street Station an hour late. Roz emerged on to the platform from her first-class carriage and was struck instantly by the cold. Her breath puffed white before her. Winter was coming, she realised, her first Christmas without Charley . . . Hot tears fell suddenly and she made haste to dry them. She couldn't cry there.

She advanced on the taxi rank where several black cabs waited. She got in the first.

'Where to, love?'

She hadn't given it a thought. She'd told Hugh she had gone to stay with a friend, so obviously she mustn't do that. Nor could she risk going to her sister's, or the two hotels she and Hugh customarily used. She remembered an article she had read about where the stars stayed, an establishment famed for its discretion.

She named it.

'Right you are.' The cabbie cocked an eye. 'You famous? I know your face, don't I?'

She went cold. It was possible he did. She and Hugh had been plastered everywhere. 'I don't think so,' she smiled, 'I'm just a housewife. It's our tenth wedding anniversary; I'm meeting my husband there. I'm so excited!'

'Oh. Nice,' said the man politely, and lost interest, as she had intended.

The hotel was in a small, cobbled street in Covent Garden, quietly set back behind black railings. Hugh never read magazines, he would never think of looking for her there.

Nevertheless when the receptionist asked for her name, she lied, and offered to pay for her room in cash, there and then, rather than leave a credit card with her details.

Her room was small and cosy and luxuriously appointed but Roz wasn't in the mood to appreciate it. She had her second hot shower of the night and went to bed, but she couldn't fall asleep.

Every time she shut her eyes, she saw Charley's sweet face. His sweeping eyelashes that had caused so many remarks about her having a beautiful baby. She had had the most perfect child, but not for long.

Her pillow grew wet with tears. She hadn't cried like that since the early days. What was the matter with her? Was it also because she was losing Hugh?

She had to get enough sleep or she wouldn't be sharp enough to evade him. She swallowed a pill and let sleep take her.

CHAPTER THIRTEEN

As Mady entered the outskirts of Charleston, she pulled off the highway into a residential street and rang John Fitzgerald's home again. This time, a woman answered and demanded to know who wanted him.

Taken aback by her unfriendly tone, Mady gave her name, hoping that would be enough, but if anything it seemed to increase the woman's suspicion. 'What's your business?' she demanded.

Mady thought she heard the click of an extension being lifted. 'I'm a freelance journalist from England.' She paused. 'Would it be at all possible to speak to Mr Fitzgerald?'

'What about?'

'It's about an old university friend of his . . .'

A man's voice asked tiredly, 'Are you from Trump Card?'

Eureka, Mady thought.

'John!' hissed the woman. 'Let me deal with this.'

'No, Louise, I—'

'He doesn't want to talk with you.' The woman slammed down the phone, but Fitzgerald was still there; Mady could hear him. She appealed directly to him: 'Mr Fitzgerald, please, I must speak to you. Someone's in prison who perhaps shouldn't be . . .'

'The nanny?' he suggested, flooring her.

'Yes, maybe. Can I meet up with you?'

In the background, the woman shouted: 'John, put the goddamn phone down!'

'Can I meet you?' begged Mady, but she guessed that a hand had gone over the mouthpiece because both voices became muffled. Then the woman broke through again shrilly, in exasperation: 'Hasn't it made you ill enough?' and the line went dead.

Mady stared in disbelief at her mobile. Fitzgerald was vital to her and she had just let him slip through her fingers. Then she saw his address written on the page of her notebook. She hadn't lost him, yet. She looked up the streetname on her map and saw that he lived less than a mile away from where she was parked. Face to face was always easier. She started the car once more.

After a couple of turns, she entered an area that was more run-down than any she had encountered thus far in Charleston. Buildings were boarded-up, rubbish was piled on to the pavements, and gusts of wind sent it racing across the road. A stray dog ran suddenly in front of her, she braked hard, and the driver behind swerved past her, his horn blaring.

She drove into Fitzgerald's street. At the top, there was a school with a fenced-in playground in which a ball game was in progress. Along the wall outside sat a string of black-clad teenagers. There was a menacing air about them, she thought, avoiding eye contact.

She remembered Moira saying Fitzgerald worked with the poor. She saw his house: an ugly, dark brick building of two storeys, with the windows boarded up on the first floor. A wreck of a car sat on the driveway. She parked opposite to consider what to do next.

A police car cruised by, and the teenagers sitting on the wall jeered. It passed her car, the occupants glancing lazily at her and away again. Its tail-lights disappeared around a bend in the road. She wondered if she was in a no-go area, and felt suddenly vulnerable: a lone woman sitting in a shiny, rental car. A target.

Something hit her rear passenger door. In her mirror she saw two youths sauntering towards her. Whether or not they were dangerous, they looked it. She'd come back in the morning, she decided; it was too soon after her call to knock on the door . . . She started her engine, and then a movement from Fitzgerald's house caught her eye.

A woman was getting into the car on the driveway. It shot backwards on to the road and screeched off.

Fitzgerald's wife, Mady thought, and without a second's further delay, slid her own car over the road and up on to the empty driveway. Fitzgerald would be in there on his own. He wanted to talk, he wanted to tell her why Alice shouldn't be in prison.

The boys hadn't followed her across the road, or if they had she couldn't see them. She approached the front door which, close up, she saw was made of steel. There was no letter box, doorbell or knocker, only a glass eyehole. What an area, she thought, admiring the priest for his dedication.

She rapped on the door with her knuckles but there was no reply. Distantly, though, she heard the sound of a television. She raised her hand to knock again, but the door opened.

'Yeah?' A balding man stood there. He was wearing a pink polo shirt that barely covered his bulging midriff.

He didn't look very Christian, was her immediate thought.

'Mr Fitzgerald? I'm Mady O'Neil. We talked on the phone just now.'

'Say again?'

She felt exposed on his doorstep. She had to get inside to make him talk. 'I wonder if I could come in?' she asked, smiling.

'What for?' he demanded suspiciously.

'To talk about Hugh Eastwood?'

His frown deepened. 'Who's he?'

'You were at university together. You shared a room.'

'I've never been to university.'

'But Mr Fitzgerald . . .'

'I'm not Fitzgerald.'

'I called you . . .'

'No.'

She frowned. 'But . . .'

'You want the preacher, don't you?'

'Yes.' She stared at the unkempt, rather threatening face before her which bore no likeness whatsoever, she now saw, to the thin, bookish boy in the yearbook. 'You're not Fitzgerald?'

'Hell, no,' he sneered and made a move to shut the door on her.

'Oh, please, do you know where they've gone?'

'Nah. They moved. Three months back.'

'But the telephone number . . .?'

'They took it with them.' He slammed the door.

Now what, she asked herself despondently. Nothing sensible occurred. It wasn't a neighbourhood where she could start knocking on doors in the evening to ask if anyone knew where the Fitzgeralds had gone. She returned to her car and found her way back to her hotel. In her room, she ordered room service and when the tuna melt came, ate it half-heartedly as she watched a new episode of an American sitcom.

She felt lonely and depressed and very tired. It was still early but there seemed little point in staying awake. She hoped sleep might inspire her. She got into bed and switched off the lamp. It was only then that she saw a winking red light on her telephone consul, indicating that she had a message.

Ben, she thought, delighted. He was missing her. They would have a good talk, put things right between them, maybe Archie would be awake and she could talk to him, like she had the last time. She switched on the light and pressed the replay button, but it wasn't Ben.

'This is John Fitzgerald. We spoke earlier. If you get this message before nine o'clock tonight, please call me back.'

It was seven minutes to the hour. Mady scrambled out of bed, found her notebook and Fitzgerald's number. She dialled it quickly. It was four minutes to nine o'clock. No one replied. She had missed him. He might not be able to call her again, that had been her only chance . . .

'Yes?' He answered swiftly.

She told him who it was.

'Yes,' he cut in. 'We should meet. Tomorrow morning, nine o'clock at the Tidewater Café.' He gave her the address, quick-fire, and she scribbled it down. 'How will I know you?' she asked him.

'I'm six-two, a hundred and forty pounds, grey hair and glasses.'

'I'm about five-four with fair hair—'

'I'll find you.' The line went dead.

She felt breathless, but exuberant also. She was about to

phone Ben with her good news when she realised what the time would be at home: ten past two in the morning. Ben would not welcome a call. She would have to wait until after her meeting in the morning to catch him at a reasonable hour. Deflated at that thought, and aching suddenly to hold her baby, she tried to fall asleep but couldn't. She watched television until eventually she dozed.

By eight o'clock the next morning, Hugh was at work. His secretary, coming in half an hour later, acted surprised to see him there. 'I thought you were in Suffolk,' she said when she brought in his coffee.

'I changed my mind.' He was on edge, waiting for a call which came at ten to nine. Alan and Rebecca wanted to see him in her office, as soon as possible.

Was the mission already accomplished, Hugh wanted to ask? But Alan had already gone. Alan and Rebecca, what a team! he thought exultantly as he marched down the corridor. Alan had clearly wasted no time in informing Rebecca of the O'Neil problem. Quite right on Alan's part. Rebecca held the reins of power. When she gave the order, people jumped.

He was admitted without preamble to her ante-chamber, then into her room. She sat behind her desk, Alan to one side; the chair intended for himself already pulled out and waiting.

They had been talking when he came in but stopped. Hugh liked that; he saw it as a mark of respect. Perhaps, if they did all he asked of them now, he might keep them on when he was Prime Minister.

'Sit down,' murmured Rebecca while, behind him, Alan closed the door. The triumvirate in session. How many more times in the forthcoming years would these three meet thus to plot and survive?

'Alan has told me of your visit to his home last night . . .'

'Good, excellent, excellent. Any news?'

'News?' Her eyebrows popped up like inverted 'V's. 'Ah, no, no news, not yet. In fact, will you outline for me again what it is that you wish him to do?'

Hugh suppressed a sigh. As ever in politics, it came down to egos. Rebecca wanted to hear it in person before she acted. Very well. Succinctly he outlined the case against Mady O'Neil.

He noticed once or twice the looks Rebecca was giving Alan – sharp little arrows – but presumed she was merely checking that the civil servant was listening. Then she asked silkily: 'What is the film about exactly, Hugh?'

He didn't want to get into that. 'Surely we discussed that the first time around?' he parried.

'The "first time"?'

He shifted uncomfortably. He had no recollection of that first conversation, but he knew it must have taken place. He had been suffering from intermittent amnesia since Charley's death; they had no such excuse. What game was Rebecca playing? Whatever it was, he could handle it. He spoke up, 'Yes, the first time. When I spoke to you about the first journalist.'

'What journalist?' she asked carefully.

'Christine Evans. The one who fell out of a window yesterday. Or was she pushed? Only we will ever know.' He winked, but Rebecca looked askance.

Come off it, he felt like saying. Don't play the innocent with me!

'I don't know what you're talking about.'

'Yes you do.'

'I assure you, Hugh, I do not.'

Hugh turned to Alan. 'Help me out here, will you?'

'I would if I could, Minister.'

They were both looking at him in the same way: pityingly, and a little apprehensive. Hugh had had enough. 'What are you two up to?' he demanded.

'We're not up to anything,' Alan purred.

'The hell you're not. We're all in this together, don't forget.'

'Hugh.' Rebecca was plucking at the loose skin on her neck. 'Are you trying to tell me you had something to do with this woman's death?'

'You and me both, sweetheart.'

She flinched. 'What have you done, exactly, Hugh? Would you like to tell me?'

What did she fancy herself as now, a psychiatrist? 'No,' he snarled, 'I wouldn't like to tell you anything! You're taping this, aren't you?' He glanced wildly around the room, looking for the hidden lens. 'Just to put it on the record, Rebecca, Alan, I'd like you to know that it won't work. You're not pinning Evans on me.'

Alan got up. 'Calm down, Hugh, or we'll have to get security.'

'Security?' Hugh felt his eyes bulge, then panic took the place of anger as he understood. 'You're ditching me, aren't you? Why? Cos I walked out on that TV twerp? He asked me about Charley. He wasn't supposed to ask me about Charley . . .' Suddenly he was weeping, he couldn't help himself. 'I thought you said it was all right, I got such good coverage . . .'

They were both staring at him, appalled.

'Rebecca,' he whimpered through his tears, 'tell me you're not dumping me? I couldn't stand it. After Charley, my career's all I've got left.'

There was a moment too long of silence before she said, 'We're not dumping you, Hugh.'

'You're not?'

'No.' She shook her head. 'We do think you might need a change of routine, though.'

He nodded. Anything she said.

In a tender tone, almost motherly, she went on: 'Weren't you supposed to be working from home today?'

He nodded again, fervently.

'Why not do that? Why not have a week or so to yourself? Spend some time with your wife?'

He frowned. He wasn't sure about that, but he saw Rebecca waiting. 'Certainly, by all means. Yes.'

'Good. You need to get a few things sorted out.'

'You're right.'

She smiled and he got up. 'Can I call you?'

'I don't know if that's wise just at the moment, Hugh.'

'Very well, I understand. You know you can rely on me.'

'Absolutely. Goodbye, Hugh.'

'Goodbye, Rebecca.'

After Hugh had left, there was total silence, and then Alan said, 'What do you think?'

'Mad as a hatter,' responded Rebecca briskly. 'There's been no sign of it before?'

'He's been on edge, certainly, but nothing to indicate this, no.'

Rebecca stared into the middle distance. 'You told me as soon as his baby died we should drop him. He wouldn't be fit for office, and I overrode you.'

Alan said nothing.

'I should have listened to you. I'm too soft.'

'You handled him jolly well at the end.'

She ignored his praise. 'I don't want him blubbing to the press. He's been privy to too much. We need to keep him on side until we figure out what to do with him.'

A look of alarm crossed Alan's face. 'You are going to drop him, aren't you?'

'Of course, but the timing's crucial. What d'you think the chances are of him topping himself?'

'High.'

'Yes. I'd like to find out who killed Christine Evans, and what this other journalist, O'Neil, is up to? I don't want any more sudden shocks if I can help it.'

'It shall be done.'

'Also, what the film was about,' she added.

'I can't imagine that will be too difficult, Minister.'

'No. We've both got plenty to do.'

Alan took his cue and excused himself.

Outside, Hugh considered briefly what his next move should be. There was no need to return to his office, indeed it was probably better that he did not. He had to assume that it, like Rebecca's, was bugged. He wondered who was responsible: MI5, spying on one of their own, or one of the dreadful new government inquirers appointed by the Prime Minister.

Whoever, Rebecca and Alan's every move and utterance was now being monitored. That was why they had played so dumb. They had had no option. But brilliant Rebecca had still managed to pass on her message, which he, Hugh had received loud and clear. He was to drop out of sight. He was to handle

Mady O'Neil himself. Rebecca was relying on him. He was to be their agent.

'Where to, sir?' asked his driver.

Hugh stared at the back of his head, considering the likelihood that he too, a faithful servant for so many years, had changed sides. 'Just drop me at Charing Cross, will you?'

In the ticket hall, Hugh found a quiet corner. First he called Suffolk: no reply, not even an answering machine. He tried all the other numbers in quick succession: the house in Surrey, Chelsea, the mobile, her work, but Roz was nowhere to be found. He wondered suddenly . . . she hadn't crawled back into the sea of her own accord, had she?

He called the woman who did their cleaning in Suffolk and explained he needed to get hold of his wife urgently but there appeared to be a fault on the line . . .?

'I'll pop in right now, sir,' the woman offered as he had hoped she would.

'If you're sure it's no trouble?' he asked smoothly.

'None at all.'

She rang back within ten minutes to relay the contents of a note found on the kitchen table. Roz was still alive then, but what of her note? Bluff, or double-bluff? Gone to stay with a friend? After Charley, Roz had cut herself off from most of her friends. He entered the station and bought himself a street atlas then boarded a Tube train.

Half an hour later, he was standing outside a house in Kilburn. At the front door, there squatted a dustbin bulging with nappy sacks. Wrinkling his nose in disgust, Hugh rang the bell.

He heard sounds coming from within, but no sign that his ring had been heard. He tried again, pressing heavily on the bell. If Roz was in there, it would help panic her.

The door opened and Ben stood there, alone.

'Hugh.' Ben looked stunned.

'Who is it?' An old woman's face poked out from a doorway, and from somewhere in the house, Ben's son wailed like a siren. Hugh's ears echoed with the sound.

'A friend,' said Ben over his shoulder. 'What do you want?' he asked Hugh, neither friendly nor hostile.

'Can I come in?'

Ben hesitated, then, 'Sure.'

Hugh followed him into the kitchen. The door closed, and mercifully the baby's cries were cut off.

Ben turned to face him. Over the years, owing to their wives, the two men had met regularly and had grown used to being civil to each other.

'So, what can I do for you?' Ben offered, not sitting down.

'Mady away?' Hugh looked meaningfully over at the clutter of dishes in the sink.

'Yes.'

'Anywhere interesting?'

'Not particularly.'

Hugh changed tack. 'D'you know where Roz is?'

'Not a clue. Don't you?'

Hugh studied him. 'She's missing. I'm worried about her.'

'Well, she's not here.'

Was that a challenge to search?

There was a peremptory rap on the door, and before either man could respond, it opened and the grandmother came in with the baby. It looked quite a big baby, Hugh thought, almost a year old? It screamed again, a banshee shriek. A shudder ran through Hugh and he remembered how he'd thought of adopting that child. He must have been mad. Charley had been beautiful, Ben's son was so plain.

'Archie needs a bottle,' the woman said, elbowing past. She got one out of the fridge and looked hard at Hugh. 'Am I to be introduced?'

Ben muttered, 'Hugh, my mother-in-law, Lydia. This is Hugh Eastwood, Lydia.'

Hugh watched the effect of his name. The woman's complexion changed from powdered pink to dark ruby red. Sobs suspended, the baby too stared at him, as if it knew.

'It was your baby that the nanny . . .' started the woman.

'. . . killed? That's right,' said Hugh, smiling, nodding into their horrified faces. He got up. 'If you're sure Roz isn't here?'

'No,' Ben reaffirmed faintly.

'I'll take my leave. Tell your pretty wife to take care of herself, old chap.'

'What d'you mean?' Ben caught his arm. His normally pale face was flushed. He looked almost threatening, Hugh thought, amused. With ease he disentangled himself. 'Steady on. I don't mean anything, particularly. Just that the world can be a nasty place. I'll let myself out.'

That ought to be warning enough, he thought, as he closed the front door behind him. He glanced up sharply. No curtain twitched at a window, no face jumped back out of sight. Roz wasn't in there. For one thing, like him, she couldn't have stood that infant's cries. For another, the house was too squalid.

He returned thoughtfully to the Tube station. He had entirely run out of options concerning Roz's whereabouts, and he was exposing himself too much. If anything happened to her – she was in such a delicate state – people would remember how he had been hunting for her.

She wasn't his immediate prey. He always carried his passport with him, which was all that he needed. He boarded a train for the airport.

CHAPTER FOURTEEN

The telephone and the alarm clock rang out at the same time. Mady sat bolt upright, trying desperately to sort out what was happening. It was seven o'clock in the morning.

She picked up the phone and heard Ben's voice. Her spirits lifted. 'Ben! How's things?'

'Okay, well, not that great.'

Archie, she thought instantly, and her heart started skipping. 'Is it Archie?' she cried.

'He's fine. Absolutely fine. Actually not shrieking at the moment.'

Thank God, she thought weakly.

'Are you there?'

'Yes, yes I'm fine.' She took a deep breath. 'What's not great?'

'Hugh's been round.'

'What? To the house?' she asked, astonished.

'Yes, issuing warnings about you. And Roz called last night, doing much the same thing.'

Mady shook off the remnants of sleep and listened. Roz's call, she could dismiss: Roz wasn't issuing warnings, she merely wanted to know Mady's progress, which was understandable. But Hugh's visit sounded more alarming.

'I hope Roz is okay. It sounds like she's run off.'

'Never mind her,' snapped Ben, 'it's you I'm worried about. Hugh knows you're up to something.'

'He's running scared,' she said thoughtfully. She felt a surge of excitement. 'That means he's got something to hide.' She told Ben about her forthcoming meeting with Fitzgerald.

'Are you sure he's safe?' asked Ben.

'He's a priest.'

'That's no guarantee.'

'How is Archie, really?' she asked, changing the subject and wanting to know.

'Ripping up the telephone directory as we speak, but at least he's being quiet about it. Your mother left an hour ago, thank God. She popped in to see her "poor abandoned grandson", quote and unquote, and to tell me it was high time I got a proper job to support you.'

Mady grimaced. 'Sorry.'

'She met Hugh.'

Mady tried to imagine that. 'How'd it go?'

'I'd say they were a perfect match.'

Mady smiled. 'I meant to say to you yesterday, I love you.'

'That's nice.'

'You're meant to say, "I love you too".'

'I do.'

'I miss you,' she added.

'Me too.'

'Can I speak to Archie?'

'I'm just second best, aren't I? Archie, your mother wants a word . . . Here he is . . .'

She heard Archie breathing. 'Hullo, my angel. Are you having a lovely time?'

'Ma, ma, ma,' Archie said, or so it sounded to her ears.

'Did you hear that?' Mady shrieked. 'Isn't that his first word?'

'Babble,' said Ben, coming back on.

'It was definitely "mummy".'

'If you say so. Listen, I'm worried about you. Will you please take care?'

'I will.'

'I need you to come back and take over babycare.'

'I will. I promise. Don't worry.'

She felt great, uplifted, and happy. After they had gone, she got ready quickly and ate a hurried breakfast in the hotel dining room. She had already checked the location of the café and set off heading east out of the city towards the town of Mount Pleasant. She caught some commuter traffic on the Cooper River Bridges, but followed her route easily enough and pulled up outside the Tidewater Café half an hour early.

It looked a pretty place, quite on its own, a single-storey, timber building on stilts, set a little distance back from the estuary on which boats were moored. As Mady approached on foot, she heard the sound of plastic cables hitting metal masts, the boats creaking and the gulls screaming, and thought it could have been Cornwall, or Dorset. There was a wildness about it that appealed to her and came as a relief after the carefully preserved cuteness of Charleston.

She went inside. It was an old-fashioned café, with a lot of yellowing pine on the walls and ceiling; one wall was festooned with little triangular sailing flags. Beach Boys music played from huge speakers and on the counter, a vast coffee urn was sending out clouds of steam. Mady ordered a cup and took a seat at a window overlooking the water.

There were few other customers. Two elderly men eating breakfast at another window table and a mother with two young children.

Mady's eyes strayed to the children. A girl of around three years old was claiming all her mother's attention while the baby sat quietly unregarded in his pushchair. He was a sweet baby, near Archie's age. He looked at Mady, and she smiled back at him. That caused obvious delight, and he waved his hand and lurched forwards, struggling to get out of his harness. Mady resisted the urge to go over and scoop him up.

'Mady O'Neil?'

She jumped at the sound of her name.

Fitzgerald stood beside her. He was a tall man, slightly stooped, and wore glasses. He took the seat opposite and she vaguely recognised his face from his student photograph, but he was grey and drained-looking, papery, fragile. He was Hugh's age, she reminded herself, it was only that he looked ten years older.

She offered him a coffee and then saw that he already had one. He didn't seem to notice her slip. He looked exhausted and she wondered if he had been awake all night, worrying about their meeting. He removed his glasses and rubbed his eyes roughly. 'You're a journalist?' he asked.

'Yes.' She produced her newspaper identification, but he gave it the most cursory of glances.

'When your colleague came to see me last fall . . .' he began.

'I'm not actually from Trump Card.'

He frowned as if that was an irrelevance, and she decided not to tell him about Evans' death unless she had to. It might put him off.

'You do want to know about Hugh Eastwood?' he queried.

'Oh yes!'

'Fine. Because I don't care who I tell it to, so long as I off-load it. You can do with it what you like. It won't be my burden any more.' He was speaking very fast. 'Maybe if I'd told that television woman last year, their baby wouldn't have died.'

Mady asked sharply, 'What d'you mean?'

Fitzgerald worked his fingers together. 'God's judgement? It's an old-fashioned idea, I know. But the sins of the father shall be visited upòn the children . . . Not that Hugh really sinned, as such . . .' He seemed about to drift off and she worried that he might be too vague and distracted to be of any use to her.

He seemed to collect himself. 'I suffer from depression,' he explained briefly. 'My last bout was a bad one, and only a year ago, so you must understand my wife's protectiveness, particularly as the cause for my depression is rooted in the very subject you wish me to talk about.'

Mady could hear her heart thumping. The surroundings, the cry of the birds, the old rock music, the children, seemed to fade away, throwing Fitzgerald and his words into sharp focus.

'I buried it, you see. I pretended, as we all did really, that it hadn't happened.' He sighed. 'Christine Evans had half the story. She knew about the club. She had circumstantial evidence about Hugh, but not the proof she needed.'

That suggested he had it. But he paused tantalisingly. When she could bear it no longer, she asked: 'What club?'

'The Go-Go Club?'

When he saw it meant nothing to her, he sighed again but continued rapidly. Mady scribbled notes as fast as she could.

The Go-Go Club had been formed at Chesterfield late in the

fall of 1979 by a group of graduates, including Hugh. It was a pro-abortion group . . .

Mady thought of Hugh's new crusade at home. She had assumed he had adopted it merely for political advantage. Perhaps she had been wrong, perhaps he had genuine feelings about it?

The Go-Go Club was set up deliberately to counter the activities of another student body, militant anti-abortionists. The latter had become a power on campus that semester following a fire at an abortion clinic in Charleston. The students hadn't been responsible – it had been the work of a group from out of state – but they encouraged the belief, at least until the local police had come calling.

'They were very full of themselves that fall,' Fitzgerald recalled, 'strutting around the campus, saying they were doing God's will. Most of them were far-right Christians. Christians,' he spat the word, 'that's what they called themselves.'

They targeted local girls who had got themselves pregnant. Homes and schools were picketed, hate mail sent, the girls' neighbourhoods leafleted. Then a student, a freshman, came to their attention. Eighteen years old, and two months pregnant, Vera Leopold found herself the victim of a hate campaign.

'She was a pretty girl, and clever. She wanted an abortion, she didn't want the rest of her life ruined by a mistake. Word got round school and the Antis made her life hell.

'That's when Hugh and the others formed their club. "Go-Go".' He frowned. 'Silly name. "Go get it out"; "Go go, be gone," that's what Hugh said it was named for. They were kind of flippant about it, at least to begin with.'

'You weren't a member?' Mady put in delicately.

'No, not my sort of thing, although I sympathised with

them. I knew what was going on from Hugh, and the others. They held a lot of their meetings in our room.'

'Was Hugh a leading light?'

Fitzgerald smiled for the first time. 'Yes, I suppose you could say that. He was quite an orator even then, and him being English had a certain appeal, a kind of sophistication the others envied. There were only twelve of them, all men, although Hugh wasn't allowed on the membership scroll.'

She looked up in surprise. 'Why not?'

'He was a foreigner. Silly university rule back then, I'm afraid, that probably was linked to racism. No foreigners in Chesterfield societies.'

The Go-Go Club swore to defend Vera from the Antis. They were her protectors: they worked shifts, one of them being with her during the day, and at night, one on guard outside her dormitory room.

'Sounds quite fun, in a way,' Mady commented.

'Yes, I think they thought that too. But then she asked them to arrange for her abortion.' He fell silent.

'It stopped being fun.'

'Exactly. I don't think it had occurred to anyone that there was a serious point to the whole thing. Vera didn't look pregnant. They had a meeting about it in our room. I was there, and Vera. They couldn't take her any place locally, the Antis had them all covered, so they decided to take her up to Virginia. One of the boys' fathers was a surgeon there. He arranged it all.'

A few days before the Christmas vacation, Vera was smuggled out under cover of darkness. The trip went well and the abortion was successful. Vera went home for the holidays and reappeared at the start of the new semester.

News of her abortion got out, and whilst not condoning it

(the university was a very traditional place in those days), the Dean was forced to take action to ensure no further harassment of Vera on campus. There was some but low-key. The fizz went out of the affair, for the Go-Go Club as well as the Antis.

The result of that for Vera meant that her guardians deserted her.

'She had got used to having them around, especially Hugh.'

'She had a crush on him?' Mady guessed.

Fitzgerald smiled wanly. 'Yes, I suppose you could call it that. She came to our room a lot. If Hugh wasn't there, she'd wait for him. She told me she didn't like being on her own, that Hugh was like a big brother to her, but she was in love with him, it was plain.'

'And he?'

Fitzgerald shrugged. Hugh was fond of her but thought she was too young for him. Three weeks into the new semester, they had a major falling-out. Hugh did not reveal any details, but the upshot was, Vera stopped coming around. Then one afternoon, about a week later, she arrived again at their door. Hugh was out, but she begged Fitzgerald to let her in, saying she had something to tell him.

'But I felt my loyalty was to Hugh. I turned her away. That's what has haunted me ever since. If I'd let her come in, let her talk, it might have been different. As it was . . .'

He stared straight ahead. 'That evening, Hugh and I went out for a drink. We got back to the room just short of midnight. The note was lying in the middle of the floor. She must have pushed it under the door. It said, "Dear Hugh, By the time you read this, I'll have done what you want. I'll be dead . . ."'

Mady caught her breath.

'And she was, or at that moment in a coma. She died the following morning. Vodka and tranquillisers. She'd meant to do it.'

A girl had committed suicide because of Hugh. That was what Trump Card had on him. The fact that it hadn't actually been his fault wouldn't have mattered. The film needn't have said he'd been responsible, but it would have been put together to encourage the viewer to hold that opinion. To have that painful history exposed on national television would be horribly embarrassing, particularly given his current crusade . . . But would it have been enough to have pushed him over the edge, to the point of killing his precious child? Vera had been depressed; would right-thinking people really have blamed him?

'Do you know who the father of her baby was?' she asked suddenly.

Fitzgerald started. 'She never said.' There had been a Freshmen's Ball, he explained. She'd been drunk, along with most people. She couldn't remember what had happened.

Mady let a pause fall. 'Was Hugh at the party?'

There was a longer pause. 'I wasn't there.'

'But he would have been there, wouldn't he? As a postgraduate freshman?'

Fitzgerald studied his watch. 'I'll have to be on my way.'

He wasn't prepared to tell her, she realised, he still owed loyalty to Hugh. He stood up.

'Please,' she cried, 'don't go yet! I've got so much more to ask you. None of this has ever come out about Hugh . . . I mean, about Vera's suicide. How did he keep it a secret? With the note? There must have been an inquest?'

'Yes, an inquest. But no note.'

She frowned. 'What happened to it?'

'Hugh was advised to lose it.'

'By whom?'

Fitzgerald gazed steadily at her. 'First by me and then by his academic advisor.'

'He destroyed it?'

'No one other than Vera wanted there to be a note. Her family didn't. Hugh didn't; the university certainly didn't. Without a note it could be argued, as it was, that Vera hadn't intended to take her own life. She'd had a little too much to drink; she was feeling low; she'd taken a tranquilliser, then forgotten and taken a couple more . . . the verdict was death by misadventure.'

Which was how Hugh had managed to keep it a secret all those years, Mady thought triumphantly. By destroying the evidence. Everyone involved had colluded in the cover-up. It made Hugh appear much more guilty.

Fitzgerald told her that, pushed by its governing body, the university had reluctantly held its own inquiry. The members of both the Antis and the Go-Go Club were reprimanded, but because Hugh hadn't been on the membership list, he had escaped even that mild censure.

Fitzgerald started training for the Baptist ministry soon after his first bout of depression. The illness had haunted him throughout his life. He gave a brittle smile. 'I'm talking to you now in the hope of warding off another bout. It's been bad, not the worst it can get, since Christine Evans called. She asked me outright about the note and I lied, as I always have. I told her I knew nothing of it.'

She had been right to say nothing of Evans' death, Mady thought. It struck her that she, like Evans, only had hearsay evidence against Hugh. She asked Fitzgerald if he would put his version of events on the record?

He shook his head. 'No way. I thought when I refused to talk to Miss Evans, it would all go away, but then I got a Christmas card from Hugh and family. That's what it said, "With love from our family to yours". There was a picture of him, with his wife and baby.'

Mady's heart turned over. 'Roz, his wife, sent them.'

'Did she? A nice-looking woman. A lovely baby.'

Mady let a silence fall.

'Maybe if I had called Hugh. Maybe if I had persuaded him to tell the truth . . . I don't know . . .' Fitzgerald trailed off.

'You don't believe the nanny did it?'

'I don't think so. Do you?'

Mady lowered her eyes. 'She claimed during the court case that Hugh was under enormous pressure.'

'Yes, I read that.'

There was a pause while she waited for him to say more. When he didn't she asked the question that had been troubling her: 'Was the trial big news over here? No one at the university seemed to link it to Hugh.'

Fitzgerald shrugged. 'Why should they? We had our own killer-nanny case going on at the same time. We had wall-to-wall coverage of that. Yours got hardly mentioned.'

'He's so well-known at home.'

'Well, he's nothing here.'

She saw him glance towards the door. 'Did he ever tell you what he and Vera had rowed about?' she asked quietly.

'No.'

'Can I just ask one more thing?'

He sighed.

'Do you know how Trump Card got the story in the first place?'

He met her eye. 'Christine Evans said it was a fluke, I remember that. She traced me through the inquest. There was an article in the local paper.'

Of course, she thought. 'D'you remember when the inquest was?'

He sighed impatiently. 'April or May, I can't be sure. Now I really must go. I told my wife I was going to the bank.'

She gave him her card. They shook hands and he left, not looking back. Mady stared after him. She needed to find a second witness to corroborate his account, but on the record. Christine Evans had got her information elsewhere, so must she. There was Moira, ever helpful, but the risk in going back to her was too great. Mady was supposed to be writing about Hugh, not probing a suicide.

She glanced at the time: 10.15. She called Jack, reaching him for the first time since she had been in the States. She told him she was making progress but still needed more leads.

'Nothing more on Eastwood?' he queried.

'Nothing I could write, yet.'

'Get on with it then.'

Thus galvanised, she approached the barman and asked for the names of Charleston's newspapers.

Halfway through the morning, Moira Branigan left the office, saying she was on the way to the library. In fact she went to her car to make a telephone call. Personal calls were frowned upon in the office.

She called her daughter at work, to make sure she was there

and not sobbing at home over the break-up with the boyfriend Moira had never liked. Her daughter sounded good, and, much relieved, Moira emerged from her car.

There was a toot behind her. A car was waiting, with its window down, its driver mouthing: was she going? Regretfully, Moira shook her head, no.

She glanced again at the man behind the wheel, bearded, nicely dressed, beautiful car. 'Oh! Doctor,' she exclaimed, causing him to turn.

She stuck her head in at his window and he shrank back in some alarm. 'Dr McCloud?' she queried.

He admitted it cautiously.

'I understand you've met our young lady researcher from England?'

He didn't now what to say; he wasn't entirely sure who Moira was for a moment, and then he remembered. But she had rushed on:

'. . . Such a sweet girl . . . I tried to help her out, but it's quite a long time ago really . . . Put an appeal out on the Alumni website . . . Did you remember Hugh Eastwood?'

McCloud listened attentively. He asked a couple of questions, being careful, he hoped, not to arouse suspicion, but Moira was only too pleased to answer anything, and in full. When eventually she moved off, he circled the parking lot distractedly, finding a space at the furthest end, which would normally have infuriated him but not now.

He called all Hugh's numbers and, not being able to locate him anywhere, left a message on his mobile answering service. He felt very anxious. He had assured Hugh that Mady O'Neil was not a threat, now he was not so sure.

He went to work, to deliver a lecture he knew by heart, but

which on that occasion he stumbled through, his mind being largely elsewhere.

Life had been a series of disappointments for Lola Beaney. She was overweight, which she blamed on her genes. She was twice-divorced and now newly separated, circumstances which she blamed entirely on her husbands, whom she also largely held responsible for the unruliness of her five children.

Her eldest was the reason she was at home now. The girl had been ditching school again, and the High School principal had called Lola at work. What was she going to do about Estelle?

What was she going to do, Lola thought bitterly? Why was it always up to her? What was wrong with the school sorting it out, or Estelle's father? She had got herself so worked up that it had brought on one of her headaches, which in turn had meant she had to leave work, getting dirty looks from her supervisor as she did so.

Entering the house now, she saw the pile of dirty crockery on the table, the milk left out to go sour on the counter. Her daughters were supposed to have tidied up before leaving for school. Meanly, Lola decided they could do it when they came home.

She fixed herself a snack and took it into the den. She switched on the computer, and checked if she had any new e-mail; for the last few weeks, she had been corresponding with a man from Florida.

She saw there was a new message on her old university notice board. She read it and frowned. They were asking for anyone who remembered Hugh Eastwood (1979–1980) to get in touch; a researcher from England wanted to speak to them.

At some length the previous winter, Lola had spoken to a British television researcher about Hugh Eastwood.

Upon hearing what she had to say, Christine Evans had been very excited. She had described Lola's disclosures as sensational and worth quite a lot of money, she had thought, in response to Lola's questioning.

Christine had impressed upon her the absolute necessity to tell no one else what she had told her. She was starting filming in the early spring, and she would be bringing a crew from England to film Lola. She had also promised to be in touch. Neither promise had been kept. With all that had been going on in her life, Lola had forgotten about it, but now . . .

Now here was that woman issuing a public appeal!

Lola's mouth yanked downward. She supposed that the producer thought she was lying. Or perhaps had deemed her too large with her glandular problem to appear on her precious programme. She would be sorry; no one else knew what Lola did about that man.

Her fingers, greasy with food, hovered over the keyboard. She would send her a message, that she now refused to be interviewed. Then she paused. Did she really want to be bothered? Did she want that woman harassing her again, taking up her valuable time for nothing? The promised money had never materialised, Lola remembered.

No. She had more important things to do. She ran her cursor down her message list and clicked on to Michael from Tampa.

The photographer had been in position on the flat roof for five hours. He had supposed the Greek sun would be hot but he had forgotten it was November. By mid-afternoon, it was descending rapidly in the sky and he lay there, chilled and despondent.

He knew that Kate Armstrong was in the Dimitris Bar opposite. He'd talked to her the night before, had confirmed with his own eyes that the tip-off was correct. At noon, just after he'd crept up on to his rooftop, he'd seen her enter the bar from the street. He hadn't been quick enough to get a shot. She hadn't come back out. But he comforted himself that soon she would.

There was only that one entrance, of which he had a perfect view. He stared at it, until his eyes lost focus, then he switched to the bar's flat roof. A line of bright clothes flapped there. All he had to do was wait, he told himself.

But the hours dragged. He dared not move around much, in case he was seen or heard. In a tiny community like that, everyone would know each other. They would protect their own. He didn't rate his chances highly if he was discovered.

Now he was not only cold and stiff, but growing worried about losing the light. He couldn't use a flash. He faced the awful prospect of another day up there.

A movement caught his eye. Down on the bar's rooftop, a door had opened. A young woman emerged, bearing a wicker basket. The photographer blinked once to make absolutely sure: it was she.

As she stretched and bent, gathering her clothes, folding them down neatly in her basket, he snapped shot after shot. When he used up the film in one camera, he picked up another, already loaded.

By the time Kate left the roof, he knew he had just made more money than he had all year. As dusk fell, he climbed carefully down into the street and used back alleys to reach his hotel.

*

The plane to New York left Heathrow at four o'clock in the afternoon. There was a connecting flight to Atlanta at nine o'clock in the evening, eastern seaboard time. Hugh estimated that by driving through the night, he would be in Charleston by the morning.

Now that he knew what he was doing, his head felt perfectly clear. He was travelling in first class, in a sleeping berth. Shortly after take-off, he swallowed two of his pills and was asleep before the aircraft had left the Irish coastline.

CHAPTER FIFTEEN

Charleston had many newspapers, the barman at the Tidewater Café informed Mady, but the best and most comprehensive was *The Bugle*. It had been around for a hundred years. If anything moved in the city, *The Bugle* had it.

An hour later, having returned her car to the hotel car park, Mady caught a cab to the newspaper's offices in downtown Charleston.

She went in through shining revolving doors and asked at reception whether the newspaper covered the Little Corinne area?

'We cover the whole of South Carolina, ma'am,' came the drawled response.

She had prepared a loose cover story in case of awkward questions but it wasn't needed. Halfway through her explanation, she was directed to the Archive Department, an airy room on the fourth floor.

A number of projectors sat on tables spaced around the walls. The sole occupant, a man busy at a word processor, introduced himself as the archivist, and asked how he could help?

She asked if she could look at newspapers from April and May 1980. Material that old was on microfilm, he informed her, and disappeared into another room. He came back with a dozen microfiches.

'That many?' she queried, surprised.

'We house all the local papers, not just our own. You've got four there.'

Even better, she thought.

He offered to help further, but she told him she knew how to operate a projector. Looking relieved, he set her up at a desk a long way from his own. When she thanked him for his help, he merely shrugged, told her it was his job, and returned to his computer, becoming oblivious to her presence within moments.

He was a far cry from Moira, she thought, which was probably just as well. She inserted the first fiche. It contained two weeks' worth of *The Bugle*, but there was no mention of the inquest.

She tried a second fiche, covering the last two weeks of April: again there was nothing. It wasn't until the fourth piece of film, dated the last week of May, that she found the first reference. It was *The Bugle*'s front page lead:

'Dead University Girl was Depressed after Abortion.'

Snappy headline, she thought, then scanned the report:

Vera's comatose body had been found at midnight by her roommate, nineteen-year-old Lola Flynn. Lola had called an ambulance but Vera had never regained consciousness. The police had also been alerted in case of foul play, but no evidence had been found, nor had a suicide note . . .

Vera's family doctor confirmed that she had recently undergone an abortion out-of-state and that he had subsequently prescribed her mild antidepressants. The university authorities dismissed suggestions from the family's lawyer that Vera had been the victim of a hate campaign on campus by anti-abortionists. 'Vera had a close network of friends and supporters,' the Dean was reported as saying.

The Bugle made no specific mention of the Go-Go Club, but now, having a date, Mady was able quickly to check the other papers too. The *South Carolina Crier* came closest to revealing the club: it talked of a group of students that had formed to protect her. This paper alone carried a quote from Vera's mother, Mrs Sylvia Leopold:

'We have lost our only daughter. Now we want to be left alone.'

Mady wanted to speak to a family member. Vera had gone home for Christmas after her abortion; if she had been at all close to her parents, she would have talked to them, her mother in particular. According to *The Bugle*, the parents lived in South Street, Charleston. It was twenty-three years before, Mady cautioned herself, but Leopold was an unusual name.

She asked her companion for a telephone directory. Wordlessly he pointed at a long shelf of them on the wall above her projector. Feeling foolish, she opened the Charleston book and leafed through. There was half a page of Leopolds, more than she had expected; still, she was prepared to try them all. One at least must be related. She ran her eyes down the column, and stopped. The second entry from the bottom listed Leopold, S., 78 South Street, Charleston. S for Sylvia, Mady told herself, it couldn't be otherwise.

'Is there somewhere I can phone without disturbing anyone?' she asked aloud.

The man directed her out into the hall. It wasn't that he was rude, she thought, just staggeringly uncommunicative. At the far end of a hall, by a window, were three old-fashioned telephone booths. She went in and dialled the number.

It had been so easy to find. Christine Evans must have called it too. That could work for or against her, Mady thought cautiously. Mrs Leopold might feel that having spoken once, she wouldn't do so again. Alternatively, having done it once, she might not find it so hard to talk again.

'Hullo?' spoke a bright female voice.

Mady asked if she was speaking to Mrs Sylvia Leopold?

'That's right.' The voice was calm and clear.

Mady explained that she was a journalist from England . . .

'What do you want to speak to me about?' asked Sylvia Leopold sharply.

'It's about your daughter, Mrs Leopold, I wonder if I . . .'

'I have nothing to say.'

'I know it must be very difficult . . .'

'I have no comment to make.' Still calm, but very firm.

'Did you speak to Christine Evans?' asked Mady in desperation.

'I am putting the phone down now,' said Mrs Leopold and did.

Mady felt shaky. It wasn't nice to be treated like a pariah, although of course it had happened to her before and on that occasion she completely sympathised. To Mrs Leopold, all journalists were vultures, seeking to pick over the memory of her child. Mady had the address but wouldn't dream of going to the house.

She returned despondently to the room. The archivist glanced up without a word and she longed for a touch of human warmth. She resumed her seat and applied her eye to the projector.

There was so little to go on from the reports. The roommate's evidence, Vera's tutor, her doctor who had prescribed the anti-depressants . . . and yet Fitzgerald said Evans had traced him through a newspaper.

'Excuse me?' she murmured.

'Yeah?' said the archivist.

'Are these all the local newspapers from back then? There aren't any others that you don't keep here, or . . .?' She let her voice dribble away as he stared.

'That's all of them, I said.'

'Thanks.'

Could Fitzgerald have been lying to her? But why would he, when otherwise he had been so helpful? Was Mrs Leopold the key? Had she talked to Evans last year, telling her how to find Fitzgerald? If she had, there was nothing more Mady could do about it. She knew the woman would never talk to her.

The report she was staring at was the *Carolina Times*: the lengthiest and also the dullest account, everything being in reported speech apart from a single quote right at the end: ' "Vera was always quiet," said her roommate, Miss Flynn.'

Thrilling observation, Mady thought, and then it dawned on her: the roommate! Why hadn't she thought of her before? As Fitzgerald had been Hugh's confidant, wouldn't Lola have been Vera's? Lola would have known Fitzgerald, and if Vera had told anyone about her row with Hugh, it would have been the girl who shared her room. Lola Flynn had to be the source.

Mady opened the telephone directory. There were two pages, two columns deep, of Flynns. Her resolve quailed.

'Thanks.' She handed the fiches back to the archivist.

'Uh huh.'

She paused, debating all the things she could say to him, but in the end saying nothing. Outside, she caught a cab back to her hotel and had her car brought up from the car park.

She headed off for the university once more, knowing she would have to think of a convincing reason to explain to Moira her sudden interest in another old student.

She was about to join the highway when her mobile rang. Trying to bring to mind who had that number – hardly anyone – she answered it.

'Mady?'

'Roz!' She froze momentarily. The avoidance of Roz while she was on Hugh's trail in the States was one of the reasons she had got a temporary mobile. How had Roz got the number?

'Are you okay?' Roz asked.

'Fine!' Mady swerved off the road on to the forecourt of a garage. A lorry sounded its klaxon angrily as it passed. 'Er, how're you?' she asked, trying to collect herself.

'Well, I've been better, to tell you the truth. Hugh's been acting pretty weirdly actually, Mady. He tried to drown me last night, if you can believe it.' She gave a little laugh but Mady failed to find that funny.

'Are you going to go to the police?' she asked.

'No.'

'Why not?'

'I love him, and I don't really think he meant to harm me.'

Mady opened her mouth to argue then thought, what was the use?

'He's not going to find me, don't worry. If I go to the police, that's it, isn't it? Everything will come out and I don't even know if he's guilty yet.'

Mady knew what her friend was saying, illogical though it seemed.

'How're you getting on?' Roz asked next.

'I'm, er, making headway.'

'Is that it? You're as bad as Ben,' Roz complained. 'He wouldn't give me your number. I had to get it from Jack.'

Damn Jack, Mady thought. Although she supposed she should have spelled it out to him, that he was not to tell Roz anything.

'Jack told me you were in Charleston,' Roz challenged.

Mady gave up. 'Roz, I'll tell you everything once I've got it, I promise.'

There was a long pause. 'You don't trust me, do you?' Roz said quietly.

'I . . . Everything is at such a delicate stage . . .'

'It's all right, you don't need to explain.' How bitter Roz sounded. The line went dead.

Mady felt terrible. Roz must feel so alone, deserted by her best friend and threatened by her husband. But Mady was there in Charleston for Roz, she argued with herself, at least partly. She chose not to dwell on the other reason: that she was there in pursuit of a story.

'Gas?' enquired a man at her car window.

'No thanks.' She drove off, leaving him muttering beside his petrol pump.

The photographs of Kate Armstrong went down the line within one hour of them being taken. At six o'clock local time in Hamburg, they were received delightedly by the German picture agency for whom the photographer was working.

Kate photographed well; in fact, in one of the shots she was actually beautiful, thinner than in her old pictures but still easily identifiable. The agency's proprietor literally rubbed his hands in glee: it wasn't just the money, it was the kudos. He was respected in the business, he was about to be much better respected.

He knew his market. He sent a brief e-mail to every picture desk in London. His agency had found the missing nanny; her pictures would go to the highest bidder in one hour's time. There would be no previews, the winner alone would see the pictures.

The response was immediate and as good as he could have hoped. The British papers scrambled over each other to get those pictures, and the price soared up and up. Forty minutes later, most bidders had fallen by the wayside, leaving just two, a tabloid and a quality, to fight it out between them. Slightly to the proprietor's surprise, it being more of a tabloid story in his opinion, the quality won. But the money was what counted.

He went to the phone to agree final terms with the winner.

The office was one of the few places where Roz felt safe and still connected to the outside world.

She was so glad, following her depressing call to Mady, that she had decided to go there. Her colleagues had not fobbed her off; they had looked pleased to see her. It was her first time back since the trial had finished, not that anyone mentioned that. The talk was all of how well she looked. She found herself smiling and complimenting others in return.

Her secretary brought her a coffee, her mail, and telephone messages: Hugh had called the previous day, looking for her. Roz gave no explanation, and she hadn't returned Hugh's call. She was there to feel good about herself, not to be dragged back down into his darkness.

Work, that room, her familiar things in it, including

photographs of Charley, had saved her after his death, and soothed her still. It was like being in a time warp. In there, it was as if he wasn't dead. As if he was still at home and when she left work, it would be to rush home to see him. She was in control. She was the editor of her magazine, as she always had been, even in those dreadful early days after Charley when she had gone about like a ghost, her mind a blank. Her staff had been fantastic, running the magazine for her, and taking over completely during the trial and its aftermath.

On Monday morning, however, in three days' time, she was due back, full-time, or else she would have to resign. That hadn't been said in so many words but the magazine couldn't continue to carry her indefinitely. That looming deadline had worried her, she acknowledged, until now; now she knew she could handle it. She was alive there, her core intact. She relished her imminent return.

There came a tap at her door and her deputy editor entered. 'Roz? Good, you are still here. We're going for a drink. Like to come?'

How wonderful to be back at the wheel of life. 'Love to!' She gathered her things together, checked her desk drawers, and went out with the others. In the elevator, the chat was cheerful and light, people looking forward to their weekends. She found that she could join in. She felt quite young again.

They headed for The Cellar, a favourite haunt. Already at just after six, the place was half-full with bankers and journalists. Instantly she recognised two men at the bar, Jack Simpson and his picture editor. What were they doing there, she wondered? And then she remembered that in the summer *The Register* had moved into the same tower as her magazine.

In the dim light and in profile Jack, at least sixty, looked rather handsome. In the past, he had fancied her and that afternoon, she remembered, when she had called for Mady's number, he'd been awfully sweet to her, and very helpful. She approached stealthily.

'Good scoop?' she enquired slyly.

He jumped at the sight of her. The other man, not seeing her for a moment, carried on talking, then he too flinched and clamped his jaws together.

'Er, Roz,' Jack managed faintly.

'What's wrong?' she asked.

Jack drained his glass, the other man left his, so urgent was his need to get away. 'Got to be off,' Jack muttered and bolted after him.

She stared. She replayed the snatch of conversation that she had overheard: '. . . awkward . . . what Bishop said . . .'

Alice Bishop. A chill moved through her. They had been talking about the case again. Would it never end?

A door flapped open inside her head. Of course she, Roz, wasn't normal. She would never be normal again. She would always be the mother of the baby that the nanny – or the husband – had killed. She would always be a talking point. Forever people would stop dead in their conversations when she appeared.

She gazed over at her own entourage. They were affecting not to have noticed anything untoward, or perhaps they truly hadn't, but they soon would. Once Mady had her story, she, Roz, would again be thrust into the limelight, not as a brilliant editor, but a childless mother, a cuckolded wife, a fool. She couldn't bear it. She saw suddenly that her colleagues were shamming: their smiles stretched, their speech artificial, their inclusion of her a burden. That was what she was reduced to. She no longer existed.

She edged away without their noticing and made it outside. It was raining spikes into the river. She stood there, watching the swirl and suck of the dark water, becoming hypnotised by it. Hugh had tried to drown her, they said that drowning was easy, it didn't hurt. If she was dead she would see Charley again. Startled, she realised her baby was mere moments away from her. Why had she never thought of that before? If only she possessed the courage to get up upon the stone parapet, pleasurably rough under her smooth fingers, and let go.

By dint of hard work and persistent bullying, Alan Hardy had acquired a great deal of information by six o'clock that evening. He duly presented himself outside Rebecca's door to be told she was on the telephone, but when she heard he was there, she had him ushered in.

'Well?' she asked eagerly before he'd had a chance to sit down. 'Minister . . .'

He kept his report brief, as she liked. First, he dispelled the mystery of Christine Evans' death. 'She was a coke addict. Her system was pumped full of it.'

Some of the tension went from Rebecca's face but she queried, 'She had taken the stuff herself, I presume? She wasn't helped?'

He shook his head. 'No, ma'am. There are no indicators to suggest that and two witnesses have said she was a regular user.'

'Glad to hear it.'

He continued, 'Additionally, there was no evidence of a break-in to her flat. None at all,' he reiterated, forestalling any question that a professional team could have been responsible.

Rebecca nodded. 'She jumped when she was coked up, that's what the police are saying?'

'That's what they will be saying,' Alan concurred carefully, 'if we want them to. At the moment the official line is they are still investigating the cause of death. It could go either way.'

'I see.'

They looked at each other. 'Hugh is convinced it's murder, isn't he?' she asked.

'He is. And he's in such a highly suggestible frame of mind at the moment.'

'Will the police play ball?' she enquired.

Alan paused tentatively. 'In return for a name or two on the Grey Team business.'

She stiffened instantly. 'Who brought that up?'

'It occurred naturally, ma'am. Evans worked for Trump Card.'

Rebecca shrank before him, and he knew why. Until the previous spring no one he knew had heard of Trump Card. Then the horrible news reached their ears that a tinpot production company had got hold of the minutes of a Grey Team meeting and were intending to make a film about it.

If they did, it would end Rebecca's career. Alan's would probably survive.

The Security Services had done what they could but the two men working on the film, both directors of the company, had been extremely surveillance-conscious. They discussed their work with no one. They swept their premises for bugs, they talked in code on the telephone. A discreet break-in to the office revealed nothing, which was in itself suspicious. Eventually, by tampering with their mail, it was discovered the company used a room in an office block to store their material. It would look too suspicious if that got burgled, so the entire building was fired. The security guard had been an unfortunate casualty, but otherwise the fire had worked like a dream. The film had been dropped.

Rebecca took a sip of water from the glass on her desk before asking, with commendable calm, 'Evans worked on the Grey Team film? I thought it was just the two men.'

'Her fellow directors. She wasn't working on it. She was working on a film about abortion. And Hugh, apparently.'

Rebecca went white. 'What about Hugh and abortion?' she rasped.

'I don't know more than that, Minister,' Alan admitted.

'Well, bloody well find out.' She glared at him. 'You told me Trump Card were amateurs. They'd stumbled on the Grey Team by accident, you said. Now it looks like they could destroy us all. What else have they got up their sleeves?'

Alan looked wordlessly back at her.

Her face glowed pink with anger, her finger tapped, waiting for the answer that didn't come. '"Hugh and abortion?" That's all we know?'

'So far—' Alan started.

'Why didn't we know last spring?' she barked.

'She worked on her own, as they all did. They were a bunch of conspiracy theorists. No one knew what anyone else was doing.' A bit like your department, he thought of saying, but didn't.

Rebecca took another gulp of water. She was calming down. 'So how do we find out what she had on Hugh? Surely she'd paperwork somewhere? Now she's dead it won't be too difficult to find out.'

'There's already been a preliminary search. Nothing found. It's possible she operated the same system as her colleagues and there'll be another hideaway somewhere, but that'll take time to find, and I don't think we'll need to wait.'

'How so?'

'I think Mady O'Neil is going to find out for us.'

'Mady . . .?'

'The other journalist Hugh wanted us to deal with,' he reminded her. 'She's in Charleston at the moment. Hugh was a student there, a postgraduate. Christine Evans was there last year researching a film about abortion that somehow entangled Hugh.'

'My goodness.'

'And Hugh left for the States this afternoon.'

She goggled at him. Truly, he thought, it was not the politicians who ran the land. 'Hugh's definitely not stable,' he went on. 'Who knows what he might do to another pesky journalist, given his track record?'

Her eyes fixed on him. 'You're right,' she breathed.

'His wife's gone missing as well, it seems.'

Rebecca swooped greedily. 'Really?'

'She may turn up of course.'

'Of course,' Rebecca echoed. But suppose Hugh had harmed her as well? Or it could be made to look that way?

'My advice on Hugh,' Alan continued, 'is we wait and see. He may well do our dirty work for us. We can always step in to lend a hand if necessary.'

'Supply a piece of background information.'

'Precisely,' he smiled at her. She was quick on the uptake; that was why she had lasted so long.

'Our police can be trusted not to talk to the press?' She was in wrap-up mode now.

'I believe so. They want a break on the Grey Team too much.'

'Who shall we give them?'

Alan raised his eyebrows.

'Hugh could be jolly useful to us all round then?'

'I believe so.'

He could see her mentally ticking off things to be done. 'Won't other journalists be sniffing around into Evans' death?' she asked.

'Don't think so. Her addiction was well enough known, and she wasn't a key player or particularly well-liked. Her death just about made it into today's papers. There's been nothing since.'

'Good. Let us see what unfolds, then.' She smiled. 'Have you had any thoughts on Hugh's successor?' They fell to discussing names and possibilities.

CHAPTER SIXTEEN

On the drive out to Chesterfield, one idea had occurred to Mady to explain her interest in Lola Flynn: that she was a distant relation to Hugh's wife. That amazing coincidence had only just come to light and now Mady had been asked to write an extra piece on the long-lost cousin.

She didn't know how good the story was but it would have to do, Mady told herself, as she walked down the corridor that led to Moira's office.

She turned the handle, but the door remained shut. She twisted it the other way. It was only then that she saw through the frosted glass that the room was in darkness. Panic rose: it was Friday, perhaps the college staff went home early . . . What on earth was she going to do? Then she saw the sign on the door. It read, 'Gone to lunch'.

Light-headed, she realised she was hungry herself. She found a sandwich bar at the end of another corridor. She scanned the tables hopefully for a sight of Moira, but there was none. She bought a vast pastrami on rye sandwich, took it out into the sunshine and walked a little way until she found a bench. No one else was sitting down, in fact people were scurrying about huddled in jumpers and jackets, but then they hadn't experienced November in England, she thought, as she basked in the sun's pleasant warmth.

She finished her sandwich and closed her eyes. It was nearly two o'clock, it would be seven in the evening back home, bath-time. Archie would be splashing madly about, chucking water out of the bath when Ben wasn't looking, his hair going really curly in the damp, and when he was dried, it would spring into little dark corkscrews.

Her head jerked to one side, waking her rudely. She longed to doze again but made herself get up. Time was too short.

Her mobile jingled and she saw Jack's number on the read-out. He told her *The Register* had bought exclusive pictures of Kate Armstrong.

'Wow,' said Mady, stunned. 'She's been found? What's she saying?'

'Don't know if she's saying anything yet. We've got a wordsmith going over there first thing in the morning.'

Mady yearned to be that person.

'We're hoping to run it Sunday for Monday, if you're ready in time,' Jack continued. 'Or have you got what you need already?'

There was suddenly no more time. 'Er, not quite,' she hedged.

'Uh-huh. Don't let me down, will you, Mady? Your story's the main reason we bought those pictures.'

There was more than a hint of nervousness in his voice, which automatically she sought to soothe. 'Don't worry. I'll call you.'

Talk about pressure, she thought, as she re-entered Moira's

building and squeezed past a group of students who blocked
the corridor. The Student Affairs office door was open now. She
could hear someone on the phone inside. Moira, she prayed,
and stepped in, but it wasn't Moira. There was no sign of her,
only a grey-haired woman Mady didn't recognise from the day
before, who was talking furtively on the phone. She looked over
crossly at Mady then resumed her call.

Mady stood there uselessly, not knowing what else to do.
Finally the phone went down, just short of a slam.

'Excuse me,' called Mady in desperation.

The woman was rummaging in her handbag and didn't look
up.

'Is Moira in this afternoon?'

The woman extracted a lipstick then turned to eye Mady
slowly. 'Moira's gone home,' she said.

Mady's lips went dry. 'Is there any way you could help me?'
she begged. 'I need to get into the vault.'

'Can't help you. I'm only the clerk.'

Mady wanted to shake her. 'I'm from England.' She tried
again. 'I really need to talk to Moira.'

'Come back Monday then.'

Mady felt her face go hot. 'Could you please, possibly, give
her a call at home? It's terribly urgent.'

'Sawry.'

She would have to phone every Flynn in the telephone
directory. There was nothing else for it. It would probably yield
nothing, Lola had undoubtedly married and/or moved away in
the past twenty years. What was she going to tell Jack?

'Hello, Mady!'

She jumped. 'Moira,' she said weakly. 'I thought you'd gone
home.'

Moira smiled as she lifted the counter into the office. 'On my way now. Just came back to switch off my computer and get my things.' She paused. 'Were you looking for me?'

'Yes! I desperately need your help.'

'Oh?' Moira looked flustered. 'I've got to get home . . .'

'Please.' Mady just prevented herself from clutching her arm. 'What is it?'

'Something else has come up. I've got to get back into the vault.'

Moira bit her lip. 'But I've got my daughter coming over.'

'It won't take long.' Mady poured out her story. It sounded good, and she saw Moira wavering. 'Can't it wait till Monday?' she suggested.

'I need it now. You can't believe the pressure I'm under. I've got to have a draft written by Sunday.'

Moira sighed. 'Okay, I'll take you over now but we'll have to hurry.'

'You're marvellous. Thank you so much.'

With minimum delay, Moira found the swipe card and they left the office. One advantage to the shortness of time was that she didn't question Mady's story. They didn't talk very much at all and reached the library quite out of breath. The vault was in darkness. Moira flicked a switch and when the lights came on, she went straight to the shelves and found the relevant yearbook.

'D'you want me to check her details on the database while you look at that?' she volunteered.

'Oh, yes please.'

Moira went over to the computer. Mady pulled out a chair and sat down. She leafed to the undergraduate section of the yearbook and flicked through until she found Lola Flynn. She was a pudgy young woman with a middle-aged face but incongruously spiky hair. She looked sulky. She had majored in Economics, her hobbies were listed as reading and ballroom dancing.

Mady skimmed over the pages to see what Vera Leopold had looked like: pretty and delicate, and very young. How Lola must have loathed her, she thought ruefully, then remembered how it had ended for Vera. Lying dead on a mortuary slab at eighteen years old.

'I've got her,' called Moira.

Mady hurried over.

'You're in luck. She answered one of our updates.'

Thank God, thought Mady, bending down to see the screen.

'Mind you,' warned Moira, 'it was seven years back.'

'That doesn't matter.' She read that Lola had married in 1987 and had three children. Her married name was Sorensen. There was a Charleston address, no telephone or e-mail details, but that was of little account. Mady took down the address and they left the building, Moira hastening back to her office and Mady to the car park.

She located the street in her roadmap and left the college, heading back to Charleston on the route that now seemed familiar to her. She took a turning for the Isle of Palms, east of the city, but before she reached anything resembling an island, saw the street sign she was looking for. She entered a grid of streets, kept going until the junction she had seen on the map, and turned right into Palm Tree Boulevard.

It was a broad street with houses painted in pastel shades and porches and neat front yards. In front of each dwelling was a palm tree. Towards the end of the road, the houses became apartments. Number 1129, Lola's, was in a building three storeys high.

Mady parked and approached. There were six apartments in the building and admittance was by entry buzzer only. She uttered a prayer and buzzed Lola's number.

It was three-thirty in the afternoon. There was no response. Lola was probably out picking up the children from school, Mady guessed. Or she might be at work. She returned to her car. Half an hour went by and a yellow schoolbus appeared. It stopped at the top of the road, and a stream of children descended, but none of them came in her direction. Cars whizzed by but no one stopped.

Mady gazed up at Lola's apartment. It didn't look very big for a family with three children, so money was probably tight.

A car bounced on to the driveway beside her, then disappeared below ground into an underground car park. Mady gazed at the windows of the building but she saw no one moving around. She got out and tried Lola's number again, but there was still no reply.

Another half-hour dragged by and tension gave way to boredom. She got out of the car and walked up and down the street a little, then imagined how suspicious she might look to local residents. She went back to the apartments again. She pressed another buzzer, and a man's voice quavered faintly, 'Yes?'

'Oh hello. I'm looking for Mrs Sorensen? Lola?'

'That's not me.'

'No. I think she lives in your building though? She's got three children.'

'I dunno.'

Brilliant, Mady thought. 'Thanks anyway,' she called gaily into the speakerphone and trailed back to her car.

Another vehicle was approaching, indicating its intention to turn into the driveway. Mady saw a woman at the wheel and waved frantically. She wouldn't stop, Mady warned herself, but she did. It wasn't Lola but a woman in her sixties, tanned and white-haired. She studied Mady for a few moments before rolling down her window and calling suspiciously, 'Can I help you?'

'I wonder if you could?' Mady approached, smiling ingratiatingly. 'I'm looking for someone who lives in this building. A Mrs Sorensen?'

The woman shook her head. 'No one of that name lives here.'

'Are you sure?'

'Perfectly.'

'I'm sorry, of course you are. But the address I have is 1129 Palm Tree Boulevard?'

The woman's eyes narrowed. 'Then I think you have the wrong address.' The window started to slide back up.

'No, no, I'm sure I don't,' cried Mady. 'Lola's got three children . . .'

'Lola?' Understanding seemed to dawn. 'You're looking for the daughter?'

'I'm sorry?' asked Mady, confused.

'Mrs Flynn lived in the apartment next to mine for eighteen years. She died last June. She had a daughter called Lola with several children.'

'Ah.' Why had Lola given her mother's address and not her own to the college? 'I'm, er, sorry about Mrs Flynn. D'you happen to know where Lola lives?'

'I've no idea.' The woman spoke disapprovingly. 'Edith had three daughters. Lola was the one who only ever visited to collect her mail.'

'Oh dear,' said Mady inadequately. Her mind raced. How on earth was she supposed to find Lola now?

The woman's mouth pursed up. 'Too busy getting divorced, I shouldn't wonder.'

'Oh?'

'She was on her third last time I heard. A realtor this time.'

Mady seized the snippet gratefully. 'D'you have any idea of her new surname?'

'Why would I?'

Mady had no answer for that. She asked, 'Would you happen to know how to get in touch with Mrs Flynn's other children?'

'No. Edith and I were good neighbours, not close friends. I must be on my way.' She started the ignition once more.

'Oh, please. D'you know if Lola lives in Charleston?' Mady cried.

'All Edith's family were local. That's what used to upset her so when Lola didn't come round. Now, if you'll excuse me?' She rolled up her window and drove down into the car park.

Mady returned to her hotel room. In the Yellow Pages, she found dozens of real estate dealers. Even whittling down the ones with Charleston addresses, still left her with over twenty.

She began dialling. The first number was unobtainable, the second answered just as she was about to give up. The woman she spoke to was charming. Then Mady explained that she was looking for a realtor whose wife or partner was called Lola . . .? and found herself speaking to the dialling tone. That happened several times as she worked her way doggedly down the list. Some people said no outright; a few sounded intrigued, most bored. To as many people as would take it, she gave her hotel and mobile number. As time wore on, she got more and more answering machines on which she left messages. At seven o'clock, she realised she was beaten. Nowhere had she found a trace of the woman, or man, she was looking for.

Her neck ached from using the phone so much. She ordered food and coffee from room service, drank and ate mechanically, then picked up the other telephone directory.

There were forty-eight Flynns. It took her two hours to go through all of them. She followed up two hopeful trails that turned out to be false. At nine-thirty, she found she was too stupefied to talk any more and too exhausted even to care. She plugged her mobile into its adaptor then into the mains to recharge it, got into bed and fell asleep instantly.

The flight from New York had been delayed and by the time the plane landed in Atlanta, Georgia, it was almost midnight. Hugh had slept soundly on the main leg of the journey, however, and when he emerged on to the quiet concourse, he felt fine.

Many of the car-rental booths were closed but Hugh had pre-booked and his car was waiting for him in the pound. Less than forty minutes after touchdown, he was on the Interstate, heading east for Charleston.

He hadn't been in America for twenty-three years. Both his wives had expressed the desire to go there, but he'd refused. His first wife had been too pliant to object; Roz had gone on her own.

He'd never told anyone about what had happened at Chesterfield. At first, he'd been sure it would come out. He had lived with that fear, which in turn had made him wild and earned him the deserved reputation as a womaniser. But the layer of years had acted like a dressing on a wound. As time had passed it had been sealed off until he'd even forgotten about it.

Now, driving through the darkness, listening to gospel shows and call-ins on the radio, he recalled that other time travelling through the night, all those years before. Himself in the back of the car with Vera, while two other members of the club had been up front going hard for Virginia. Vera had been so quiet – scared, he guessed; he would have been – that he had put his arm around her shoulders for comfort and she had nestled into him, soft and warm, and then kissed him.

He liked her, she was very pretty, only she was such a kid, young even for her age. That night, though, the drama of it, the illicit nature of their fumblings in the dark, had combined to make her irresistible. They'd brought each other to shuddering climax on the back seat. He had wanted to do more, but she'd grown coy and pushed him off. The other two, concentrating on the bad roads, hadn't appeared to notice.

When she had returned to college after the abortion, and the holidays, she had wanted to pick up where they had left off. He had tried to fob her off but she had been so keen, and he'd felt sorry for her, and so he'd seen a bit of her, until he'd got fed-up. When he had told Vera it was over, things had gone very wrong indeed.

It had taken all of Amos McCloud's support to pull Hugh through and get him out of that mess. Hugh, with the arrogance of youth, had never questioned himself about Amos's motives, until at a final parting dinner, Hugh had drunkenly thanked him, and asked him why he had been so good to him?

Amos had kissed him on the mouth and said, 'I love you.'

Amos had helped him then, and would help him now. The road was empty ahead and Hugh put his foot down.

*

The duvet was flung back, the lights switched on.

'Get up, Bishop,' rapped a voice.

Alice saw two figures in her cell, a man and a woman, both warders. She had no idea of time, only that it was dark outside. She was terrified suddenly that she hadn't hidden her pills from the night before: that they might be lying in her bed.

'Outside,' ordered the man.

In the corridor two more guards were waiting. She was told to stand against the wall. She counted the seconds. If the pills had been in her bed they would have found them by now.

She was wearing only her T-shirt and she tried to pull it down over her pants while the screws stood there, staring at her. She wrapped her arms around her body.

'Arms down by your sides,' said one.

The clock on the wall read twenty minutes past five.

Inside she heard them searching. They could still find her pills. A sheen of sweat broke out upon her. She tried not to visualise her hiding place in case they could read her mind. She was going crazy, or was she?

They were dragging furniture away from the wall. There was only a table, a chair and her bed. They had sharp eyes, they were used to prisoners' tactics. What would they do if they found her pills? How would they punish her? What more could they do?

They came out. She steadied herself for the onslaught, but they said nothing as they passed her. They hadn't found them. It would be all right.

Five minutes went by, then ten.

One of the two guards took out a cigarette and lit it. They didn't speak to each other or to Alice. They kept her there, standing stiffly upright, for another hour, then ordered her back to her cell.

It was a mess, everything upturned, her photographs ripped from the walls, the bed covers torn off, the mattress on the floor. But the skirting board hadn't been moved.

'Tidy up this shit-hole,' barked the butcher of the guards and Alice did as she was told.

The winter sun was bright that morning, coming in low through the shutters, and Kate woke early. Beside her, Dimitris slumbered on as he would for another couple of hours: he had been very late coming to bed. Kate could not bear to lie still.

She got up, made herself some coffee and tidied their small apartment, conscious all the while of not wanting to wake Dimitris. She was hungry and there were only tins in the cupboard; she had eaten the last of the fruit the day before. At nine, she slipped out into the street to go to the nearby supermarket.

There weren't many people about, only gulls cawing and the smell of the sea. As she turned the corner, she saw the sea, midnight blue it looked at that time of the morning, and very still. She loved it there. She swung her purse as she walked. As she turned the corner, she heard footsteps behind her and whipped round, but it was all right: it wasn't the golden-haired tourist, but an oldish man with dark hair. She walked on, calling 'good morning' to a couple of shopkeepers and a friend who was loading her children into her car.

At the supermarket, she bought what she wanted and stepped out again into the sunshine.

'Kate?'

Even as she turned, she knew the mistake that she had made.

The dark-haired man said swiftly, 'It's all right. I'm a journalist; I'm not going to hurt you.'

She wanted to run, but her legs wouldn't work. Her bag of groceries fell from her arms and as he bent to retrieve them, she came back to her senses.

'Leave me alone,' she croaked, edging away from him.

He followed her. 'I know where you live and work, Kate. We've got pictures. D'you want Dimitris to know what you did?'

Her throat constricted. 'I . . . I didn't do anything,' she whispered.

'No? Then why did you run away?'

She could only stare, hypnotised. He came right up close so she could see how the wrinkles cut deeply into his face. 'You were there, that morning, with Alice and Charley?'

The scene flashed back. The beautiful baby lying dead to the world. 'Yes,' she whispered.

'D'you want to help Alice?' asked the journalist.

She took a deep breath. 'Yes. But I'm not going back there.'

'You won't need to,' he promised. 'You're a witness not a suspect,' and she believed him.

Someone passed whom she knew who nodded at her. The man noticed too. He suggested they go for a coffee, back at his hotel, so they could talk.

She hesitated only a moment before acquiescing. She didn't know what else to do, and it would be a relief to talk, and if it could help Alice . . . She had never meant to hurt Alice, her one true friend. She thought of her in prison, and started to cry.

The journalist hurried her away into the town, to the smartest hotel, where he had a suite. In his sitting room, he poured her coffee, adding milk and sugar as required.

He asked her if she had seen any coverage of the story?

Truthfully, she replied that she had skimmed a newspaper

story, but she'd been too shocked to take any of it in, just the fact that it was Alice.

That seemed to please him.

He asked her permission to tape-record the interview. It was pleasant to have one's opinion sought as if it counted. That feeling increased as the journalist explained the importance of what she said, that it could be crucial in freeing Alice and sending the guilty person to jail instead.

'So, Kate, are you willing to go on the record?' he asked.

'Yes, so long as I'll be left alone afterwards.'

His eyes tracked away but she didn't notice. 'Absolutely. In fact, by talking to me exclusively, you're ensuring other journalists will stay away. They won't be interested once they see it in our paper.

'So from the beginning,' he urged, as with one hand he switched on his recorder. 'You arrived at the Eastwoods' home on Wednesday evening, May the thirteenth . . .'

Once she had begun, the memories came back. The lovely house, all those antiques and paintings; Alice's neat little room in the basement, the gorgeous nursery where they had peeped in on the sleeping baby. He hadn't stirred all evening although Alice had gone up to check on him twice.

They had stayed in the kitchen, mainly, talking. Alice was half-envious of Kate's plans to resume travelling, although she was very happy in her new job. She loved Charley and she was in awe of Roz and Hugh because of their jobs and how rich they were.

'Was she jealous?' enquired the journalist.

'No. She's not that sort of girl. She thought she was lucky to have got the job, that's what I meant.'

She had adjourned to Alice's room half an hour before the

Eastwoods were due home. After they came in, Alice joined Kate, then the parents came down to the kitchen where they rowed.

'A bad row?' put in the journalist.

'Yes. It was a bit frightening.'

'Oh?'

'They were so angry. They sounded as if they hated each other. I remember thinking, I wouldn't have liked it there, no matter how famous they were.'

The row had only ended with Roz going to bed. Kate and Alice had fallen asleep. Kate had woken in the night when the baby cried. It had been around five in the morning. There had been a real commotion, and she had thoroughly woken up, as Alice had. Hugh had been crashing around in the kitchen, and then he'd thundered up the stairs. 'I said to myself, I wouldn't like to be his baby,' Kate recalled.

There was silence in the hotel room except for the tape spooling and the journalist writing.

'Did you hear the baby cry any more, either after that, or before?' he asked.

Kate shook her head. It had taken her a long time to fall asleep again but obviously she had because the next thing she remembered was hearing the front door slam: Hugh going to work, Alice, already up and dressed, had explained.

When Kate had joined Alice in the kitchen after Roz had left for work, Charley had been lying in his bouncy cradle on the floor. Kate had been eager to meet him now that he was awake. According to Alice, he was the brightest, most alert, most advanced five-month-old ever, so she had been expecting something rather special.

'And?' prodded the journalist.

'He was sweet, sure, but he didn't look very alert to me. He seemed a bit unresponsive, to tell the truth. When I picked him up, he lay there staring up at the ceiling. He wasn't even holding his head up very well, which they ought to be by that age. Alice said she thought maybe he was going down with something. She put him to sleep in his buggy.' Kate paused.

The journalist asked what happened next.

Kate shrugged: nothing. She left the house shortly afterwards.

'Did you see the baby again? After you and Alice had gone up to the front door?'

She shook her head.

'Are you sure of that?'

She felt herself grow hot. It was as if he'd been there, watching. 'Oh,' she exclaimed. 'I did just pop back down to get something I'd forgotten. The buggy was blocking the hall, and I had to edge round it.'

'Did you touch Charley?'

She gazed at him. Had there been a secret camera, filming her? Her throat felt dry. 'He looked so sweet. I . . . I rubbed his cheek but he didn't wake or anything.'

'You didn't pick him up?'

'No,' she said, although she remembered she had thought about it.

'You didn't shake him?'

'No,' she whispered.

'Good, excellent!' he enthused. 'Sorry I had to ask you that but there was that other case in New Zealand, wasn't there?'

Her fighting spirit rose. 'I didn't hurt Simon, either.'

'Did Alice?'

Who did he think he was? 'No, definitely not.'

'Who do you think killed Charley?'

'I've no idea,' she said, although she did have an idea, but, accused herself, she wasn't about to blame anyone else.

He switched off his tape recorder. He told her that she had been fantastic, that she had been more help to Alice than she knew. She was glad of that but now she wanted to be gone. She was exhausted and already getting worried about what she'd done.

His telephone rang, making him jump.

'I'll just get that in the other room,' he said, quickly rising. 'Why not read the newspaper reports,' he suggested, indicating a stack on the coffee table.

As soon as he'd gone, she thought of bolting through the door, but to get to it in the vestibule would mean passing his bedroom door, and she didn't want to be caught sneaking out.

She picked up a newspaper. The headline read, 'Baby Charley case: The Missing Tape'. She hadn't the stomach to read it.

She tried to hear what the journalist was saying but she could catch nothing beyond a murmur.

She glanced down at the newspaper, and despite herself read the first paragraph and then the rest of the story.

When the journalist came back in, she murmured, 'I saw a tape in his study, that morning.'

The journalist stood still. 'Whose study?'

'The man's. I went into the wrong room,' continued Kate. 'I thought it was Alice's but it was Hugh's study. They were next door to each other. I wasn't looking where I was going. I stepped inside and felt something under my foot. There was a shirt lying on the floor. I'd stood on something in the breast pocket. I was scared I'd broken it. I picked up the shirt and took it out. It was a tiny tape. It had a blue sticker on it.'

The report said nothing about a sticker, but she remembered it vividly.

'Are you sure?' asked the journalist and she saw she had unnerved him and was glad.

'I am,' she said and went out, leaving him staring.

The court reporter who had covered the trial was on his way to work when the newsdesk called him.

He was able to answer the query immediately: the Eastwoods had colour-coded the cassettes from the hidden cameras in order to avoid confusion. Yellow for the kitchen and family room and blue for the nursery.

Jack Simpson gave a little moan of ecstasy when he heard, then setting aside his principles, he did what he'd been told to do if there were any major developments on the story, and called the newspaper's owner at home in Auckland.

Peter Collins, who was entertaining politicians that evening, was delighted. He went back to regale his dinner guests with the news and failed to notice one of them slip away to make a telephone call to London.

That was how within the hour, Alan Hardy was tipped off about the new piece of evidence against Hugh. It was damning, he and Rebecca decided, and set in motion the plan they had earlier muted that would effectively finish Hugh's career in politics.

CHAPTER SEVENTEEN

It was seven o'clock in the morning: too early for estate agents to ring, Mady reassured herself as she left her hotel room. Nevertheless, she was in the lift before she stopped listening for the sound of her telephone.

She needed a respite. She had been awake in her room for two hours, worrying. She entered the dining room expecting it to be a quiet oasis at that time on a Saturday morning, but found it teeming with loud, cheerful people in golfing gear. The South Carolina Dental Surgeons' Annual Convention, she was informed. She was invited to join them but politely declined and ate her breakfast quickly and alone.

Crossing the lobby on her way back to her room, she heard her name being called by a receptionist. She had a telephone call. She took it in a hooded booth around the corner. When she introduced herself, a man's voice said, 'Yeah, hi. It's Mark Beaney here,' and waited expectantly. She racked her brains but she had called so many people the night before . . .

He continued testily, 'Settonlake Realtors?'

'Oh yes?'

'You wanted to find Lola Flynn's husband. You're speaking to him, or one of them. I'm her third ex.'

Her stomach fell like a lift dropping twenty floors. 'Thanks so much for calling back.'

'You some sort of friend of Lola's or what?'

She had already rehearsed her answer. 'I'm over here from England and I need to trace her.'

'More,' he demanded abruptly.

'I'm a researcher. A journalist. I believe Lola might be able to help me. It's about something that happened when she was at college. There was a suicide. Lola knew the person . . .'

'Probably drove them to it.'

Mady didn't know if he was joking. 'Would you be prepared to give her my number and ask her to call me?' she asked hopefully.

'Nope.'

'But . . .'

'I don't want any contact with her. I was just checking you weren't about to give her a million dollars. I'd hate for Lola to have gotten lucky and forgotten to tell me. You want her number?'

Mady wrote it down. He gave her the address too. 'You're staying downtown, aren't you?' he went on. 'At The Plaza?'

She agreed that she was.

'If you hurry, you'll catch her at home.'

'I'm sorry?'

'She works Saturdays, leastways she did. She leaves for work around eight-thirty.'

It was five to eight. She thought of calling Lola and begging her to wait, but that would give her the chance to say no. She went outside and found a cab. The driver estimated it would take around twenty minutes to reach the address. He set off and they hit traffic.

To stop herself screaming, Mady read her shorthand notes, then checked her mobile for mail. She had a new message, from Jack.

'KA saw tape in HE's shirt,' it read. 'Pls file yrs asap.'

Kate Armstrong had found the missing tape? And in Hugh's shirt? What more convincing evidence could there be? Mady felt sick. She had started to feel sorry for Hugh. Now she realised he hadn't been so out of his mind when he killed Charley that he had forgotten to remove the film from the spy camera. It had been careless of him to leave the tape in his shirt pocket, but presumably he hadn't been expecting a visiting nanny to go snooping through his clothes.

She wondered exactly what Kate had said? Wouldn't it be argued, she reflected, that Alice could have placed the tape in Hugh's shirt? Without the tape itself, there was still no proof against Hugh. Alice could be retried and reconvicted.

Hugh's past would shed light on why he had done it. She sent back a message to Jack. 'Copy by this eve,' and sent it.

She looked at the time. It was twenty-eight minutes past eight and the cab was stuck at red lights. What would happen if she failed to get hold of Lola? or if Lola wouldn't speak to her?

The lights changed, the cab took off. It was twenty to nine before they pulled up outside a bungalow in a northern suburb of Charleston. There was no car on the driveway.

Resolutely, Mady walked up to the building and pressed the door-chime. No one came. She surveyed Lola's home. The paint was peeling and the flowers in the windowboxes were dead. Bits of toys lay strewn about in the front yard.

'Yeah?' A teenage girl stood squinting at Mady in the doorway. Mady saw an immediate resemblance to the young Lola.

'Is your mother in?' she asked.

The girl regarded Mady truculently.

Yes or no would do, Mady thought in desperation. 'Or is she at work?' she prompted.

'Mom!' yelled the girl over her shoulder, making Mady jump. Lola was there, she told herself exultantly.

'Lady to see you,' called the girl and disappeared with a bang into a room.

Mady waited but Lola didn't appear. She watched the second hand sweep on her watch: two minutes passed. She called out the woman's name but there was no reply. She took a tentative step inside and heard a radio coming from the back of the house. Calling out again, and again receiving no reply, she followed the sound into a vast, cluttered kitchen. The radio was blaring on a counter. At the far end, by an open door, stood a very overweight woman in a jogging suit who was feeding a toddler strapped into a highchair.

'Excuse me?'

The woman spun round. A bottle of baby food fell to the floor. 'Who the hell are you?' Lola demanded breathlessly.

'I'm sorry if I frightened you. Your daughter let me in . . .'

'Estelle!' roared Lola but there was no response.

The little girl in the highchair started to wail and Lola told her to shut up. Another child came in, whining 'Mom . . .' and stopped dead at the sight of Mady.

'You can get out. I'm not buying anything,' snapped Lola.

'I'm a journalist,' Mady explained. 'I'm here researching a story about what happened at Chesterfield . . .'

The other woman cut her off. 'You're that researcher, aren't you? The one on the college website?'

Taken aback, Mady admitted she was. Both children stared at her.

Lola shook her head. 'I've got nothing to say. I already spoke to a British researcher.'

'Christine Evans?'

'That's right.' Lola scowled. 'She never came back to film me. You from her outfit?'

'No.'

'I'm not going through it again. No way.' She eyed Mady sideways. 'Not for nothing.'

Mady thought quickly. She was supposed to get permission from Jack before offering money for a story, but she knew roughly how much the paper would pay for an exclusive, and if she went off to phone Jack, Lola might not let her in again. She had several large notes in her wallet for just such an eventuality. She named a sum.

Lola pouted.

Mady increased it slightly.

'I've got five kids to support,' Lola whined.

'I'm sorry, that's the best I can do.'

Lola sniffed and bent to pick up bits of broken baby bottle.

'Mom . . .' began the older girl.

'Be quiet. Cash?' Lola asked, straightening up.

'If you like.'

'I could do with it. I've had to take another sick day today with my headache.'

Mady murmured sympathetically.

Lola deposited the bottle shards in the bin. Peremptorily, she told the older girl to clean up the rest of the mess and look after the baby, and Mady to follow her. They went out through the open door, down a few steps and into a lean-to conservatory that had been made into a study. Plants were dying on the windowsills.

Lola sat down on a swivel chair and indicated a shabby wicker one for Mady. It was grossly uncomfortable.

'So, what d'you want to know?' Lola eyed her beadily.

'Everything.'

Lola's eyebrows shot up. 'Didn't that other woman tell you anything?'

'Very little.'

Lola sighed mightily but once she started, she made a good interview subject. She was bright and quick and it helped that she had recently relived the events for someone else.

She described herself and Vera as being very different, but as freshmen and roommates, they had become close. During the first semester, Vera had started dating Hugh Eastwood.

'Dating?' queried Mady. John Fitzgerald had never been so specific. Perhaps he hadn't known.

'That's right.'

'As in sleeping with?'

Lola gave her a long look. 'Someone got her pregnant, didn't they?'

'Did she have any other boyfriends?'

'None that she was interested in.'

'But there were others,' Mady pushed. She needed to know.

'Yes, one or two.'

'Why should it be Hugh who got her pregnant?'

'She wasn't a slut.'

'No, I wasn't suggesting—'

'There was a party for freshmen,' Lola interrupted. 'I didn't bother going but Vera did, and Hugh was there.'

'I see.' Mady wrote that down: the vital piece of evidence that Fitzgerald either hadn't known or had withheld.

'Yep. She didn't get back to our room until eight in the morning.'

'Was she okay?'

'You mean did it look like she'd been raped?' Lola took a deep breath. 'Nope, not to me. But that's what she later claimed.'

'Hugh raped Vera?' Mady asked weakly.

'That's what she said. Not then. It was after the vacation, six days before she killed herself. She came in one night crying, saying Hugh had said he didn't want to see her any more. Then it all came out.'

'What exactly did she say?' Mady asked carefully.

'That it had happened that night.'

Mady waited.

'She'd got drunk at the Freshmen's Ball; they had started fooling around and things had gotten out of hand. She had wanted it, then not wanted it. She had been a bit scared of him. He had got pissed off and forced her. Her wrists had been red from being held. Didn't I remember how red they had been?' Lola rolled her eyes.

'Did you?'

'Like I'd remember five months later how her wrists were? No, I didn't remember. So, they couldn't have been anything special. She said she had woken in one of the student rooms. She had been naked, with semen on her legs. Later when she tried to talk to Hugh about what had happened, he laughed it off.'

'Did you believe that?'

'I wasn't sure. Until he paid her off.'

Mady's mouth went dry. Hugh, the super-clean politician, had got a girl pregnant, encouraged her to have an abortion – callously setting up the Go-Go Club to use it as his shield – and then paid for her silence. It had been about to be exposed on national television; he would have been finished. On top of that, a baby crying on and on. She could understand why he had lashed out.

'Vera blackmailed him?' she asked Lola carefully.

'That's right. She said, "I'm going to make him pay," and she did. Ten thousand dollars.'

A lot of money back then. 'How d'you know that?'

Lola smiled. 'I saw the cheque, in his handwriting. She got it the day before she died. You would have thought it would have made her happy, wouldn't you?'

Mady said nothing. Was blackmail where it had ended? 'You found the body?' she asked.

'Yeah, I found it.'

'There was no doubt it was suicide?'

Lola gave her a long look. 'You think maybe he did it? I'd believe most things of that man, but I don't think so.'

'No?'

'I was with her when she bought the vodka that morning. We went into Charleston together. I thought she was going on a spree but she only wanted booze. I should have thought. I mean, she wasn't a drinker, but I thought, she wanted to get smashed. Why not? She never said . . . I'd no idea . . .' A look of horror passed over Lola's face. 'It was that same bottle that was lying beside her when I found her. The vodka and the bottle of pills on the floor.'

'You weren't to know,' Mady said quietly.

'No. No, how could I?'

'Was there a note?' Mady asked.

Lola stared at her.

She repeated her question.

'Christine Evans asked that exact same question,' Lola ruminated.

'What did you reply?'

'I said no.'

Mady knew she had more to say and resisted the desire to push.

'I thought, why should I tell her what happened? What's in it for me?'

Less pleasant, Mady thought, but kept her expression neutral.

'Then after she'd gone, it weighed on my mind. I was going to call her and tell her, then I had marital problems.'

Mady started to say something but Lola interrupted: 'But you're paying me, aren't you?'

Mady agreed that she was, inwardly wincing at how bad that sounded, chequebook journalism.

'So, I'll tell you—'

Mady's mobile rang. Unable to believe its bad timing, she grappled for it in her pocket and switched it off. She apologised to Lola. 'What did you say?'

'I said, there was a note.'

Mady's heart beat faster. 'You saw it?'

'Not the finished article, no.'

'What d'you mean?'

'Vera had had a few shots at it in her diary; it was lying open on the bed. "Dear Hugh, When you told me it was over, I wanted to die . . ." "My baby died, so why shouldn't I?" She'd written things like that and crossed them out, and then there was a page torn out. It was for that day's date: February eighteen.'

Mady knew she was speaking the truth. Her evidence was as conclusive as it could be without the note itself. She asked what happened to the diary.

'It went,' Lola said simply.

'Did the police take it?'

'No. I put it in my bag before I called the police.'

'Oh?'

'I wanted to protect her.' Lola spoke more softly than before. 'I knew it was suicide; I didn't want the police to know or her parents if I could help it.'

'That was nice of you.'

'She had a nice family.' A brief silence fell.

'Did you give evidence at the inquest?' Mady enquired, thinking there had been no mention of it in the newspaper reports she had read.

Lola shook her head. 'The police said I didn't have to, which was just as well. I'd been told I mustn't.'

'By whom? Your parents?'

Lola shook her head.

'The university?'

'In a manner of speaking.'

'What do you mean?'

'My academic advisor warned me off.'

'What had he or she got to do with it?'

Lola gazed at her. 'He was Hugh's advisor too. His buddy-counsellor.'

Mady remembered Fitzgerald saying Hugh's advisor had told him to destroy the note. She hadn't thought to ask him who that advisor had been. She asked Lola now.

'Amos McCloud,' she replied promptly.

For a moment, Mady failed to recognise the name, then she exclaimed, 'Dr McCloud? The Ethics teacher?'

'He wasn't a doctor then,' Lola retorted.

'But he wasn't at Chesterfield then!'

'Yes he was.'

'But he told me . . .' She had a flash of the scholarly man in the charming room. 'Amos McCloud. Tall and thin?'

'Yeah.'

He'd been lying to her? 'You say he warned you off?'

Lola nodded. 'He came to see me the morning after I found Vera. I was on tranquillisers. My parents were coming to take me home. McCloud wanted to know everything I could remember. What Vera had said to me; if she'd written a letter, if I'd seen that? I told him about the diary. He asked to see it.'

'You gave it to him?'

'Yes. I was glad to. I didn't want the responsibility of it. I gave him that, and the cheque from Hugh. She hadn't cashed it. It had been lying beside her diary on the bed.'

Mady had wondered about that cheque.

'McCloud said it was better I forget everything and rest. I thought he was concerned about me. He wasn't, of course.' Lola's bitterness returned.

'How do you know?'

'When I came back, he threatened me.'

'What d'you mean? How could he?'

'He was my academic advisor.' Lola fiddled with her wrist-watch strap. 'I was naïve, I was only nineteen, I didn't know how the system worked. To me, McCloud was like a kind of god. He said he didn't think I should dwell too much on Vera; it could be detrimental to my grades. I shouldn't allow myself to get distracted with giving evidence to the inquest, or talking to people about what Vera had said to me. He said I should let him handle everything and concentrate on my studies or else I might fail and get thrown out.'

'He said that?'

'Words to that effect, yes. I knew what he meant.'

So McCloud had blackmailed Lola. What a viper's nest the little university had been. 'You kept quiet?' she asked softly.

'Wouldn't you?' Lola snapped. 'I needed to pass. And then, after a bit, I sort of forgot about it. Life goes on. It wasn't until Christine Evans came here last year asking questions . . . Is her film still happening?'

Caught on the hop, Mady stammered that she wasn't sure.

'Tell her I'm waiting to be filmed,' Lola said sourly.

'Er . . . right.'

'It was she who suggested it, not me. She was so grateful. "Elated," I remember her saying. She hadn't even known Hugh had been in the Go-Go Club until I told her.'

'Oh?' said Mady, interested, and thinking what a sensation it must have been for the producer.

Christine had been researching a film on the history of the pro- and anti-abortion movements in America, Lola went on. 'Antis' had been easy to find, pros more difficult. She had tracked down a Pro-Abortioner in Atlanta who had been active since the eighties, and who remembered the Go-Go Club — because of the name — and a bit about Vera.

Christine had found out more in newspaper archives, which was how she had traced Lola, initially writing to her mother, whose address Lola sometimes used to screen mail. She had also supplied Christine with the name of another student who would corroborate the story. Would Mady like it, Lola asked?

Eagerly Mady accepted, but to her disappointment, the name was only John Fitzgerald.

'He's a pastor,' Lola went on.

Mady thanked her.

Lola asked for her money, Mady paid her, and was escorted to the front door. 'Good luck,' Lola said unexpectedly.

Mady got back into her taxi. She checked her mobile, and saw that she had a text message from Moira. 'Pls call,' it read simply, and gave a telephone number. She dialled it.

Moira answered breathlessly. She was full of apologies. A message had arrived the previous afternoon, an old student who remembered Hugh . . . She ought to have called Mady in the afternoon – she'd intended to, but with being in such a rush and her daughter being there, it had slipped her mind until that morning . . .

'What was the message?' Mady interrupted as politely as she could.

'Oh yes! It was an e-mail, Mady, from an old student who remembered Hugh. Frank Hart? He'd read my message on the website. His e-mail came in just as I was packing up to leave. I was in such a hurry . . .'

'What did the e-mail say?' implored Mady.

'That he'd fought the same battle as Hugh, whatever that means . . .'

Mady's heart beat faster. The same battle? Couldn't that mean he was a fellow Go-Go Club member? More evidence, she thought gleefully, more corroboration. Luck was running with her at last.

'He, er, wanted to speak to you last night, that was the only thing,' Moira went on in a small voice.

Mady's hopes fell. 'Oh?' she managed.

'It said, "Must speak soonest. Before tonite." As if he was going away. I'm really sorry, Mady,' she rushed on, 'I truly meant to call you . . .'

'Don't worry,' Mady assured her, although she felt like lead. 'Did he leave a number?'

'An e-mail address,' Moira supplied eagerly. 'I've got it for you . . .'

Too late, Mady thought, but she wrote it down, thanked Moira profusely and hung up. Why couldn't Moira have remembered, she asked herself bitterly? Without doubt, Frank Hart's interview would have been superb, answering any queries, sealing the story. Now she would have to do without it.

It was almost not worth sending the e-mail. Nevertheless, back in her hotel room, she plugged in her laptop, tapped in a brief message and sent it.

Five minutes later, as she was debating whether to drop in on Dr McCloud's home or call him first, an electronic bleep sounded from her laptop. She had a message.

Frank Hart wrote: 'Don't worry, I've been delayed and am still here. Lots to talk about. Are you free for lunch?'

Whispering a prayer of thanks, she wrote back, 'Am free whenever, wherever!'

He replied within minutes, suggesting his home at twelve-thirty? He gave her directions, and a description of the house, saying it was about forty minutes' drive from Charleston. She promised she would be there.

It was not yet ten o'clock. She was too keyed up to sit still. She walked round to McCloud's house, imagining his reaction to the awkward questions she intended to put to him, but when she rang the doorbell there was no answer. The house was empty. She walked back to her hotel.

*

It was a rainy November afternoon. By three o'clock the light
was quite gone from the sky and in order to see anything it was
necessary for Roz to switch on the lamps in the hotel bedroom.

She hadn't drowned herself the night before. She needed to
know how it was going to turn out and she wouldn't if she
wasn't there. She had booked into another hotel, nothing like
as luxurious as the first night's, but it had done, she had slept
all night and half the day, perfectly undisturbed because
nobody knew she was there. Now she felt lonely. She switched
on her mobile phone to see if there had been any messages and
saw, to her surprise, that there had been several, most from the
same unfamiliar number.

As she was trying to guess who it might be, her mobile rang
again. Mady, she thought instantly, but it wasn't Mady.

'Is that Roz?' came a man's voice cautiously.

She agreed it was, and asked who was speaking?

He told her, Alan Hardy, and when she hesitated, he
reminded her that he worked for her husband.

'He's not here,' she said, wondering why he was calling her
mobile and not Hugh's.

'Oh? You're quite all right?'

It struck her as an odd question, then she asked herself: did
they know she hadn't been home, that she was running from
Hugh? Were they hunting for her on his behalf? She hung up.
Her heart was pounding. She knew from Hugh how slick the
Security Services had become. She had been mere seconds on
the phone but would that have been long enough with today's
technology for them to trace her?

Hurriedly she gathered her things together. As she was about
to leave the room she glanced down into the street below. She

saw no one sitting in a car, or loitering on the corner, but that didn't mean they were not there. They could already be in position, the call to her mobile a device to put her off the scent while a team took up position outside her hotel door. She felt horribly afraid. Where could she go? Where was safe? If only Mady was there, she thought, all recent antagonism evaporating. Mady always had such good ideas . . .

She paused. Why, Mady's house was her perfect bolt-hole!

She put her eye to the spyhole in the door. It provided a fish-bowl view of the corridor. She could see no one out there. Steeling herself to be seized nonetheless, she opened the door. No one pounced. She hurried down to the lifts and went straight into one that was waiting. When she emerged on the lobby floor, she asked the doorman for a taxi. As she got into the back of the cab, she glanced over her shoulder: as far as she could tell, no one followed, but it wasn't until the taxi drew up outside Mady's home that she began to feel safe.

She walked quickly up the path and rang the doorbell. A light came on in the hallway. 'All right,' called Ben crossly, and she heard the sound of a lock turning.

For the first time, she wondered if he would let her stay. Over the years, she had not always been sure that he liked her.

'Roz.' He looked dumbfounded.

'I'm sorry. I ought to have called. Oh Ben, I . . . I'm so scared . . .'

'Is it Hugh?'

'Yes.'

'You'd better come in,' he offered unenthusiastically.

The hall was piled high with boxes. She remembered about Ben's work and wondered what it would be like to be there without Mady; how long would Ben let her stay? But he had to let her stay because she couldn't go back out there . . .

From the kitchen came the thin wail of the kettle. Ben asked: 'What's Hugh been up to now?'

'He tried to drown me.'

He stared. 'Are you serious?'

'Absolutely. I think he's put some other people on to me.'

Ben glanced sharply towards the door.

'Don't worry. They haven't followed me here. Look, I . . . er . . . I don't like to ask but is there any way I could stay here?' she said in a rush. 'I won't get in your way . . .'

He looked appalled.

'Please? Only, I don't know where else to go . . .' Her voice quavered.

'Okay, okay.' The kettle shrieked. 'We'd better get back in there.'

She followed him along the narrow hall, down the step into the poky little kitchen . . . The shrieking stopped.

'Remember your Aunty Roz?' Ben asked the baby in the highchair.

Roz stared at Archie, and he, round-eyed, gazed back. She had forgotten Archie would be there – of course he would; he lived there! She had volunteered to babysit him but . . . that had been over the phone. Now he was right in front of her, holding his hands out to be picked up. She hadn't held a baby, or been alone with one, since Charley died. She didn't know if she could handle it. Mady had understood that without need of words, but Ben was a man, he wouldn't. He had already turned away to do something at the microwave.

'If you don't mind sleeping on the sofabed?' he offered gruffly over his shoulder.

She turned gratefully from the baby. 'Oh, no, not at all. Thank you so much. And please, if there's, um, anything I can do to help out?'

His back failed to register a response, then he said more brightly, 'Actually, Roz, there is something. I need to get a new printer, my other one busted last night. There's no way I could take Archie up to the Tottenham Court Road, he'd scream his head off, but if you could keep an eye on him for me . . .?'

She heard herself say, 'Of course,' but inside she felt wooden.

'It would be a tremendous help.' He lifted the baby out of the chair. 'Hear that, son? Your aunty's going to look after you.'

Roz's face muscles ached but Archie looked genuinely delighted. She had a sudden sense then of being outside herself, looking down and seeing the three of them, like the perfect nuclear family. She was the perfect mother, Ben the perfect father . . . Ben was passing Archie over and she couldn't move, her arms would not rise to take him.

'Here you are,' said Ben, and the bubble burst. She took Archie in her arms, felt the softness of him, that adorable baby smell. She hugged him tight. She wanted never to let him go.

'Are you okay, Roz?'

She was crying. She was holding a baby again.

'Oh, God. Sorry. Look, I won't go . . .'

She shook her head and wiped away her tears. 'I'd love to look after him – if you'll let me?'

'Of course I'll let you. If it doesn't bring back . . . I mean . . .'

How sweet he was, stumbling and awkward. How very unlike Hugh. 'It won't upset me,' she promised him. 'I'll look after you,' she addressed the baby, 'won't I, angel?' and Archie looked into her eyes with love.

*

The psychologist's name was Dr Briers but he wanted Alice to call him Tony, if she felt comfortable with that?

She nodded. Anything to make him happy, to make the hour go swiftly and without mishap. She wanted to be sure that she was back in her cell in time for her evening pill.

He hoped she didn't mind him coming to talk to her on a Saturday afternoon, he went on in his super-friendly fashion, but it was the only time he could guarantee being free every week?

'I don't mind,' she said, thinking, what did it matter if she did mind? What option did she have but to see him?

Such sessions were usually filmed, he explained, but in her case he had decided to dispense with that in case it brought back unhappy memories of the trial.

She said nothing.

'I am very interested in your circumstances, Alice. The suppression of what one has done, or not done . . .?' His voice petered out hopefully but she remained silent.

He would like to take her back to her childhood. To the very first time she could remember doing anything wrong, and what had happened to her as a consequence?

She told him how when she'd been six, she'd taken her mother's engagement ring off the side in the kitchen and swopped it at school for a plastic bangle. It was true.

'Yes?' he breathed. 'Yes . . .' Writing down every word with his thick black pencil. 'And what happened when Mum and Dad found out?'

She stared back at his piggy eyes behind their glasses. 'Nothing,' she said.

'Really? They weren't cross at all?' If his eyes popped out any further, they'd come right out across the desk, she mused.

'No,' she said. 'I didn't tell them.' She remembered her mother collecting her from school, how she'd been red-eyed and frantic, and at home her father had been unpinning the stair carpet in case the ring had somehow slipped under there. She had been too frightened to admit to what she had done.

'You didn't tell them,' he repeated, licking the tip of his pencil till his tongue was black. 'What did that do to you?'

She'd had sleepless nights, but she wasn't about to divulge that to him. 'I got used to it,' she said.

He wrote that down in capital letters and underlined it deeply.

'Thank you for telling me that, Alice,' he murmured and she shuddered at his awful intimacy. He asked her if that had been the start of a pattern of behaviour?

'A pattern?'

'Yes. Hiding things from those close to you? From yourself?'

One misdemeanour by a timid child didn't equal a baby-killer. But there was no point in antagonising him. She said slowly, 'I don't think I hide things from myself.'

He set his head to one side. 'No?'

'Did you steal as a child?' he went on, but before she could respond, his bleeper went off. Swearing, and without a word to her, he left the room.

She heard him on his mobile out in the corridor. His voice faded as he walked away. She wondered whether the warder who had brought her there was standing guard outside the door. Probably not. They were in the hospital wing, which had its own staff. Visiting guards liked to linger in the office to chat rather than stand about staring at a closed door in a draughty corridor.

Right then, Alice told herself, she was probably not being watched. She stared at the spyhole in the door for long enough to provoke any guard into action, but nothing happened. She was on her own. But what did that benefit her, she thought in despair?

She couldn't escape. There were bars on the windows, guards at either end of the corridor. The bare room contained an empty shelf. She saw a dead fly on it. Opposite her was the plastic chair on which Briers had sat, on the metal desk before her were two plastic cups of water. She got up, conscious that at any moment she might be called roughly to account, and went round to the psychologist's side. There were two drawers, both locked. There was nothing else of the slightest interest in the room, except his fat black briefcase, sitting open on the floor.

She extracted a file, thinking as she did so that if he could see her, he would say she was acting out her criminal tendencies. Unable to sit still for a moment without getting into mischief or worse.

The file was about her: the psychiatrist's report that had been submitted by the prosecution at trial. She flicked through it, words springing out at her without meaning: depersonalised, pathological, psychotic.

She put it back in the briefcase. As she did, something at the bottom of the case got knocked over. It was a little brown medicine bottle. She took it out. The label read 'Temazepam'. She rooted around at the bottom, and found three more identical bottles of sleeping tablets. For the psychologist himself, she wondered, or his patients? It didn't matter: she slipped one bottle inside her shirt and resumed her seat.

Seconds ticked by in which she looked at her cup of water

and calculated how long it would take her to swallow all those pills. Two or three minutes, unless she gagged? Not long, but she had no idea how long he would be and if he came in and caught her that would be it: all pills confiscated, herself on suicide watch, never trusted alone again for six years.

He came back in without knocking and resumed his intimate questions. She tried to concentrate and supply him with credible answers and it must have worked because after an interminable-seeming length of time, he declared that the session was over and that he felt it had gone very well, didn't she?

She nodded.

He looked forward to seeing her next week, he concluded as he handed her over to her warder who was, as she had guessed, ensconced with the medical orderlies at the front desk.

She walked away, expecting at any moment to hear his shout, but the doors kept shutting behind her until eventually she was back in her cell. Her tranquillisers arrived at four o'clock, without explanation, two hours early. Her supper, sandwiches, came twenty minutes later. She guessed it had something to do with it being the weekend, but she didn't ask, she wasn't interested.

She waited for as long as she could, which was only ten minutes later. She went under her duvet and opened her bottle of pills. She swallowed six, taking her time, not wanting to gag. When those were safely inside her, she took another half dozen.

CHAPTER EIGHTEEN

The route to Frank Hart's home lay partly along the coast. Mady drove with the sunroof open, admiring the distant grey sea and the wild sand-dunes and revelling in the fact that everything was falling into place. After the next interview, she would call Hugh to challenge him about his past, and to ask him what bearing it had on Charley's death? And that of Christine Evans? Then she would write her story, and send it, as she had promised Jack, by that evening.

The case against Hugh, coupled with Kate Armstrong's revelation, was building piece by piece. Once her story was published, it would only be a matter of time before Alice Bishop was released, and Hugh charged.

That thought sobered her. Hugh had sat at her dinner table. She had wept to see him break down so utterly at Charley's funeral. He'd been part of her life for years. What was she about to do to him, and through him, to Roz?

But he shouldn't have killed Charley. He shouldn't have let Alice take the blame. If he had been honest from the start, if he had owned up, pleaded mitigating circumstances, he might not have gone to prison.

She entered the town that Frank Hart had described as being less than two miles away from his home. It was a long drag of depressing-looking stores, pull-ins and fast-food joints.

Her mobile phone played its theme tune, and she pulled into the kerb to answer it.

'Mady O'Neil? It's John Fitzgerald. We met yesterday . . .'

'Of course. Is everything okay?'

'I just wanted to let you know . . .' he paused. 'Amos McCloud – he was Hugh's counsellor . . .'

'Yes. I know.'

'Oh? He called me last night.'

Her stomach knotted. 'He did?'

'For a chat, he said. I'm afraid I didn't believe him. He hasn't spoken to me in more than twenty years: why should he call now? He wanted to know if anyone had been in touch with me about "old schooldays".'

'Did you tell him?'

'No, I did not.'

She took a deep breath. 'Thank you.'

'I felt I ought to warn you.'

Mady asked, 'You knew him quite well?'

'Yes, he was non-tenured during our graduate year, not even officially on staff, as I remember.'

That explained his absence from the staff-roll.

Fitzgerald asked, 'How's it going?'

'Very well, thanks to you. I'm just off to do a final interview now.' It occurred to her that he would have known Frank Hart and she mentioned his name.

'Frank?' Fitzgerald repeated stiffly.

'Yes. Was he a member of the Go-Go Club?'

'He was. He died about ten years ago.'

She felt cold. 'But he e-mailed me just now . . .'

'Not he. Both he and his son were drowned in a freak accident on the river. Our families were quite close,' Fitzgerald added.

Her blood raced. Who had sent the message?

Fitzgerald said awkwardly, 'I guess you know how to look after yourself?'

She gathered her wits. 'Yes, thank you.' She ended the call.

She was afraid, but she had to go on. She had to find out who had sent her those messages and the only way to do that was to keep her appointment. She looked at the dashboard clock. It was half past eleven. She drove out of the town and followed signs for George Island, crossing a bridge over a marshy waterway. The island looked scrubby, although the road was busy enough with cars. Signs dotted the roadside for condos, holiday homes and rentals. She saw an advertisement for luxury 'beachcomber' homes and turned right, falling in behind an oil truck. She kept her eyes on the mileometer: according to the directions, the road she wanted was almost exactly one mile from that turn-off.

The land ahead sloped away to the sea and, looking down, she saw a blue-roofed house on the shore. That was the house that Frank Hart, or whoever it was, had described. It was the last house in a row of three. The red Honda he had described sat on the drive.

Mady carried on past the narrow lane that would take her down to the shore and entered a bend in the road with a promontory over the sea. She pulled in and got out. Below her, pine trees descended to the beach. She climbed a low wall and weaved her way through, emerging suddenly on to the sand.

It was a beautiful spot, clean and unspoilt, with bits of driftwood strewn about and rocky outposts marching into the sea. She skirted the headland and saw that the first of the three houses was only a hundred yards away. She ducked into the lee of the hill in case he might be looking for her. He would be expecting her to arrive by car, not along the beach, but as she got nearer, the blood was hammering in her ears so hard that she could scarcely hear properly.

She came to the first dwelling. Like its neighbours, it was built on stilts and in the area beneath it, she saw a neatly stacked log store and a canoe hanging down from a main beam. The house was shut up for the winter, she surmised as she slipped past it, into the shadow of the next building. Beneath it was an old Jeep and barbecue equipment, and, on the far side, daylight. She stepped back to check the house again. The windowsills were clear, the curtains open, every door tightly shut. There was no sign of life. She ducked under the building and walked half-bent to the other end where she stopped and crouched down.

The Honda sat on the drive in front, the handsome rear of the house faced the sea. There was a window and door in the side which directly faced her, the door opening on to a wide porch that ran round the house.

It was five past twelve. The e-mailer might reasonably be expected to start looking out for her now, but again, at the front of the house, not at its side. Eventually he would realise she wasn't coming and at some point, he would emerge. She would see him and gauge whether to approach him or not.

She wondered how long her wait might be, and also if she might be seen from the side window? She retreated to a pillar where a washing machine stood. Out of the sun, it was cold and she shivered. She heard gulls crying and the roar of the sea. She looked at her watch: three minutes had passed.

A car drove up. She peered out, thinking that the e-mailer had summoned another guest to the meeting, but the new car was coming down the driveway of her house. Doors slammed and she saw people's legs.

'I'm sticking the beers in under here,' came a man's voice.

'Yeah, the icebox is going to be way too full,' agreed a woman.

The man approached. He bent and Mady saw two great crates of bottles appear, one balanced on top of the other. She prayed that he would shove them in and leave but he came in after them, pushing them in front, grunting with effort. She tried to inch her way around to the other side of the pillar and her movement caught his eye. He looked up sharply and his face went white.

'Who the hell . . .?'

'Tod? Can you get my platters in there as well?' called the woman, and then also crying out: 'Who's that?' in a quick, frightened voice.

'Please, it's all right—' Mady started.

'I'm going to call the police!' shrieked the woman.

Mady took a step backwards, intending to make a run for it, but the man snatched at her arm. 'Hang on there,' he growled.

Another man called out, 'Mrs Osborne, are you okay?'

'Oh, Doctor! We've got an intruder!'

She mustn't be caught and handed over. She wrenched her arm free and ran, ducking beneath the low roof until she reached the other side. Out on the sand she looked back and saw figures appear from beyond the house. She recognised Amos McCloud, and then Hugh. Hugh wasn't in England, menacing Roz, but there, with McCloud, luring her to that remote house for what purpose? She knew far more than Christine Evans, and she knew what had happened to her.

Hugh started running, breaking her spell, and she put on an extra spurt. She rounded the bend and dived into the cover of the pine trees. She heard behind her Hugh's voice shouting, 'She's up there!' – and McCloud more distantly answering, 'She's heading for the road. Get in the car!'

She plunged up the hill, her lungs bursting, her face getting scratched by branches, and arrived at the top, spent. She fumbled desperately for her car keys, but she couldn't find them. She thought she must have lost them in the headlong race, now she was trapped here. She tried her jeans pocket and her fingers closed around the plastic fob. She nearly wept. Her automatic locks popped up, and she jumped in. She shot the car into reverse and pulled out, going in the direction away from the house.

She checked her rear-view mirror and saw it was clear but she knew they would come that way. She put her foot down. A road sign flashed by, 'Welcome to Beachcomber Valley', and there was a speed limit of twenty miles per hour. She raced through at sixty and caught sight of a red gleam in her mirror far back: their car was coming. She put her foot flat down and the needle climbed to eighty, eighty-five . . .

She glanced back; they were getting nearer. Even as she watched they were closing. They were perhaps fifty feet away now, and flashing their lights. Were they crazy? Did they really expect her to pull in meekly?

Before her, another bend was coming up and she thought: if it would just take her back to the highway, where there was more traffic and people about, they wouldn't dare to harm her.

She braked as she entered the bend, and saw the sea dazzling before her and the sharp rocks. She knew they would be on her bumper in moments: would they push her into the sea?

The bend finished, the road flattened out, not taking her back to the main road as she had hoped, but running along the shore. She saw yet another bend coming up. Surely it would loop back to the highway? There was nowhere else for it to go. Somehow she had to keep ahead of them for a little bit longer . . . She glanced in her mirror and saw them, their lights still on, but further back than she had expected. Her heart skipped. Had they given up? Was their car about to break down? Or was it a device to make her stop? She kept going hard for that final bend. She rounded the corner and froze. Ahead of her, the road narrowed to a single track that opened up into a wide area which in turn petered down to the sea. She guessed that in the summer it would be a car park. There had been no warning. She applied her brakes and, on the sandy gravel that the road had now become, her rear end swung out into a skid and her car stalled.

She sat dazedly. They would have known what lay beyond that bend and that was why they had slowed down. She looked out of her window and saw them coming sedately towards her, their lights still on. They stopped short of the gravel and turned their car so that it was now blocking the road. The sea on one side, a hill on the other. What was she going to do?

She saw them sitting there, watching: Hugh closer, staring out of the passenger side at her, and, she fancied, smiling. They knew she was trapped, that there was no one else around. They couldn't have engineered it more perfectly. She wondered if they had a weapon. They could dispose of her body right there, into the sea . . . No one would ever know.

She pulled herself together. They hadn't got her yet. She heard the ding-ding-ding of their door opening and McCloud emerged. He stood by the driver's side, cupped his hands around his mouth and called out: 'Let's talk.'

Her car was her only protection, and her one weapon. She restarted the ignition, and pushed the gear stick into drive. She swung the car round until it was facing theirs, then put her foot down hard on the accelerator. She catapulted back on to the road, stalled once more, and started the engine again. She saw McCloud hop back into his car, and Hugh not smiling any more, but staring wildly at her. She raced for them. The sea was too dangerous, so she headed for the hillside, where there was a little space, but hopefully her passenger side would take the brunt of the impact and knock their vehicle out of her way.

Their car jumped into life. She had a split second of seeing Hugh's panic-stricken face right up close to her window, and then their cars hit.

There was a sickening screech of metal upon metal, and for one terrifying moment they were locked together in a dance, both cars careening towards the hillside as she fought to stay in control. She steered for the sea, keeping her foot on the gas, there was a wrench and suddenly she broke free. Their car spun away behind her, smashing into the barrier, but she was past them and zigzagging crazily down the road.

She regained control. They were still stuck in the barrier, incapacitated for a moment. Her passenger side was damaged, the door caved in and the wing smashed; also, from the bonnet, which looked badly dented, she could hear a high-pitched whine that hadn't been there before. She became aware that her ribs hurt on her right; she'd crushed herself into the wheel, but it wasn't too bad, she told herself, she could cope with it. She rounded the first of the bends, then the second. They hadn't caught up with her yet. She saw a car coming. It slowed as she approached and she saw the man from the other house at the wheel. He glared at her but, after a second's hesitation, he continued in the direction she had come from.

She passed the turn-off to McCloud's house. The highway was less than a mile away now. Then a movement caught her eye. In her rear-view mirror, she saw the Honda coming. She felt sick panic. From a distance it looked as if no damage had been done to it. She raced for the highway. There was a lorry coming but she bolted out in front of it, causing it to swerve.

Its klaxon blared but she speeded up and overtook one car after another until the lorry vanished behind her. In spite of the damage to her car, she was travelling at eighty, and the town wasn't far away. Once there, she would be safer still. The car in front wouldn't move out of her way, so she overtook it on the outside. She saw the Honda in the middle lane, four cars back. Its front bumper was gone, the passenger side was a mess, but clearly McCloud and Hugh had survived.

The road rose up over the sea. They were two cars back now but she could see their red nose edging out of line, trying to catch up with her. Were they so angry that they would smash her into the barrier as she had done them? The town lay straight ahead. Its speed limit was fifty and she was doing seventy and still overtaking. Why didn't a police car stop her? She saw traffic lights dead ahead, and those lights were red. Before them waited three lanes of traffic.

She couldn't wait at lights. They would be upon her. But she had to slow down. As she was coming to a halt, the lights changed and the body of traffic surged forwards. She headed straight for the town centre, but she couldn't go faster than the rest of the cars. She glanced round and they were right behind her. There was another set of lights coming up. As she approached they turned to red and she jumped them.

She heard a siren wail but didn't know if it was for her, or something else entirely: she didn't have time to look. She saw a parking sign, and followed it up a ramp into a car park, entering a tight driving circle with tiers leading off. She couldn't see if anyone was behind her now, but she thought it likely that McCloud and Hugh had seen where she had gone. She had very little time to disappear. She drove out on to the second tier, went a whole circuit of that floor before finally spotting a space. She swung into it, picked up her bag and, with an effort, because her side hurt badly now and the door itself was so stiff, got out. When she saw the amount of damage done to it on the outside, she wondered how it had remained in place. It wouldn't shut again, so she left it hanging and set off, walking quickly.

She felt vulnerable on foot and in pain. She reached a door marked 'Exit', went through into a stairwell and walked down the cement steps. She heard footsteps behind her, the heavy tread of a man, but told herself they could be anybody's. She hurried out into a mall.

Bright shop lights and the mass of people startled her. She remembered it was a Saturday lunchtime. There was a chance that she would be safe in the throng, but equally she might come upon them at any moment. She had to find somewhere safe to think what to do: whether to call the police, which might jeopardise her story, or to gather her wits sufficiently to contact McCloud by e-mail and conduct the interview that way. She saw a coffee bar which was not too busy and went in. Her side ached dreadfully now. A family left a table by the window and she took it. She would call Jack first to ask his advice. She got out her mobile.

'What can I get you?' A smiling waiter appeared.

'Coffee, please.'

'Cappuccino, latte, espresso . . .?' His list went on and on. She felt weak and dizzy. She asked for a cappuccino.

'Caf or decaf?' He wiped at the table.

'Caf.'

'You'll have something with it? The special today is really good . . .' He explained it laboriously to her.

She wanted to scream. 'Just the coffee.' Her mobile rang. On instinct, she answered it.

'Hi, I'm Dawn Portman,' said a loud, friendly voice in her ear. 'I'm calling about your message.'

'I'm really sorry, this is a terrible time . . .'

'It came in the post today with the Chesterfield newsletter?'

She didn't need any more old students who remembered Hugh. 'Actually, I'm a bit frantic at the moment . . .'

'I knew Hugh,' the woman laughed, 'you could say, intimately.'

Another old girlfriend. 'Could I possibly take your number and call you back?' Mady asked.

'We dated. The summer of nineteen-eighty.'

The date penetrated Mady's brain. That summer would only have been a few months after Vera had killed herself. Hugh might have confided in Dawn.

'He was rampant.' Dawn laughed again, then sobered. 'Poor guy. He'd been through a rough time. There'd been a girl who'd killed herself.'

'Oh?'

'She'd got the hots for Hugh, but he didn't feel the same way.'

'You're sure about that?'

'That's what he told me, but hey,' she laughed again, 'we didn't do much talking.'

'You don't think there's a possibility he might have been the father?'

'The father?' Dawn didn't seem to understand.

'Of the baby?'

There was a pause. 'Jesus, no.' Dawn drawled. 'No way.'

Mady frowned. 'How can you be so sure? I mean, just because he said he didn't sleep with her . . .'

'He was sterile, honey.'

Her heart hammered. 'What?'

'He showed me the medical report. He didn't want to use contraception with me, see? He said he didn't need to because he'd just found out he was sterile. He'd wanted to make some cash out of being a sperm donor, but he'd gotten rejected cos his sperm were no good. "Sure," I said, "I've heard that one before", then he showed me the report.'

'What did it say?' whispered Mady. If Hugh was sterile then he wasn't Charley's father. Who was?

'Jeez, I can't remember. Just that he'd about zero chance of fathering a child – less risk than using a condom. It was good enough for me.'

Mady's mind swam. Roz had deceived her. She must have been having an affair, or . . . had she used a sperm bank? Why hadn't she confided in her? And Hugh! Hugh must have known throughout Roz's pregnancy that the child wasn't his. Why hadn't he said anything? Had his love for Charley been a pretence? Had he killed him out of revenge?

Out in the mall, someone screamed. She looked up and saw Hugh standing at the window, his hands spread-eagled on the glass. He seemed to be covered in blood. It was all over his face, his neck and on his shirt and jacket. He looked quite mad. People seeing him were looking horrified, clutching their children and moving off quickly: some were running. An alarm bell wailed out and, by a pillar, Mady saw a security guard talking furtively into his radio.

But he couldn't save her. It was too late. Hugh had left the window, smearing blood upon the glass. He was coming for her.

A child at the next table shouted, 'Look at that man, Mommy!'

Hugh was in the doorway, bloody and swaying, one hand deep in his jacket pocket. People screamed and scrambled out of his way; chairs were overturned in the panic, but Hugh kept coming, oblivious to it all, that hand jammed firmly into his pocket.

What did he have in there? A gun?

He was less than three feet from her. His eyes were wild. If she had ever doubted he was capable of killing, those doubts were gone now. He croaked hoarsely, 'I've got to talk to you.'

'Yes.' She found she couldn't move. She thought if she did exactly what he wanted, he might not kill her.

'You're not going to ruin me,' he muttered and pulled his hand from his pocket.

She dived to the floor, hitting her head on a table leg and feeling instantly dizzy, but she kept moving, knowing she had to get away. He was coming after her still, pushing aside chairs and tables.

'Freeze!'

She crawled under a table against the wall. She had boxed herself into a corner, and now it was too late. Her head spun sickeningly. Time slowed. There was commotion all around her, people running and shouting. She saw her table being raised and she cowered on the floor, whimpering. She saw Archie's face. She had wanted so much to bring him up.

A steel hand gripped her arm and twisted her round. He wanted to see her terror before he shot her.

'You okay?' yelled a policeman. The café was full of police with guns. Hugh was slammed up against a wall; they were cuffing him now. 'Ma'am?' asked the policeman more concernedly.

'I'm fine,' she whispered and blacked out.

Mady and Hugh were taken to the same hospital, which was also coping with crush casualties from the mall. Mady was found to be suffering from mild concussion and two cracked ribs, and she was kept in hospital overnight; Hugh had sustained multiple cuts to his face and hands in the car crash but after those were stitched he was released straight away into the custody of the local police.

There was confusion at first about what to charge him with. Initial ideas of attempted murder dissolved when it was found that he had not been carrying a weapon, in fact the only items discovered on his person were a wallet, house keys and a notebook in his jacket pocket. He was held temporarily on charges of disturbing the peace. Dr Amos McCloud, who had been booked jumping stop lights in the town, was charged with reckless driving.

Hugh would say nothing to the police, nor, frustratingly, would Mady.

The story ran on all the American networks that night: a senior British politician had run amok in a shopping mall, causing mass panic. Over twenty people, including a female British journalist, had suffered minor injuries.

The next day, following a series of telephone calls, all charges against Hugh were abruptly dropped. He was put on a flight to London that night, and arrived at Heathrow at six o'clock on Monday morning. He was greeted by a wall of TV lights, cameras and clamouring journalists.

'Minister, did you kill your baby?'

He froze. Someone thrust a copy of that day's *Register* newspaper into his hands. 'Eastwood's Connection to Three Deaths' ran the splash headline:

Hugh Eastwood, the politician tipped to be the next prime minister, has in the past been the blackmail victim of a pregnant girl who later killed herself . . .

Eastwood learned that his secret was to be revealed on national television one week before his baby son was fatally shaken. The TV producer who intended to broadcast the film was found dead outside her home last week.

Alice Bishop, the nanny convicted of Charley Eastwood's killing, was found unconscious in her cell on Sunday morning, suffering from an overdose. She is in a coma.

Her friend, Kate Armstrong, the 'lost nanny' witness, has come forward to corroborate Bishop's claims. Furthermore she alleges that she found the missing tape, a crucial piece of evidence, in Eastwood's shirt on the same day that Charley was injured.

'Did you destroy that tape, Minister?'

Hugh took a swing at the reporter but failed to make contact.

'Does your wife stand by you, Minister?'

The colour drained from his face.

At that moment, two plain-clothes police officers elbowed their way through the journalists, took Hugh gently by the arm and asked him to accompany them to the police station for questioning.

He was interrogated for three days, and allowed home each night to his Chelsea house. Roz was staying elsewhere and refused to talk to him.

On the fourth day, as he was leaving for the police station, a journalist called out, 'Minister, is it true you've been asked to resign?'

He said nothing, but an hour later in the police station he broke down, sobbing, saying that he had always known Charley wasn't his, but that he had loved him; if he had hurt him, he had no memory of it, he'd never meant to harm him . . .

The interviewing officers exchanged glances. There was always satisfaction in nailing a big bastard.

That morning, Thanksgiving in America, Hugh Eastwood was charged with killing his wife's child and, two weeks later, Alice Bishop, fully recovered, was released from the prison hospital and allowed to join her parents at a London hotel.

CHAPTER NINETEEN

Five months later, the trial of Hugh Eastwood was in its final stages of preparation. Eastwood was charged with murder and faced a life sentence. Alice Bishop, Kate Armstrong, Lola Beaney and Mady O'Neil were to give evidence for the prosecution. For the defence, Roz was the surprise, star witness. She believed her husband was guilty, but of manslaughter, not of murder, and she intended to say so.

She had the nation's sympathy, although many considered her a dupe. Hugh was a vilified figure. Not only had he killed her baby, but he had allowed a blameless girl to go to prison on his behalf. It was a matter of happenstance that she had not succeeded in killing herself.

Professionally also, Hugh's star, so recently in the ascendant, was now eclipsed. In the week following his arrest, the political editor of *The Register* was asked to meet an old Home Office contact for drinks at a Bloomsbury bar. The contact passed him a brown envelope containing highly sensitive information on an organisation whose very existence had until then been denied: the Grey Team.

The documents purported to be minutes of meetings held by the Team, three civil servants and a politician, Hugh Eastwood. Two of the civil servants' names had been blocked out so efficiently that it was impossible to read who they were. The third man had died two years before in a car crash.

The first minutes were dated six years ago. The name, the 'Grey Team', was decided upon because their job was to work in the dark to discredit members of the Opposition. They were aware that their existence was clandestine, that the Government would distance itself from them if anything should go wrong.

Their first assignment was to intimidate the Opposition's top financial backers. The chairman of a major mobile phone company was picked upon first. He was anonymously informed that the Department of Trade and Industry were investigating some of his offshore interests. If he was friendlier to the Government, it was implied, the DTI's interest might wane.

The chairman withdrew his funding of the Opposition within forty-eight hours. The Grey Team went from strength to strength. They had telephones bugged; in the run-up to the election, they broke into the Opposition's headquarters and put a virus into the mainframe computer so that the system crashed.

Then they turned their attention to the Opposition leader himself. He was an unmarried man in his middle-fifties who claimed he was straight; simply unattached. He was extremely popular with the voters, who liked his forthright approach. The Grey Team tried to find a male lover to shock the middle classes. Being unable to do so, Hugh himself, the minutes showed, decreed that the man should have paedophile tendencies. A suitable young man in his twenties was found and paid. He revealed to a Sunday tabloid that the Opposition leader had sexually abused him as a child.

The leader denied everything, began to sue, then suddenly committed suicide.

When *The Register* published the story, including large chunks from the minutes, Hugh resigned. He could do nothing else; his career was finished.

Apart from the murder charge, police were also investigating his involvement in the mysterious death of Christine Evans and his possible connection to, or at least knowledge of, a fire that had killed a security guard at her film company's archive.

In the end, there was little that the public did not believe Hugh Eastwood guilty of. Only Roz stood by him, visiting regularly, boosting his morale.

She had become much stronger since his arrest, when Mady had expected her to fall apart.

'I think I always knew, you know?'

Mady nodded. Her friend didn't weep and cling any more. In fact, it was Mady who depended on her, not least for babysitting. Roz was fantastic with Archie.

'. . . so it was a relief, really.'

They were sitting on Mady's tiny patio, having a glass of wine. It was Thursday evening, and Hugh's trial was due to begin on Monday morning. The evening was chilly but pleasant; a blackbird was singing. Ben was out and Archie was in bed. Both women's lawyers had warned them not to discuss the forthcoming trial, which was impossible.

'Roz . . .'

Her friend looked up.

'Have you thought any more about the paternity stuff?'

Roz frowned and didn't say anything. She had never told Mady or anyone else who Charley's father was. Mady had only asked once, not long after her return from the States, and had received no reply. It was one thing to stonewall her, Mady thought, but once the trial got under way, the subject was going to come up – it was a key plank in Hugh's defence – and Roz was going to find herself at the centre of very intrusive media speculation.

'You could say it was a sperm bank,' Mady suggested.

'Yes, I could,' Roz said tightly.

'Was it?'

'Stop it. I'm not going to tell you.'

'Doesn't it make you mad that Hugh let you think for all those years that you were the infertile one?'

'No. I got even, didn't I, with my cuckoo?'

Mady shivered at her turn of phrase. Then Roz said softly, 'You see, I've always loved him. Now he needs me, I've never loved him so much.' She looked Mady straight in the eye. 'There's nothing I wouldn't do for him.'

It was a challenge, Mady thought. 'Has he told you what he did with the tape?' she asked with an air of insouciance, and she saw Roz flinch.

'No.'

Hugh had told the police that the missing tape, the one that Kate Armstrong had seen, was hidden in a box in the loft of the Chelsea house. It wasn't. The only item discovered in the insulating padding he described was the television satellite box, admittedly shaped like a full-sized videotape. But the surveillance cassettes were tiny, palm-sized. The prosecution was going to allege that either Hugh or Roz had destroyed the film. They were planning to say Roz had colluded with

Hugh, and that any evidence she gave for him was therefore suspect.

'Did you destroy it?'

'No.' The colour drained from Roz's face. 'Look. I'm not talking about this, okay?'

'Okay.'

'I'm going now.'

'Roz . . .'

'We're talking about my husband killing my child, okay? It's bloody heavy stuff.' She spoke with more force than Mady could remember. She felt sorry. Not long after, they parted rather stiffly with each other.

It was only at eight-thirty the following morning that it became apparent that Mady and Ben had each presumed the other wasn't working that day.

'You're always at home on Fridays,' Ben protested.

'Not always. Not today.'

'I've got a meeting to go to.'

'So have I!'

Archie, fifteen months old, was sitting on the kitchen floor holding a bottle of tomato ketchup with a flip-up lid.

'I told you two days ago,' Mady said carefully, controlling her own anger because Archie was present, 'that I'd have to go in today for my editorial meeting.'

'I don't remember,' muttered Ben.

'You said nothing at the time! I presumed you'd be here. Who's going to look after Archie?'

Ben shrugged. 'Can't your mother come over?'

'She's done it twice this week already.'

'Big deal.'

'Sorry?'

'Nothing,' he snapped. 'How about Roz?'

'She's got a job to go to,' Mady retorted.

'Really? I thought she lived here.'

'Ha bloody ha. How about your mother?'

'It would be midday before she got here. My meeting is at ten.'

'So's mine,' Mady set her jaw. 'I've got to go in.'

'Me too.'

They glowered at each other.

'Why can't you take Archie in with you?' Ben asked.

'Why can't you?'

'Oh, for God's sake! I'm trying to convince a bank to extend our loan on the grounds that I'm running a sound business from home and I turn up with a shrieking infant?'

'Well, how about me? It's my last editorial meeting before the trial!'

'You are his mother!' Ben shouted.

'And you're his bloody father!'

'I think it's maybe time you made some choices . . .'

'I like that! Who's been keeping us afloat for the last two years?'

'. . . either we get a nanny or you cut down your hours . . .'

'Why mine?'

'Because if my business is going to take off . . .'

'I've got to kiss my career goodbye? Is that it? You selfish bastard.'

An adult coughed and they both whipped round. Roz stood in the doorway of the kitchen. 'Hi,' she said brightly.

Mady had given her a key to the house, slightly against Ben's wishes but he had warmed to Roz in recent months and he agreed that if she needed to escape from the media during the trial, she could come to them. It was only that he found it a bit unnerving, he said, knowing that Roz could walk in at any moment.

Now Mady wondered how long she had been standing there; what had she heard?

'I'm not going into the office until this afternoon,' Roz went on as if everything was perfectly normal. 'There's something I've got to pick up that's kind of crucial . . . Anyway, I thought I'd just pop in and see if you needed me by any chance today? I rang the doorbell but I don't think you heard me . . .?'

They beheld her as their saviour. Ben was the first to recover. 'We certainly do, don't we, love?'

Mady wouldn't look at him. It would take her longer than that to forgive him.

'We've both got to go out this morning,' Ben explained, 'so it would be fantastic if you could do Archie?'

'Love to,' said Roz. 'Oh my God!'

'What?' said Mady in alarm.

'Look at Archie!'

He was covered in blood. Mady stopped breathing. She couldn't move. Ben ran forward and snatched him up. 'It's only tomato ketchup!'

'Oh God, for a moment I thought . . .' began Roz.

'Me too,' said Mady. She felt weak with relief. 'You're fantastic.' She turned gratefully to Roz. 'You really don't mind?'

'Of course not. Come here, big boy.' She took Archie from Ben's arms. 'We'll go and see the ducks, shall we, while Mummy and Daddy go to work?'

Archie seemed to think that a great idea. He squirmed delightedly.

'Go on, you two,' Roz ordered. 'Shoo.'

'Thanks.' Mady kissed her and then Archie, and then, colliding in the hallway with Ben, him too.

'I forgive you,' he whispered.

'Bloody nerve.' She smiled.

They separated into their own cars.

Mady's meeting, final planning for the forthcoming trial, lasted one hour. She was supplying most of the background material. After the meeting was finished, she returned to her desk to take a copy of everything she had written to date.

As a prosecution witness, she had forged excellent relationships with the police. Hugh had told the interviewing officers – who had told her – that he had always doubted he was the father of Vera's baby, but he had been so drunk the night of the ball he couldn't remember, and when Vera had come making her allegations, he'd been scared. He hadn't known then he was sterile. He had run to Amos McCloud, his advisor and friend and it had been Amos who had told him not to take the risk, that an allegation of rape could ruin Hugh before he had started, that he, Amos, would take care of everything. He had lent Hugh the money to pay off Vera.

Amos McCloud had offered to come to England as a defence witness; the defence team had politely declined.

Hugh had a way of making people want to help and believe him, Mady ruminated. She knew the prosecution were going to suggest that Roz must have heard something that night, which Mady knew she had: those three cries. She didn't know whether Roz had told anyone else; she hadn't asked her. Mady had told no one. Either deliberately or subconsciously, Roz had concealed what had occurred that night. Under cross-examination from the prosecution, how would she stand up? How would she appear to the court? A faithful wife or a conspirator? That was what Mady feared most for her friend, that in standing by Hugh, she could end up in the dock herself. She had tried to persuade her to change her mind about giving evidence but Roz had stood firm.

'I'll do anything for him, Mady. You see, I still love him.'

Those were the last words of the interview Roz had given Mady for the backgrounder. Mady stared at them on the page. It was more or less what Roz had told her the night before. There was nothing Roz wouldn't do to help her husband: suppress memories, destroy evidence . . .

Had she seen the tape? Mady shuddered at the thought. Had she seen it, and destroyed it, to protect Hugh? That would have been the obvious thing to do – if she could have suppressed her disgust and outrage as a mother. But could any mother, Mady asked herself, seeing her spouse kill her child, really have been able to destroy the only piece of evidence that would ever bring him to justice? Wouldn't her subconscious – prompted by maternal rather than uxorial instincts – have overruled that final act of loyalty?

She felt cold at the prospect of what she was imagining. If she was right, Roz would have hidden the tape away somewhere somewhere that it would never be found, that she would never be tempted to look at it again herself, unless she needed to . .

Not the house, that had been searched again from top to bottom by the police.

Her office? Mady's heart skipped a beat. Roz had a safe at her office; in it, she'd told Mady, she kept love letters from her old boyfriend, Hugh being jealous of even an old flame. The safe was set into the wall behind a painting; the combination was

1066. 'You're the only person that knows that,' Roz had joked with Mady, 'so if anything should ever happen to me, you'll find all my treasures there.'

Hadn't Roz told her at the house that morning that she had to go into work that afternoon to pick up something crucial?

What else could it be but the tape? On the weekend before the trial, Roz, her husband's best defence witness, was going to finally destroy the evidence . . .

Mady had to stop her. She had to find out if she was right, or if her imaginings were only that. Roz's office was ten floors above her own. She headed for the lifts.

CHAPTER TWENTY

On numerous occasions Mady had visited Roz's office, but always to meet Roz there. She appeared brightly before Roz's secretary's desk. The woman recognised her at once.

'Hi.' Mady smiled warmly. 'Roz asked me to drop by to get something for her.'

'Oh. Sure. I'll get it for you if you like?'

'No, no, that's okay. It's to do with, er, Charley . . .' She hated herself, but the ruse worked; the woman's face crumpled.

'She told me which cupboard they'd be in,' Mady went on swiftly. 'She said there was quite a bit of personal stuff in there. She wanted me just to flick through . . .'

'Sure. Okay. I'll let you in.' Quickly, the secretary unlocked the door and Mady stepped inside.

She closed it after herself. She mustn't be long. She moved around behind Roz's desk and lifted from the wall a charcoal drawing of a nude. The small safe faced her, with its simple combination dial. She moved it clockwise, one . . . it clicked loudly, it seemed to her, but she kept going, zero, six, six . . . the metal door popped open.

Her mouth felt dry. She inserted her hand and pulled out the contents: a fat stack of envelopes, a theatre programme, photographs of Roz and another man. No tape. Mady ran her hand around inside the safe, there was nothing else there.

She'd been wrong. Crazy in her thinking. Hugh had destroyed the tape, not Roz. She replaced the contents of the safe and shut it. She would leave now. Roz would never know what Mady had suspected her of.

She took one final glance around the room. There, over by the floor-to-ceiling windows was the shelf on which sat the silver-framed photograph of Charley, taken a month before he died and showing a bright-eyed, alert little baby with a beaming grin.

Beside it there lay a palm-sized video camera. Mady stared. She recognised that camera, she had one the same. She and Roz had bought them together, just after Archie was born. It would serve a dual purpose for her, Roz had said: she would be able to check up on the nanny, it took the same size films as the spy cameras at home.

Mady felt her stomach turn.

She looked quickly about the room. There was very little furniture in it; the secretary kept the files outside in her ante-office. Just the desk, really. Mady returned to it, and pulled open the top drawer. It was cluttered with personal belongings, stamps, a set of keys, aspirin, lipsticks, an old tube of mascara, and right at the back, a little cassette-cover.

Her heart turned over. It had been there all the while, anyone could have found it. Was that what Roz had been hoping? That someone would find it, view it, absolve her from any other awful responsibility?

Poor Roz. How long she had had to wait. But Mady was here now, she would do it; she would hand it over. Hugh would have to change his plea to guilty, Roz wouldn't have to give evidence and the court case would be over in a day instead of stretching on for weeks.

She picked up the little tape. She looked at the blue sticker. Before she sent Hugh to prison for a very long time, she wanted to view the film herself and she needed to do it quickly before she changed her mind. She could take it home, she had the camera there, but Roz would be there and the other camera was here. It wouldn't take a minute. She flipped open the lid and inserted the cassette.

There was a rap at the door, and before she could turn, it opened.

'Roz, why didn't you tell me—' The man stopped mid-sentence.

Mady stopped too, the camera in her hand. She recognised him vaguely, one of the management chiefs.

He looked at what she was holding.

'Just something for Roz,' she murmured. 'I'm her friend, Mady O'Neil.'

He coloured. 'Oh yes. Mady.'

He knew her name although she didn't know him. He introduced himself. 'I'm Martin Roper. I'll . . . er . . . leave you to it,' he said and withdrew. The door closed.

She didn't have time to wonder about him; she didn't know how long it would be before he thought it strange that she was there viewing a video film in Roz's office, before he made the connection between Roz and a missing tape . . .

She put the tape in and switched on the machine. The spools played. The pictures appeared on the little screen in her hand.

Alice was in the nursery, singing away happily to Charley a

she folded clothes into the drawers of the chest beside his cot. Then she picked up the baby, gently, lovingly, and carried him out.

The film, action-activated, stopped. The next frame was at night, Roz putting Charley to bed. Although it was night-time, the lamplight was sufficiently powerful to see what was happening in the room. Roz went out and Hugh came in. Mady's heart thumped. Would this be it?

But Hugh simply stood gazing down at the sleeping baby, then he leant forward over the cot and kissed him. 'Sleep tonight, my darling,' he whispered.

Mady's blood ran cold. In context, that was a terrible warning.

The film stopped. It was still dark when it started again, with Roz coming in, sleepy, acting on automatic pilot, feeding Charley, then replacing him in his cot. The same sequence occurred again – two night feeds, Mady realised: the night before Charley had been injured.

The next morning appeared: Hugh getting Charley up, and then later, Alice coming with him into the room, changing him, cuddling him. The film started and stopped, and then eventually it was night-time again. The night in which Charley had been hurt. The same routine as before except now it was Hugh stumbling into the crying baby, reaching out, picking him up, giving him a bottle. Once it happened, twice . . .

Mady stopped the film. She didn't know if she could bear it, to watch Charley being shaken to death. As soon as it started, she told herself, trembling, at the very first sign she would stop the film and run, take it to the police, hand it over.

She pressed the play button again. Hugh fed Charley then put him back into his cot and left the room. Of course, thought

Mady dully; it was on the third occasion that he had snapped. She watched the screen.

Charley was crying, on and on. 'Stop, Charley, stop,' whispered Mady, tears streaming down her face. The nursery door opened. She couldn't bear to see it, she turned away, and then back again. Hands held Charley, shaking him back and forth. He was so tiny, so helpless, and whoever was hurting him like that was so terribly angry, heedless of what they did . . . and the voice, so filled with hatred, the face . . .

Still holding the camera, Mady ran for the door.

At the park with the ducks, several people, mothers mainly, had smiled at Roz and Archie and they had smiled back: Roz, the doting mummy with her angelic little boy.

Only he wasn't angelic. He had been bad, very bad. He had caused Ben and Mady to row, Ben to say those awful things to Mady, that she must give up her career, that she was a mother first. Babies did that. They divided parents, they ruined careers.

Roz had fought so hard for her career and, in the long absence of a baby, it had become hers. She had been in line for promotion to Group Editorial Director, the pinnacle, when it had happened: she had got pregnant. She knew now that it wasn't Hugh's; the father therefore was Martin Roper, the Financial Director, with whom she had had a casual, delightfully illicit affair the previous year: love letters, dirty photographs, it had been like being a teenager. Martin Roper, whom she had overheard on her return to work from maternity leave, stitching her up with the Chief Executive.

'With a young child, she's not going to have the energy for the job,' Roper had warned.

'She's not going to like it.'

'Oh, she's besotted. She brought him into work the other day. Just like any other woman: give them a baby, and their brains go to mush . . .'

People assumed so many things about mothers, that they were the givers and protectors of life. Why should they always be, Roz wondered? Why should they always be passive, the put-upon? Could they not also be takers? They could.

Dear, sweet Mady who had been such a precious friend to her, as well as her protector, although she'd been largely unaware of that role. Mady had sounded at the end of her tether that morning. Roz knew how that felt, how much better off Mady and Ben would be without the responsibility, the drag on the relationship.

Now Archie was crying again. He'd been tearful ever since she had put him firmly but kindly into his cot and left him there.

She mounted the stairs. 'I'm coming,' she called softly.

But he kept crying, on and on.

She opened the door to his room. She went to pick him up, but he cowered away from her, as if he knew. But he was only a baby, he couldn't run away. She bent and picked him up. He was much heavier than Charley had been but like Charley that night, Archie screamed in her face. He put both hands on her chest and shoved her away.

'Don't,' she said sharply and knelt down with him on the floor. He shrieked all the harder, and she seized his upper arms.

Ice-cold fear ran in Mady's veins. There were no spaces in her street. She double-parked and ran, fumbling at the front door to get her key in the lock.

'Roz!' she screamed as she entered the house. She heard a sound upstairs and she pounded up, past one flight and then the turn to the top landing. Roz was standing in Archie's room, facing her, holding her son rigidly in her arms. Her face was perfectly blank.

'Give him to me!' she screamed.

Roz offered no resistance.

Archie opened his eyes. He began to cry again, but dry hiccoughing sobs. Mady held him close. 'Oh my baby, my darling.'

'Mady?' said Roz wonderingly. 'What . . .?'

Clutching Archie, Mady backed away from her. At the stairs she turned and ran down into the hall where she dialled first for an ambulance, and then the police.

EPILOGUE

On arrival at hospital a brainscan was carried out immediately on Archie. It showed no obvious damage but he was kept in overnight for observation. The doctors told Mady and Ben that his age had saved him. Had he been a baby rather than a toddler, Roz would probably have killed him.

Her trial took place the following December. She was charged with murder and attempted murder, and pleaded guilty to both, on the grounds of diminished responsibility. She was ordered to be detained indefinitely at a hospital for the criminally insane.

For several months she kept up a disjointed, one-sided correspondence with Mady, at times denying what had happened, at other times reliving it:

'Charley cried out and Hugh didn't hear so I got up, and went in. He suddenly looked so like his father! Just like Martin Roper, and Martin had hurt me. So I picked Charley up. Then he was still. I don't know how long went by. Then I remembered about the camera. I had to get rid of the film. I took it out and put the other one that was in the shoebox into the camera instead. I didn't know what to do with the film. I wasn't thinking straight; everything seemed strange. Panicky and floaty at the same time, you know?

'I put the film into the pocket of Hugh's shirt, you know I always liked wearing his shirts in bed? Then I thought, suppose Hugh found it there? Where could I put it where no one would look? Hugh's study, I thought! No one ever goes in there. I nipped downstairs and put the shirt on a chair in there. It must have fallen off on to the floor, I suppose, for Kate to have stood on it . . .

'When I went back to the house that day to get things so we could stay at the hospital with my baby, I put the tape in my handbag. No one searched me. Why would they?'

Perhaps she had longed to be found out from the start, Mady thought. Perhaps she had intended to confess, before Alice presented such an easy scapegoat. First Alice, and then Hugh.

Mady did not reply to Roz's letters and did not go to see her; she could not, she was too afraid. She doubted she would ever have a best friend again.

Hugh was like a lost man. He visited his wife at first, but she treated him like a stranger and as time went by she lost herself more and more in the life of the institution. She seemed happy there. Hugh found the change in her too painful to bear and stopped visiting. He devoted his energies to clearing his political name. He wrote his version of the events that had taken place at Chesterfield University, a truthful account that was published in a Sunday newspaper and won him widespread public sympathy. He had never been involved with the Grey Team although he had known of its existence. The 'secret papers' leaked to the media were shown to have been fabricated, probably by Hugh's former aide, Alan Hardy, who resigned early in the new year. Rebecca Moynihan had become Shadow Home Secretary when her party lost the general election.

Hugh left politics and returned to the bar. His first case involved defending a surgeon. The man had been charged with attempted manslaughter after reversing his car into a group of Pro Life protesters outside the private London clinic where the surgeon carried out abortions. Hugh defended the man vigorously and won. During the case, he became engaged to, although never married, a young woman doctor from the clinic.

Alice Bishop returned to Hastings in New Zealand where she got a job on a local newspaper as a trainee journalist, her scant wages being supplemented by the income from her auto-biography, 'Nanny Not to Blame'. She became a good journalist, eventually marrying a local boy and having a daughter of her own.

Kate Armstrong went back to Laros where she resumed her life with Dimitris.

A year after Roz's trial, Ben's company was starting to do well. He took a short lease on an office in the City and employed a secretary but still worked from home occasionally. Mady took over his old office in the basement: she found that as long as she was on a separate floor within calling distance if she was needed, she could work quite contentedly with a nanny in the house.

Archie loved the nanny and she, him. Occasionally Mady felt jealous but told herself it was far better she felt that way than worried that her child was being ill-treated or neglected. The nanny lived out: neither Ben or Mady felt they could face a stranger in the bathroom in the morning.

It was Saturday morning in January. Archie, nearly three years old, and due to start nursery in a week, had climbed out of his own bed during the night to join Ben and Mady in theirs.

Mady woke first, on the edge of the bed, and thought about shifting Archie off her pillow on to Ben's side, but didn't want to wake the sleeping child.

She studied his outline in the dim morning light: his still curly hair, those terrific eyelashes and perfect tawny skin. She adored him so that tears welled up. The thought of hurting him was horrible.

'Hi, you,' murmured Ben, awake on the other side. He propped his head up on one hand.

'Do you think he'll ever forgive me?'

'Of course he will.'

'But he's so little, and it's such a betrayal.'

'Mady, children have been betrayed in this way since the dawn of time. He'll get over it.'

Mady wiped away a hot tear. 'But suppose it damages him? Suppose he changes completely?'

'He won't.' Ben extended a hand and brushed her cheek. 'He's going to love his new little brother or sister.'

Mady was six months pregnant. Archie woke up. 'There was an octopus in my bed,' he explained gravely.

'A likely story,' derided Ben.

'Did it scare you, my angel?' soothed Mady, kissing the little face.

'Archie?'

Archie turned to Ben.

'D'you want a baby?'

'Yes,' said Archie firmly.

'Okay, that's a done deal. Let's go and make mummy a cup of tea. See,' Ben said smugly, 'it's easy.'

'You tricked him,' Mady smiled.

'I certainly did.'

'I love you.'

'Me too you.' Their eyes lingered for a moment.

'We're so lucky . . .' began Mady tremulously.

'Daddy, I can open the front door,' yelled Archie, and both parents leaped out of bed.